REVOLUTION TIME

Paul G. Varnas

ANAPHORA LITERARY PRESS

AUGUSTA, GEORGIA

Anaphora Literary Press
2419 Southdale Drive
Hephzibah, GA 30815
http://anaphoraliterary.com

Book design by Anna Faktorovich, Ph.D.

Copyright © 2016 by Paul G. Varnas

All rights reserved. No part of this book may be reproduced in any form or by any electronic or mechanical means, including information storage and retrieval systems, without permission in writing from Paul G. Varnas. Writers are welcome to quote brief passages in their critical studies, as American copyright law dictates.

Edited by Christina Wordham

Cover Image: "The March to Valley Forge" by William B. T. Trego (1883).

Published in 2016 by Anaphora Literary Press

Revolution Time
Paul G. Varnas—1st edition.

ISBN-13: 978-1-68114-232-6
ISBN-10: 1-68114-232-5

Library of Congress Control Number: 2016901305

REVOLUTION TIME

PAUL G. VARNAS

Chapter 1
June 5, 2014

How to Avoid a Family Vacation

The noxious smell emanating from the back of the Range Rover put a damper on Eddie's adrenaline rush. It was like an ugly scratch on a new Ferrari. He was still excited by the sheer audacity of what they were doing. He just wished that the car didn't smell so bad. The source of the smell was the three buckets of rotting fish that were vital to the success of the plan. He absentmindedly tugged at a lock of his long dark hair and tried to ignore it.

Eddie was a bit of a prankster, but had never been in trouble. He and his friends had pulled a number of stunts, like turning a Mrs. Henderson's Fiat on its side, stealing other teams' mascots and then there was the pig caper. They released three piglets into the halls of the high school and painted numbers on their backs: 1, 2 and 4. The administration looked for the fourth pig for days.

This prank was different; it was a crime—possibly even a federal crime. Getting caught would not result in a reprimand or suspension from school, it could land him in jail. But Eddie was smart and cocky and getting caught was never an option. "With great risk comes great reward," he thought to himself.

Ted was driving, erratically. He was, by nature, reckless. He also loved everything gangsta and always talked like he was preparing to star in a rap video. He wore an oversized sports jersey and his baseball cap was worn backwards and tilted to one side. Eddie thought it odd that it was a Blackhawks jersey; wondering how many African American hockey fans there were in Chicago. Ted was probably the only gangsta hockey fan in Illinois.

Beans was a key component to the plan. Beans sat in the back seat of the Rover, tapping away at his laptop. His real name was Virgil Bienino; he had a name that sounded like he was in the cast of the Sopranos, but was as far away from looking the part as could be. He was 14 years old, but so short and skinny that he could pass for a 4th grader. He wore thick horn-rimmed glasses and had a thick, jet black hair that he combed back. He looked like a miniature Clark Kent. Beans was Ted's neighbor and was a computer genius. Eddie owed some of his 4.0 GPA to Beans. On more than one occasion Beans had hacked into the school's computer and "adjusted" Eddie's grade.

Beans had an expensive Nikon SLR around his neck along with what looked like a thin rubber necklace; it pinched his nostrils together. Beans explained that swimmers and divers used to wear them to keep water out of their noses. "Smart move," thought Eddie as he opened the window a crack, trying to get away from the smell.

"Man, yo' is OD-ing to come up with this caper; but you my ace-even if you cray. Know what I'm sayin'" Ted said as he accelerated and passed an Audi from the right.

From the back, Beans said, "You're crazy to come up with this plan, but you are my best friend, even if you are crazy, so I am in this with you," without looking up from his computer.

"Got it," said Eddie, teeth clenched and hands digging into his knees as Ted swerved and cut off a minivan. Beans was in the habit of translating for Ted.

Earlier today, Eddie had the beginnings of an idea to keep his parents from taking him and his sister, Angie, to Greece for the summer. It was a little crazy and Eddie wasn't entirely serious when he told it to Ted, but Ted was on board. He said they were 'for sure jumping the couch,' but that he was 'alls about it.' "Jumping the couch, for sure," thought Eddie. Jumping the couch was Ted's way of saying a crazy act—like Tom Cruise jumping on Oprah's couch. This caper was a lot crazier than that.

"Ted! Take it easy!" Beans complained from the back. "You're going to spill that crap." They had just merged to the Kennedy Expressway from the Edens, heading south into Chicago. Ted had crossed three lanes of traffic—blissfully unaware that there were other cars on the road. That "crap" was the six buckets of rotting fish parts and two buckets of motor oil.

Eddie said, "Plus the whole plan goes down the drain if you get pulled over."

"Gotcha bro—no five-oh," said Ted. Then he actually slowed down.

They were on their way to the Greek Consulate on St. Clair Street, in Chicago. It was in the Streeterville neighborhood, just east of Michigan Avenue, near Erie, close to Northwestern Hospital. The Greek consulate wasn't anything like you'd imagine an embassy to be. There were no walls surrounding it, and no guards at the gate. It was just a little bigger than a Chicago 3-flat, with doors at street level. Access was ridiculously easy.

The plan was simple: they were going to convince Eddie's parents that Angie was a fugitive wanted by the Greek government. To accomplish that, they were going to commit an act of "ecoterrorism" on the consulate.

Angie was a bit of a tree hugger, as Eddie liked to call her. The Greek government was about to begin drilling for oil in the Adriatic Sea—amidst protests from environmental groups, fishermen and people vested in tourism on the nearby island of Corfu. Eddie had heard Angie explaining the situation to their mother. Actually, he heard her ranting about how the Greek government didn't care about the environment. That's what gave him the idea.

The plan was to dump the fish and motor oil in front of the door of the consulate and spray paint the word 'murder' on the door. Beans would take pictures of the whole thing and use Photoshop to put Angie's head on Ted's body. Ted was chosen because he was large and solidly built and could pass for Angie in a blurred photo. When they got back, Beans would make a fake front page for the Daily Herald, with Angie's picture on the front page (blurred, but recognizable to Eddie's mother). They would also forge a letter from the consulate asking Eddie's mother to bring her daughter in for questioning. The letter would be angry and suggest that anyone committing such an act in Greece would receive prison time. Eddie would then suggest that the safest place for Angie would be at their Uncle Sol's farm in Wisconsin.

When they arrived at the consulate, they parked in an alley between the building and the restaurant next door, backing in. Beans put his computer into his backpack and took up his camera. All three put on ski masks in case there was video surveillance. Ted carried two buckets of fish, Eddie carried a bucket of fish and a bucket of motor oil. They dumped the contents in front of the door and Ted took out the spray can and wrote 'murder' on the door. The whole thing took about a minute. Beans took pictures the whole time.

They were headed back to the car when they heard the single bark of a police siren. A squad car was on Erie, about 50 feet away, moving fast toward them. They threw down their buckets and squeezed past the car into the alley. The other two ran down the alley, but Eddie stopped and opened the back hatch of the Range Rover.

The cops got out of the squad car to give chase. They were both in their 40s and a little overweight, but were surprisingly quick. Eddie took the other bucket of oil out of the Range Rover and spilled it on the ground, then ran as fast as he could to catch up with his friends. The three of them took off down the alley. Squeezing past the Range Rover slowed the portly cops down a little—by then the three boys were at the end of the alley. Once the cops squeezed through the gap between the Rover and the building walls that framed the alley, they began to give chase. They both went down hard when their feet hit the oil.

The boys reached Huron Street and turned toward Michigan Avenue. "Split up," cried Eddie, "And meet up by the Bean." Ted took off his jersey and mask and calmly walked south on Michigan in his t-shirt. Eddie put on a jacket and walked west and Beans headed north. Beans ducked into a Walgreens and bought himself a bright blue Cubs t-shirt. By the time the cops got off the ground, the three boys were gone, and no longer fit the description that the policemen had given over the radio. Unfortunately for the boys, the police had their car.

Millennium Park was about 10 blocks south of the consulate. The "Bean" was the centerpiece of the park. Its real name was the Cloud Gate, a public sculpture by Indian-born British artist Anish Kapoor, so nicknamed the Bean because of its shape. It was made up of 168 stainless steel plates welded together, and its highly polished, mirror-like exterior had no visible seams. It measured 33 by 66 by 42 feet, and weighed about 100 tons. You could see your reflection in it—distorted like in a fun house mirror. Within a half hour the three friends were standing in front of it. Ted went underneath, and looked up and grinned at his fun house reflection in the Bean, "Aw yeah! I'll buy that for a dollar. Know what I'm sayin'," Ted said with a little chuckle.

"You're happy?!" Eddie said incredulously. "The police have your car! We're busted! I won't have to go to Greece. I'll be in jail!"

"Frilldo, I'm Finna go back to my crib. You in? Chill, my man. I hit the digits and tole five-oh my ride got jacked. We cool," Ted said as he pulled out his phone. "We got Uber."

Beans translated, "He called the police and reported the car stolen before we left. We're taking Uber to get home."

Eddie just stared, his mouth open. Everyone always thought that he was the daring one. "My God, reporting the car stolen was a gutsy move," he thought to himself. "Uber is fine," he finally said.

While they were waiting for the driver, Ted said, "Man, you be busted if your ma does an Onion check." This confused Eddie.

Then Beans explained, "Your mother will find out the story if phony if she goes online. An 'Onion check' is to search for a story, like a phony one in the Onion, and find out it isn't true."

Eddie said, just as the car arrived, "No worries. My mother doesn't go near a computer. No emails, nothing. We even still get paper report cards." The car pulled away, heading for the north suburbs.

Chapter 2
June 6, 2014

A Trip to Uncle Sol's

Seated at the kitchen table, Angie took off her Cubs cap and flicked at a fly on the corner of her Chicago Tribune. It was the Friday paper. Angie loved the Friday paper, with all of the extra sections about entertainment, food and happenings in the city. She went back to her article. It was large feature about a team from Duke University that had uncovered hidden treasure from Blackbeard, the pirate, on an island off of North Carolina. The article was a pleasant escape for her. It had been a miserable school year and the rest of the paper was full of articles about ISIS, global warming, a turtle die-off in Long Island and other newsy items that drove home the horror and hopelessness of life in the 21st century. She finished the page she was on and leafed through the paper on her way to the jump page. On page 10 she noticed an article about the Greek consulate being vandalized by environmental activists. "Good for them," Angie muttered to herself.

She ate a spoonful of her bran flakes—"ugh," she thought to herself. The box had to have more flavor than these flakes. They were soggy; she had been trying to choke them down for the past half-hour. Her mom was on a health kick—for Angie. Angie had been gaining weight, so all junk food was banned from the house. She missed her Cap'n Crunch cereal. Angie had a stash of Twix bars, Doritos and Cheetos in her backpack, but her mom was right across the table. She didn't dare try to get anything out of the pack. She was stuck with the bran flakes. The article made her wistfully think of pirates and Cap'n Crunch. She made a face at the spoonful of limp bran flakes. Her mother watched her daughter's struggle and said, "You're becoming a young woman; you'll thank me when you shed those extra pounds. The boys will appreciate it, I know."

"Yes, mom," she said. Then she quietly muttered to herself, "Mom is definitely a 'cereal killer'." She noticed the box of Cap'n Crunch peering out of the kitchen garbage and smiled at her pun. Angie had a pale complexion and a face that was full of freckles.

She possessed an unruly mop of bright red hair, and bright green eyes. And, truth be told, she was heavy. She wore sweat pants, which she preferred, and her belly rolled over the elastic of the pants. She looked down at her belly. "I am fat," she thought to herself. It bothered her, but not as much as her mother's efforts to get the weight under control. She guessed that being thin would be more comfortable, and it might even make her more popular, but certainly could not be worth giving up the foods that she loved. Angie was a little bit of a rebel, especially now that her previous academic performance landed her in Elm Grove High School—or Dante's Fifth Level of Hell, as she liked to call it. Being 10 years old in high school was not a lot of fun, since the other kids often picked on her.

She went back to the article about Blackbeard. She took a sip of orange juice—at least IT had some flavor. The article said that *Queen Anne's Revenge* ran aground on a sandbar near Beaufort, North Carolina. Before that, Blackbeard unloaded treasure on one of the nearby keys. According to the article, the treasure was located at a key that was now the location of Burton Woods Coastal Reserve. The fly landed on her ear, she brushed it away and took another bite of the mushy and tasteless cereal.

The Duke University team uncovered chests of gold coins, precious stones and other valuable items, including solid gold drinking vessels, plates, pearls, and gold ingots. The value of the trove was estimated to be in the hundreds of millions of dollars.

Although Angie was part of a generation that had absolutely nothing to do with print media, she loved newspapers. She loved the yards of paper, the black and white pictures and the color ads. She even liked that her fingers became stained with the black ink when handling the paper. Sometimes she felt like she was born in the wrong decade. Her great-grandfather used to read the paper with her on his lap. He also would watch Turner Classic Movies with her and she felt very connected to the 1930s and the 1940s. She even liked big band music. Newspapers made her think of the movie, *His Girl Friday*, starring Cary Grant and Rosalind Russell. It was one of her favorite movies; they don't write dialog like that anymore. It made her love the idea of the savvy newspaperman, especially a good looking one, like Cary Grant. Rosalind Russell was his ace reporter, a strong and smart woman. Blogs and newsfeed were simply not as good as newspapers.

Living in those days would have been much better than life in the 21st century, which was absolutely horrible. There was a growing list of problems being badly handled by a government that was growing more dysfunctional by the minute.

She went back to the article; even life in the 18th century would be nice. She would prefer the 1930s, but the 18th century held some attraction to her. There were virgin forests and no pollution. True, she would miss some of the creature comforts—and Cap'n Crunch Cereal wouldn't be invented for another 200 years. But if she had to choose between her crowded, dirty and dangerous world and a clean American wilderness, it would be no contest.

In high school, being fat, young and smart translated into not much popularity. She ate lunch alone. The other kids teased her and mocked her behind her back. She felt that it was because she did not possess that which would make her valued in her peer group—good looks and an interest in the mundane. She pretended not to care. She could not think of a single person in her class that she would want to impress, but it would be nice to be better liked. Eddie would say that her lack of popularity was due the fact that she judged everyone and did not really care about the people around her. Angie was fairly convinced that there was nothing she could do to gain acceptance from kids who were more than five years her senior.

The fly came back. She swatted at it in earnest and went back to the article. Pirates were fascinating—the ultimate rebels. She remembered watching *Captain Blood*, starring Errol Flynn with her great grandfather. Flynn was a relative unknown before the film; the movie made him and Olivia de Havilland stars. In the movie, Captain Blood was not the typical bloodthirsty pirate. It turns out that neither was Blackbeard.

Even today, the name Blackbeard summoned the image of a terrible and bloodthirsty monster. In truth, he was a shrewd and calculating leader. Blackbeard spurned the use of force, relying instead on his fearsome image to elicit the response he desired from those he robbed. Contrary to the modern-day picture of the traditional tyrannical pirate, he commanded his vessels with the permission of their crews and there was no known account of his ever having murdered or even harmed those he held captive. He did, however, cultivate a bloodthirsty image. He even lit fuses in his beard to make himself look more fearsome when conducting a raid. It was a good business strategy for a pirate to be feared; it made victims less likely to resist. Angie swatted at the fly again with her hat.

***

There was a single, sharp ding from the phone on the nightstand. It woke Eddie and he opened his eyes; he was exhausted. He had gotten home very late. They actually got away with it! All that was left to do was to convince Mom that Angie would not be safe in Greece. The ding that had woken him was a text from Amy: "What are you up to?" He fought the urge to tersely write 'sleeping,' and opted for 'nothing much.' He definitely wanted to stay on Amy's good side. She, after all, was the reason for last night's little adventure.

The goal of last night's escapade was to spend summer at Uncle Sol's house. Sol was his dad's brother. His real name was Salazar, but he shortened it to Sol (thinking that 'Sal' sounded too much like 'Sally'). Uncle Sol would tell Grandma that he changed his name because he was her "sun". Grandma, on his father's side, was an old hippie. That was the fun and offbeat side of the family. Even his dad, serious and busy as he was, had a little bit of a fun and rebellious streak. Eddie also knew that his dad's name wasn't really Ben. He also was given a strange name by grandma—but it was a closely guarded secret.

There was a lot of freedom at Uncle Sol's place since he didn't really 'supervise.' Also, there was usually something interesting going on. It was always a good time. Also, being in Northern Wisconsin in the summer was nicer than being in the Chicago suburbs. It wasn't as hot or crowded. There also was plenty to do there, swimming, fishing, even hunting, and the best part was that it was still close enough for Amy to visit.

Sol's house was the only place where Eddie and Angie could stay if they didn't go to Greece. Sol was their only relative, not counting Uncle Steven who was in the Marines, currently stationed overseas. Mom didn't really trust Sol. He was too odd and she thought that he was irresponsible and a bad influence. Eddie was sure that if there were kennels for children, his mom would opt for that instead of trusting Uncle Sol, the mad scientist.

Uncle Sol had a brain like a sponge and a contagious exuberance that drew people in. The man used to raise ostriches, had a working loom in his living room and even played blues harmonica. Eddie thought he was interesting, but Mom just thought he was strange. He learned the harmonica as a lark, for no other reason than he thought it would be a cool thing to do. He spent a year in Chicago studying with Nigel Mack, a well-known blues artist. Sol had played Nigel's recordings for Eddie. The blues was not exactly

Eddie's kind of music, but the man had talent. Sol always said that it was funny that Nigel was Canadian bluesman—from the hard scrabble streets of Saskatoon. Eddie didn't get the joke.

Uncle Sol really enjoyed himself—life was fun and interesting to him. He never seemed to work and he was always involved in some kind of project—and not all of his projects were successful. The battery was a good example. He spent over a year trying to develop a permanent battery, THAT didn't go very well.

When Uncle Sol talked about his battery, he would get really excited and animated. Actually, he became excited and animated about most things he talked about. Maybe that was part of why Mom called him crazy. His eyes would get big and he'd talk really fast with his arms moving and grabbing props to illustrate his points. But the battery sealed Mom's opinion of him, and it was the reason Sol was living in a trailer. His battery blew up his house.

It was a huge explosion—it actually registered at the seismograph station in Missouri, over 1,000 miles away. There was a crater where the house once stood. Homeland Security spent a week interviewing him and Vernon. Uncle Sol took it with his usual good humor, "We never had a basement and now we do. We don't even have to pay an excavator to dig a basement for the new place," he would say. Fortunately, no one was hurt.

Eddie got out of bed and looked at his treasures. Beans had made an exact representation of the front and back pages of the Daily Herald. The cover story was about the vandalism at the Greek consulate. On the front page was one of Beans' pictures. Angie's head was Photoshopped onto Ted's body. The quality of the photo was of poor enough quality that a stranger would have a problem identifying Angie, but clear enough that their mother may suspect that she was the culprit who threw rotten fish on the consulate's doorstep. His other prize was another work of art from Beans. It was a postmarked letter on consulate stationary saying that an informant identified Angie as the vandal and that they had security footage that showed her committing the act. It demanded that Angie be brought to the consulate for an interview. It also said that she surely would have gotten jail time if she committed this crime in Greece.

Eddie went out onto the roof from the dormer window in his room. He laid down on his belly and slid down the slope of the roof. He slowly lowered himself, hung from the eaves and dropped to the ground. He took his prizes and placed them in the mail box. His phone dinged again. He ignored it for the time being. He went around to the side of the house to make sure Angie and their mother were still in the kitchen. Making sure that the two were suitably occupied, he snuck in through the front door.

***

Angie was engrossed with her article when Eddie came into the kitchen for breakfast. He grabbed the Cubs cap off of her head. She jumped up with a yell, "Hey, my hat!" Eddie, for some reason, was always mean to her.

Eddie tossed her cap back, toasted himself a bagel, and took a seat across from her. "Whatcha readin'?" he asked.

"They found Blackbeard's treasure," Angie said. "Over $100 million in gold and jewels. It's like a movie—with pirates and a treasure hunt." She carefully tore out the article and put it in her backpack.

Eddie was only half paying attention. He spoke as he responded to Amy's text, "Blackbeard, eh. I heard of him. Bad dude—murderer and a pirate. Killed hundreds of people, didn't he?" Eddie said with a mouthful of bagel. Angie just rolled her eyes.

"Finish breakfast and you should begin packing. It is only a few days before we are 'wheels up'," their mom said with a grin.

Angie took her backpack and went upstairs. Eddie sat at the table and finished his bagel. Upstairs, Angie took about 10 minutes to pack a pair of suitcases. She changed from sweatpants to jeans, grunting as she buttoned them around her waist. She then grabbed her backpack, took out a handful of Cheetos and shoved them into her mouth. She headed downstairs, wiping her yellow-stained hands on her jeans.

***

Downstairs, Angie walked into a very strange scene. Her mother was reading a letter, and holding a photograph (Bean's Photoshopped picture of Angie dumping fish at the consulate). Angie did not know what was in the letter, but she could see her mother getting angrier by the second.

Her mother looked up from the letter and said, "Young lady— GET OVER HERE!"

Angie was utterly confused, and a little frightened because of her mother's tone. She wasn't reading about the grades; so that couldn't be what she was angry about. There was a Greek flag on the corner of the envelope she was holding...strange. Her mother was so livid that she was shaking. She held up the letter and said, "What do you have to say about this?"

Angie had no idea what her mother was so upset about. She just stood there with her mouth open. Then the strangest thing happened, her brother came to her rescue. "God, mom—chill," he said. Angie did a double take to see if that was really her brother. His words seemed to quench Mom's wrath a bit.

Angie's eyes got wide when she saw that he was holding her grades in his hand—how in the world...? It turned out that Eddie had gone online and printed them. "Well, I had 10 good years," she thought to herself, sure that between the grades and whatever was in that letter, her mother would simply kill her.

Eddie continued before their mother could say a word. He put an arm around his sister and said, "Mom, you may not realize it, but you have but poor Angie under a great deal of pressure." It was their mother's turn to stand with her mouth agape. Eddie took advantage of the silence to keep his patter going. "Mom, Angie has had it hard. You made her go to high school. Did you know that she was miserable there? She even blew some easy classes so her grade point would drop—hoping that you would let her go to school with people her own age."

He paused and hugged his sister. "My poor sister was so lonely that she threw herself into trying to help the environment. I feel really bad for her, and maybe some of her behavior is partially my fault—I could have been nicer and more supportive of her." He turned her head towards him and said, "Sorry, Sis," and gave her a hug.

At this, Angie pushed him away and said, "What are you two talking about?"

Eddie jumped in before their mother could speak. He put his arm around Angie again and pulled her close. He held up the newspaper with Angie's picture on the cover and said, "My poor sister was just acting out—she is not a criminal. It's all the stress. Mom, please don't let her go to jail. She just really just wanted to protect the environment."

Angie removed his arm and turned to face him, "Jail? Environment! What the heck are you talking about?"

Eddie was not to be deterred. He continued his monologue, "We should take her to Uncle Sol's place in Wisconsin, where she will be safe. We can keep her away from the Greek authorities and neither the Chicago police nor Illinois State Police will not be able to reach her there."

Eddie had a gift. Call him a con man, a BS artist, a flim-flam man or whatever term you cared to choose. He could not only sell ice to Eskimos, he could have them sitting at the North Pole, waiting for delivery six months after they had paid him in advance. Truth be told, a fair percentage of his high grade point average was due to his, well, communication skills. Teachers loved him and if there was slack to be cut, it got cut for Eddie. They always bought his excuses, gave him second chances and generally gave him the benefit of the doubt. Even old sourpuss Mrs. Henderson, the math teacher, had a soft spot in her heart for Eddie. Lucky for him, she never found out who turned her Fiat on its side.

One of Eddie's skills was his ability to read people. It is unlikely that he could describe any thought process or even consciously knew why he would react in certain ways. But he could change his strategy instantly based on observations (that he wasn't even aware of) of his "mark." There was a subtle change in their mother's body language, a slight relaxation of her muscles and a softening of her facial features. Eddie had a thought, just below the conscious level, which said, "She's buying it."

He continued, changing his tone, "God, Mom, this isn't your fault. You want the best for both of us, and we love you for it. Angie could have a heck of a career, you could see that and of course you wanted her to succeed. She could go to Harvard—or anywhere. She is almost guaranteed to be top in any field she chooses. Of course you and Dad wanted her in high school at 10. It made sense, it put her on the fast track to success. But it was just a little too hard. The important thing is that we protect her from the mistake she made last night. In Wisconsin she will be safe from the authorities, and I can stay to keep an eye on her."

**

Their mother went into the bedroom to call their father and tell him about these new developments. She told him about the vandalism, listened a minute and said, "I know that you think Sol would be good with the children, but he seems so, so… irresponsible. The man blew up his own house. I think we need to cancel the trip and deal with this." She paused to listen, "Yes Ben, I know it has been a long time since you have been able to take time off. Yes, I know you originally wanted this to be a second honeymoon. But I think we would be leaving at a bad time."

On the other end of the line, their father was sitting at his desk and talking on the phone, looking at his computer screen. He was on the Chicago Tribune's website. There was a story about the vandalism at the Greek consulate. Someone was protesting oil drilling in the Adriatic. It also went on to say that there are no suspects. Clearly, Angie did not vandalize the consulate. He kept this fact to himself.

He said, "We really should just take them to Sol's. In Wisconsin, there is a good chance that they won't have to talk to the authorities. I have a feeling this whole thing will blow over. Sol is much more capable and responsible than you think. If there is any problem with the authorities, Sol has a great lawyer; he can get the fellow who helped him deal with Homeland Security after that battery incident. It will be fine. I don't think that much will come from this. Besides the trip will be more romantic without the children."

He hung up the phone and said to himself, "Well played, Eddie."

A coworker came in with some papers and asked, "What's up, Ben?"

He answered, "It looks like my kids REALLY don't want to go on a family vacation. Ellen and I get a second honeymoon instead."

The coworker said, "Don't take it personally. Kids that age have their own lives. They probably don't want to be away from home that long."

***

Within the hour, the family was in the car, Eddie in front and Angie in the back—still confused. Apparently Eddie had gotten her into trouble and then came to her rescue and got her out of trouble again. This must have fit his agenda, because they were not going to Greece. Angie wanted to be angry, but things had worked out so well. She didn't want to go to Greece either, plus there was a good chance that she would not be going to Elm Grove High next term. She did nothing to explain or to defend herself. "If it ain't broke, don't fix it," she thought to herself.

Angie wondered why there were pictures of her vandalizing the Greek consulate. What was Eddie up to? She was pretty sure he was behind the pictures, but did he commit the vandalism? Was there really any vandalism? You could never be sure with Eddie.

At least she didn't have to go to Greece to be dragged around by her parents, with her mother preaching to her about diet, posture and goals; misery that would be punctuated by awkward visits with relatives that they did not know. Wandering around looking at broken statues in the heat would be the highlight of the trip.

It also looked like there was a chance that she wouldn't have to go back to high school. Still, she was pretty sure she should be angry with Eddie, but things had worked out rather well. She decided to keep her mouth shut.

They reached Sol's driveway in just under four hours. Eddie sat up, unplugged his iPhone from the car charger, turned it off and put it in his pocket. Angie had an iPhone, but it was not as important to her as it was to Eddie, who was always tweeting, texting and using social media outlets that Angie had not even heard of. She agreed with Uncle Sol, who said that their generation had nothing to say, but hundreds of ways to say it.

After traveling up about a quarter mile of bumpy gravel side drive, they reached the house—or what was left of it. To the left of where the house had stood was a large mobile home. Next to the trailer was a crater that was already occupied by four concrete walls, making up the basement. Vernon, Uncle Sol's assistant, was arranging large planks along the basement walls. He looked up and waved, his bald head turning red and shining in the summer sun.

About 50 feet from the trailer, up a small hill, was a big red, old fashioned barn. Part of the property had been a working farm at one time. Two dogs were laying in front of the barn, sunning themselves. They stood for a moment, gave a cursory bark and lay back down.

Sol stepped out onto the porch to greet them. He was a big man, 6'4", with stooped shoulders and long arms. He was not an athlete, but he wasn't fat either. He was a man who spent a lot of time in front of computers, sitting at a lab bench or peering through a microscope. He had an unruly head full of salt and pepper hair, and a bushy mustache that hid both of his lips. He held out his arms as they pulled up—grinning and giving a rare view of his lower lip and teeth. "Ellen! How wonderful to see you!" he greeted her as she climbed out of the car. He stepped forward, wrapping his long arms around her, lifting her off of the ground as he gave her a crushing hug.

Ellen tried to step back and lean away—the result was that her arms and legs flailed like an animated rag doll. "Ugh, uh, yes Sol. Good to see you too." She grimaced. He let go of her; she barely kept her balance. She busied herself smoothing and arranging her clothes. Sol was gregarious and physical, and clearly made their mother uncomfortable.

"Angie!" Sol bellowed. "How is my little genius?" He scooped her up and spun her around.

"Uncle Sol!" Angie exclaimed as she hugged his neck and kissed him on the cheek.

Sol put her down and went around to the passenger side of the car where Eddie stood. Eddie quickly put out his hand to shake — thus avoiding one of Sol's crushing hugs.

Vernon had come over from the basement. He was only a little taller than Eddie, about 5'6". He was bald, with a fringe of grey hair in a ring above his ears and around the back of his head, it merged into a silvery beard that was well trimmed. He had a big pot belly and looked a little like Santa Claus. In spite of the heat, he wore overalls and flannel shirt. Vernon could be shy, at least around their mother. But there were other times, when he felt comfortable, he could be quite talkative with a very dry sense of humor. But with Mom present, he did not make much eye contact. Nodding, he walked over and said, "Hello folks."

"Hello Vernon," said Ellen. "It's good to see you again."

"Likewise, Mrs. Fitzgerald," Vernon said with his eyes fixed on a point on the ground six feet in front of him. After an awkward pause he said, "I gotta go back to work." He turned and headed back to the basement.

"He sometimes struggles socially," Sol said, half to himself. "But the man is a genius and knows how to make things work. He gives life to my ideas by taking care of the nuts and bolts." He gestured toward the trailer. "Come, lunch is almost ready."

"I'd love to Sol," Ellen said. "But I want to get back to the city before it gets too late."

"Of course," said Sol, not really expecting her to eat with him. He knew that she'd rather have McDonalds in the car than eat here. "Let me help you with the bags." Looking over his shoulder at the children he said, "I made spaghetti."

"Don't feed them too much carbohydrate—Angie is watching her weight," Ellen said as she hugged her children. She admonished them to call her immediately if they saw anything too weird. Eddie wondered how long it would take her to get back from Greece to save them if they did call with a problem.

Angie was glad to be at Uncle Sol's. He was a lot of fun to be around and he never lectured her about her grades or her eating. Plus, it was beautiful here. It was like a forest preserve—it even had a large pond, or was it a small lake? There was a rowboat and even a raft in the middle for swimming. Uncle Sol bought the property after his first invention, glasses that made any movie 3-D. Several inventions later, he had built a huge house full of computer equipment and a full laboratory. Angie was sad the lab was gone, she had learned so much there, but it looked like Uncle Sol was rebuilding.

Eddie and Angie hugged their mother and said their goodbyes. She waved at Uncle Sol, got into the car and drove off. Sol motioned toward the door, "Come in, we can eat soon." Then he yelled over his shoulder, "Vernon, she's gone. You want to come in and have some spaghetti?"

Angie looked at him. "Why doesn't our mother like you?" she asked.

"Oh," said Sol, "I wouldn't say that she doesn't like me. She probably wouldn't like to hang out with me for the afternoon, and she thinks I am a bad influence. But if I was in trouble, she would help. We are just very different. That is why she married my brother and not me." He chuckled.

They stepped inside with Vernon following. The trailer was large, about the size of a ranch style house. It had four bedrooms, Uncle Sol pointed out. "Sit, sit." He said to Eddie and Angie, motioning toward the table. Vernon also sat down.

He went over to the stove and put some noodles into a pot of boiling water. "So how is school going for you two?" he asked.

"I am doing well—all A's again," said Eddie.

"Of course you are. Is that your doing or is it due to your friend Virgil?" asked Sol pointedly. Eddie looked at him, wide-eyed with shock. Sol suddenly switched gears and asked, "How is the baseball going?"

"The team placed second in state, but we should win next year. I am hitting 340," said Eddie, relaxing a little. "There's a summer league near here, I was hoping to try out." His phone dinged, and he smiled and said, "Uncle Sol, is it ok if we have friends come to see us up here?"

"Of course your friends are welcome to come here. As far as baseball is concerned, your playing is very impressive. As is happens, I know one of the coaches. We have even talked about you. I am sure he will be happy to have you," said Sol. "No pitching though? I've seen you pitch; you're very good."

"Uh," said Eddie. He was busy answering a text. He finally looked up and said, "Pitchers don't play every day. I switched to left field. They let me because I hit pretty well, and I can steal bases."

"Just like Babe Ruth, except for the base stealing part, I suppose," said Sol. "He started as a pitcher, you know, when he played for the Red Sox." He turned to Angie, "How about you, Angie? How did your year go?"

"Mom was upset about her grades. Not to mention the fact that Angie just got into a little trouble," said Eddie.

"Still the little rebel, I see," said Sol as he stirred the noodles. "You can do better than that in your sleep. Take an extra 10 minutes a day out of your life and get all A's next term; they'll leave you alone. You aren't going to change anything by failing on purpose. The system is what it is."

"That is not the problem," said Angie. "I am miserable in high school. Kids are mean to me. I figure that if I fail, they will put me back in the 5th grade. Plus, my BROTHER is the reason I got into trouble." She glared at Eddie.

Sol said, "You won't get to go back to 5th grade. It's more likely that they will send you to the school shrink. They know how smart you are. Failing will get you labeled as having problems. As will getting into 'trouble'—with or without the help of your brother. I don't know what to tell you about the kids in your class, except that things do get better. You might consider going the other way, get great grades and place out of high school. I think you would like college."

Vernon saw that Sol was almost finished cooking and said, "Can you two set the table?" Eddie grabbed dishes and silverware. Angie took a large salad from the counter and got some bowls.

"It sounds like you two have had an interesting year," said Sol. "Let me tell you that Vernon and I have had a very interesting year ourselves. We started a project that puts the battery to shame."

Eddie thought that would not be hard to do, considering that they were eating in a trailer instead of the house that was destroyed by the battery. He remained silent.

Vernon nodded and said, "This is amazing—even for you, Sol. Tell them."

"Vernon and I have solved the mystery of time!" Sol exclaimed throwing his arms wide and nearly dropping the large bowl of pasta.

"Solved is putting it strongly," said Vernon. "There are still a few wrinkles." He shook his head, "Sol, you are a genius. I could never come up with the things you do, but you need to pay more attention to the details."

"Yes, yes, yes," said Sol. "But these are minor issues."

"Not so minor," corrected Vernon, "We really need to work on control."

The table was set, and Sol came over with the pasta. "Yes, you're right of course, Vernon. Besides, I have you to help with the details. The important thing is that the big problem has been solved. We have broken the barrier!" He began dishing the noodles onto plates. "Time!" exclaimed Uncle Sol, as he placed a dish of spaghetti in front of Angie, "Is like a plate of spaghetti."

"Yes, Sol, but it is of no practical use unless we figure out how to control it. We need to proceed cautiously. Also, you have to think of the noodles as being in constant motion." Vernon turned toward Angie and Eddie and said, "He doesn't even like spaghetti. He has been dying to make this point; so he made spaghetti."

"We think we're inside one straight noodle—still in the box, but that isn't so. The noodle curves and twists and touches other noodles. We are inside a twisted noodle," Sol continued excitedly. "It touches other noodles. If our noodle was hollow, AND..." He paused for emphasis, eyes wide, hands outstretched (moving like an orchestra conductor), grinning and giving a rare view of his lower lip and teeth, "...we could tunnel through to another noodle, we would end up in a different time and place! You can travel from noodle to noodle and eventually get anywhere or any time that you want to."

He went to the stove and got another a pan full of sauce and served some to Eddie. "So if I wanted to see mom and dad in Greece, I could just burrow through my noodle?" Eddie smirked.

"Or....if you wanted to go to Italy and see Leonardo da Vinci in the year 1489, you could do so," said Uncle Sol, leaning in toward Eddie, in a low conspiratorial tone. "I have built a device that will allow you to do exactly that."

"No way!" said Angie.

"Way," said Sol.

"Sol, I think you need to stress that using the device is not practical yet. We cannot control where we go or guarantee that we can return," said Vernon. Vernon then excused himself and left the trailer, saying that he would be right back.

They began eating, with Eddie making comments like, "Look, I just swallowed the Roman Empire," and, "There is some extra tomato sauce on the French Revolution." Vernon returned with two dogs, and took his place at the table. Sam and Dave were two large dogs of indeterminate breed. You could see some Labrador, some German Shepherd. Dave's snout looked like he might have some Boxer in him. He had short brown hair. Sam was almost black, with longer hair. They rushed to the table. Sol gave them each a meatball. "I know they are not to eat from the table, but the diet they're supposed to have reminds me of prison food." He patted each dog on the head as they wolfed down their prize.

"Why did you give them people names?" asked Eddie.

"Oh Vernon," said Sol. "We so need to educate these youngsters. The dogs are named for the greatest of all soul duos, Sam Moore and Dave Prater. They brought the sound of the black church to pop music. They worked with Isaac Hayes and David Porter, who produced and wrote the songs. They used Booker T. and the M.G.'s as backup musicians. They are responsible for a few of the greatest soul hits ever." He pulled a harmonica out of his pocket and played a few bars of "Hold on, I'm Comin'."

Vernon began to sing in his deep, melodic voice, with a bit of a raspy quality to it:

> Don't you ever feel sad
> Lean on me when times are bad
> When the day comes and you're down
> In a river of trouble and about to drown
> Just hold on, I'm comin'
> Hold on, I'm comin'

Sol stopped playing and looked at the children staring at him and Vernon. "Vernon, I fear our little culture lesson is lost on these two. They probably prefer rap music from Puff Daddy or Snoop Dog, or maybe some indie stuff from Green Day."

"Those guys are old," said Eddie. "I like Oomph and Wiz Khalifa."

"Don't let Mom hear you listening to Wiz Khalifa. I've heard his lyrics and she would not be pleased. Rap music is an oxymoron anyway." said Angie. "I like big band music, but your music isn't too bad, Uncle Sol."

"Big band, good grief. That's you, the hippest girl from 1937," said Eddie.

Angie said, "The '30s and '40s were the peak of American culture. What we have now is crap."

"We'll play you some recordings while you are here. It's great music. I even have some Booker T and the MGs," said Sol. "Right now I have something to show you." Uncle Sol went into another room and emerged with what looked like a large saucer hanging from a cord around his neck. "Let me present the Chrono Kinetic

Device, or CKD," Sol said proudly. "Chrono, means time. Kinetic means movement."

Angie giggled, "You look like Flavor Flav," she said.

"This is not to eat," said Sol, somewhat confused. "It has no flavor."

"No, Uncle Sol, Flavor Flav is..." Eddie began to correct him, but then thought better of it and was quiet.

Sol took the CKD from around his neck and handed it to Angie. "So we could use that to go see Leonardo da Vinci?" asked Eddie.

Uncle Sol sighed and said, "We are close. You can travel though our time 'noodle,' but pinpointing time and location has proven to be a challenge. Where and when you end up would be sort of a surprise."

"And," said Vernon pointedly, "we can't be sure of returning home. AND, Sol we don't EVER want to use the device UNTIL we do more research. Besides to go that far in both time and distance may take more than one 'jump.' Also, it is more like a plate of worms than spaghetti. The 'noodles' are in constant motion."

Angie sat in her chair, with her backpack in her lap, holding the device. She was transfixed. In spite of the thinness of the device, it looked a little like an old time television in black and white. The screen looked three dimensional. There were wavy lines of light all through it. There were bright spots where the lines intersected.

Eddie jumped up and said, "Let me see!"

"Just make sure that you don't touch the..."

Eddie reached for the CKD and placed his hand on it.

"...screen," said Uncle Sol.

There was a loud "pop" and the children disappeared. "Crap!" exclaimed Sol. "Ellen is gonna kill me."

Chapter 3
August 25, 1776

Eddie and Angie Take a Little Trip

"Oh my God! Oh my God! Ohmygodohmygodohmygodohmygod!" Angie screamed and dropped the disc. She looked around, eyes wide with panic. Then she looked at Eddie and punched him in the chest. "You moron!" she cried. "Why did you have to touch it? Now we're lost!"

They were in a forest; it was not too dense. They were at the edge of a clearing. Across the clearing, there was an encampment at the top of a hill and about a half mile to the west. Eddie dug into his pocket, got his iPhone and turned it on "Where are we?"

Angie said, "Besides, I don't think the issue is 'where we are,' the issue is 'WHEN we are'. The thing is a time machine, after all."

Eddie was frantically working the controls of the phone. "I can't get a signal," he said. "My map on the iPhone doesn't work."

"It never did," said Angie.

"Try yours," Eddie said.

"Can't," said Angie. "It's on Uncle Sol's table. Besides, I wouldn't be able to get a signal either. Look!" Angie stared up at the camp and pointed. "Oh…my…God." The camp was more like a fort. It was behind an embankment—earthworks. There were cannon and men looking out over the meadow towards them. They were wearing what looked like tricorne hats and they held long rifles. They were not modern soldiers.

Angie held the CKD and studied it. "We better take care of this. I have a feeling we are going to need it."

Eddie looked down at the iPhone, "I'm powering it down to save the battery."

"Good idea—you may want to make a call later or surf the net," Angie said sarcastically. "Maybe we can order a pizza."

"It has aps—they may come in handy," retorted Eddie.

Angie and Eddie sat in the little clearing, staring at the screen of

Uncle Sol's device. The screen did kind of look like spaghetti, if spaghetti was alive. It was full of wavy lines that pulsed and moved. Wherever two lines intersected there was a bright dot of light.

"I bet that where those lines intersect are different locations in time and space," mused Angie.

"Let's touch one and get out of here," said Eddie, reaching with his finger.

"No!" shouted Angie, turning away from him with the device. "What if we end up in the middle of a war or at the bottom of the ocean? We have no idea where or when we'll end up."

"I think we are already in a war," said Eddie. "You don't usually find that many guys camping with weapons unless there is a war, or it's deer season in Alabama."

"Yeah, but..." She never finished her sentence. A barrel of a gun pressed against her cheek.

Two men were staring down at them. One man was dressed in a full blue frock coat with what looked like officer's insignia on it. He was tall, thin, about 40, not a handsome man. He had craggy features and a large nose and rat-like eyes that were a little too close together, his face seemed to be molded into a permanent sneer. He held a pistol against Angie's cheek. The second man had sandy blonde hair and broad shoulders. He was not as tall as the man holding the pistol, and was as handsome as the other was homely. He was big, but looked very young. Angie thought he was the most beautiful human being she had ever seen. His blonde hair was tied tight in a knot at the back and blue-grey eyes. She thought he looked a little like Naill from One Direction, if Naill were a body builder. His loose jacket did little to hide his strong and powerful arms and chest. Angie just stared at him, transfixed, with her mouth open. "Hello," she mouthed.

The tall man with the pistol grabbed the backpack and the device. He eyed both items with a perplexed look on his face. It was like he just found something from Mars. He came to himself and asked, "Why are you spying on our camp?"

Angie ignored him, staring at the blonde man. "My name is Angie," she said to him, as if the other man did not exist. The blonde man just nodded and smiled. Angie blushed and became nearly as red as her hair.

"Oh, lieutenant," said the blonde haired man, "they're just children." He paused, "Very strangely dressed, I'll warrant, but children nonetheless. I don't think they can do us any harm."

"He has a kind face," Angie thought.

"Simmons, mind your place," snarled the man in the uniform. "They don't belong here and they may be up to no good." He cocked his pistol.

Eddie got up and faced him, "Yeah, right. I am James Bond the dangerous 16-year-old spy."

Angie snapped out of it. She got up and said, "Actually, he is more like Austin Powers." She wanted to say "Maxwell Smart," but figured Eddie wouldn't get the insult. "You really don't have anything to worry about from him." Where she was terrified just a few minutes ago, now she felt strangely serene. She spoke without breaking eye contact with Simmons, trying to sound confident and knowledgeable. He took her pack and they motioned for her and Eddie to go to the camp with them. They got up and began walking toward the fortification. Simmons was in front of the children and the other man was behind them.

"Will you guys just lighten up," said Eddie. "We're just lost. You wouldn't by any chance know what year it is?" The two men just looked at him strangely.

"Judging by the clothes and weapons, it's sometime between 1756 and 1783," said Angie, aside, in a low voice. "Either the American Revolution or the French and Indian War. They speak English, but are not English regulars, so they're American troops in one of the two wars. That also means we can rule out the years between 1764 and 1775. My money is on the Revolution, probably early in the war because we are in the North."

"Be quiet," growled the man in brown. "We're taking you to the General. You could be spies reporting to General Clinton about our fortifications."

"Clinton!" thought Angie. She was right, it was the early part of the Revolutionary War.

They made their way along a path toward the camp. The young man remained in front of them, and mean one behind. They were taken to a tent with two sentries in front. These men had full uniforms of the Continental army.

"Revolution," Angie whispered to Eddie.

The tent was big enough to stand up in. There were two men at a table with what looked like maps in front of them. One of the men stood. He was well over six feet tall, in a spotless blue uniform with piercing blue-grey eyes and sandy brown hair. He had the largest hands and feet she had ever seen.

"Oh my God," thought Angie. "It's George Washington."

He was tall. He stood erect and looked strong—regal, almost.

His face was slightly pock-marked. Angie remembered reading that he had once had smallpox. He was not the old man that was in the Gilbert Stuart portrait, but he did have the same tight-lipped look. She was suddenly disappointed in the artist. Gilbert Stuart did not capture the sense of the man at all. This man was majestic, aristocratic. He was huge. He commanded respect by his very presence. Gilbert Stuart made him look like someone's grandmother.

The angry, ugly man in the blue coat spoke, "Sir, we caught these two spying outside the camp." He handed Washington Angie's backpack and the CKD. "They were carrying these."

Washington opened the backpack. He took out the open bag of Doritos, sniffed them and made a face. He put them back. He took out a couple of Twix bars and studied the package. He put them back. He rummaged through the back, saying nothing. He held up the disc, studying it for a moment. He put it in the backpack and placed the backpack down on the ground.

Washington looked up and Angie thought that she saw a glint of recognition in his eyes. He spoke, with minimal lip movement and not showing his teeth; although his lips did curl slightly upward into a smile. "I am sure you are right, Lieutenant Collins. It seems like the Red Coats are recruiting them young these days," he said. Pausing and looking back and forth between Eddie and Angie in an appraising manner, he continued, "And... dressing them strangely."

Angie watched him speak. The lack of lip movement was a little strange, but then she remembered that Washington had always had trouble with his teeth.

Eddie stepped forward. "General Washington," he began (Angie was a little surprised that he had figured out who it was), "we're just lost. We came upon your camp by accident."

"Where are you from?" asked the general.

"Chicago," said Eddie. "But you probably know it as Fort Dearborn. Chicago is a Native American word. I think it means 'onion'."

"Eddie," Angie said in a harsh whisper, "Fort Dearborn won't be there for another 30 years, and he has no idea what a 'Native American' is—they're Indians to him." When Washington's steely gaze fell on her she became quiet.

"Er... um, I might have the name wrong. We live on the frontier. Fort Pitt," Eddie remembered that was an actual settlement in Colonial times. "We saw a *deer born* there—at the fort. We fed it onions." he said, trying to cover up his slip of the tongue.

"Then WHAT, in Heaven's name are you two children doing on

Long Island?"

"SUPPLIES! Yes, that's it. My dad came for supplies and brought us."

General looked at him and frowned, "400 miles to get supplies?"

Angie noticed two things: Eddie was getting more confident and General Washington wasn't buying it. She started to get very nervous. Eddie was usually much better at lying than this.

"It's my birthday, you see," Eddie continued. "My dad was taking us to the city.... for my birthday. We figured we could load up on supplies."

Angie wished he would shut up. What would that trip take these days? Two weeks? A month? Who travels for a month for their kid's birthday? Not to mention how they were dressed. Eddie was wearing a red Chicago Bulls tee shirt and jeans. His Nikes must look like they came from another planet to these people. Her top was a bit plainer than his tee shirt, but she wore running shoes and jeans as well. Even the fact that she was a girl wearing pants was unusual. They must really look strange to 18th century eyes. Saying they were "not from around here" didn't begin to cover it. Trying to sell the idea that they were on a shopping trip from Pittsburgh was simply ridiculous.

"Eddie," she hissed.

Eddie, on the other hand, was feeling confident and that he was doing really well—thinking on his feet and giving them a plausible story. "We're here for a week, but we got separated from our dad. He must be worried sick. We should go so he can find us." He looked at General Washington hopefully.

Washington turned his head toward Angie. His gaze burned into her. "Who are you and where do you come from?" he said in a sterner, slightly louder tone.

Angie gulped and stared down at the ground. She was frightened. She stammered in a voice that was almost inaudible, "M..M...M... Mr. President... I... I... I can tell you everything, but just you. You have to have everyone else leave the tent."

"Sir! That is not acceptable," protested Lieutenant Collins. "At least keep a guard."

Washington made what could have passed for a smile and said, "Two unarmed children, Collins? It could be a bit dicey, but I think I can take care of myself. Would you gentlemen give us a few minutes alone."

The men left the tent and Eddie and Angie were alone with the

General. "Now," he said, "Who are you two and where did you come from?"

"Fort Pitt," said Eddie.

"Stop it, Eddie," Angie hissed. "He's not buying it."

Outside of the tent, Lieutenant Collins turned to his colleagues and said, "Well gents, I am off to write to my girl."

"Write big—she must have poor eyesight if she is taken with the likes of you," one of the men said, laughing.

Collins held his temper and shared the laugh with the men, and traded an insult. "You could never be with her, even with poor eyesight, your stupidity would be obvious to her." His joke fell flat, but he did not notice. He parted company with the other men, laughing as he walked away. He moved up the mud path, past the next four tents. Looking over his shoulder, he ducked between the tents. He got on his belly and crawled to the back of Washington's tent. He lay very still, listening.

Angie sat down in one of the chairs vacated by the officers. "I am afraid that what Eddie was telling you may be a little easier to believe than the truth. If you look at how we are dressed, you know that something is very different about us. What I am about to say will sound impossible, but I promise you that I can prove what I am saying."

Washington nodded, watching her intently. Eddie sat down, astounded that she was going to tell him the truth. He wondered if they had insane asylums in the Colonies yet. They may get to see the inside of one.

"We're from the future; more precisely, 238 years in the future." She cringed a little, waiting for him to scoff at her. He just sat there, watching her intently. She continued, "Our uncle invented a time machine, but it doesn't exactly work right. My idiot brother triggered the mechanism by accident and it placed us just outside your camp, but we really cannot control it. We don't know how to get home." She paused, looking for a reaction from the general. He knit his brows slightly, but gave no indication of whether he believed her or not. She continued, "If you let me show you something, I can prove it to you."

Washington nodded. She retrieved the iPhone from Eddie and turned it on. "With this device I can call or send a message to anyone with a similar device. I can look through something called the internet, which contains millions of pages of information. I can't do any of that here, of course, but I can show you other things on the device and you will see that it clearly is from a different time."

She held out the phone to show him. She tapped the icon for Angry Birds. "This is a game where you launch birds so they can knock down pigs. The idea is that the birds are angry at the pigs, so they knock them down." She launched a bird and knocked down a stack of pigs.

Washington chuckled as the pigs fell down. Angie said, "You have to know that such a device could not possibly exist UNLESS it was from the future. Come here and move your head close to mine." Washington obliged her. Angie held up the iPhone and took a selfie of the two of them, showing the results to the general. "See, it takes pictures," she said.

Washington chuckled and nodded. "Surely not even English industry could produce such a device. If you are from the future, you know how our fight for freedom turns out."

Angie said, "Oh, you win. It is a long war—it goes until 1783. It's our longest war until President Bush gets us into Afghanistan, unless you count Vietnam." She held up her hand, "Don't ask about Vietnam... What is today's date?"

"August 25, 1776," replied Washington.

"Things are going to get bad for a while," said Angie. "Really bad. Congress is going to doubt you. General Lee is going to try to get your job. You really just get your butt kicked until later this winter. The battle for Long Island is a disastrous defeat. But don't worry. It gets better. For now, the British have put a lot of troops on Long Island—20,000, I believe. They got here during an earlier storm. It is going to rain a lot this week. A big storm on the 29th, I think. That one is important, it will allow you to escape the island, in spite of the British navy. In the fog and rain you gather everything that floats and move your army across the East River." She paused and looked off in the distance, concentrating. "You will be lucky to escape Long Island. Nothing goes right until Christmas when you cross the Delaware at Trenton and launch a surprise attack on a bunch of Hessians on Christmas Eve."

Washington nodded, "I have no doubt that we will have trouble standing against the British here. Congress, in its infinite wisdom, insists that I defend an island against an enemy with the most powerful navy in the world."

Angie said, "Don't feel bad, Congress doesn't get any smarter—even in our day."

Eddie said, "You sound like dad."

Washington said, "Thank you for your information, it is very precise."

Angie and Eddie looked at him, eyes wide and mouths open. "You believe HER, and you didn't think we were from Fort Pitt?" asked Eddie incredulously.

"Let's just say that I don't disbelieve her," Washington said.

"Look at us, Eddie," Angie said with exasperation. "We don't look like we're from the 18th century. What other explanation is there?"

Washington nodded in agreement and said cryptically, "There is another reason that your story could be true, and we should spend some time sharing information. As you can see, I am a little tied up right now, but we should dine together in a couple of days."

They stopped talking when they heard a gunshot.

Chapter 4
June 6, 2014

Sol and Vernon Panic, but Come up with a Plan

"Sol, how close are we to having completed the other prototype?" asked Vernon with a little panic in his voice.

"It's done," Sol said, "But that isn't going to be much help. First of all, we don't know where they went. Second of all, we really haven't figured out how to control where we'll end up. The best we can hope for is to randomly go back in time and hope we run into them. Of all of the infinite possibilities of time and place, you'd have a better chance of spitting out the back door and hitting the moon. Even if we found them, we wouldn't know for sure how to get back here, so we'd just be lost together. This is shaping up to be quite the challenge."

"Challenge?" said Vernon. "You lost your nephew and your niece."

"I know, I know. We will just have to find them," said Sol. "Either that or relocate ourselves into another time to avoid the wrath of my sister-in-law."

"It's not completely hopeless," said Vernon. "They are pretty smart kids. They may figure out how to choose their destination."

"The key is for us to develop some control," said Sol. "We may not be able to find them, but we could leave clues to help them."

"We are close to developing control," said Vernon. "But what you are suggesting is to leave the equivalent of missing kid milk cartons over the span of—I'm guessing—a couple of centuries."

"Not as crazy as it sounds," said Sol. "If I know Angie, she is quite the history buff and will seek out notable figures—especially if she can meet them before they become famous. If we come within a couple of decades of where they end up, and we leave clues with the right people, we have a real shot at getting them home. Also, an individual could be in possession of the notes for decades, but still meet the children within days of their departure."

Sol and Vernon went out to the barn, which was about 50 feet from the trailer. It had been outfitted it as a temporary lab. They set up their work. They put other prototype was on the workbench next to a computer, and attached it to its USB port. Next to the computer they placed a pile of pebbles; each of the pebbles had a number on it written with a yellow Sharpie. Vernon stared at the screen working the keyboard. Sol was next to him making notes on a legal pad.

"All we need is one to show up near here, and I can mark it," said Vernon. "If we can find something close to 'here and now' on the screen, we can color code the spot. I think blue would be a nice color for the spot. Then, no matter when or where you are, you can get back to here and now by simply touching the blue spot. Well, not exactly now. If we spend a day away and touch the blue spot, we would arrive tomorrow. Time will still progress linearly from the time we leave. The point is, we can always get home." He placed a pebble on the screen and it disappeared. They looked around the lab... nothing. "You should hear a 'pop' if it lands near here. Good thing it makes a noise, otherwise it could land in a far corner of the barn and we would not know it."

Sol set up a couple of video cameras to record all of the activity on the two screens. "We should have been doing this months ago. If we could map the CKD the children would not be lost. Focusing on rebuilding the house was not a good idea."

"The house had to be completed in the warm weather. Besides, we were not planning on using the device until it was properly mapped. Eddie was just a bit impulsive—you couldn't have predicted what happened," said Vernon. He reached out and placed another pebble on the screen. They both looked around the barn and listened. Nothing.

"I should have known" said Sol. "The boy is a bundle of untapped energy. Even when he was little he was into everything. I really should have kept it out of reach. It's just that I was too excited and wanted to show off my new 'toy'. I never thought of the consequences of him setting off the device."

"It's who you are, Sol, but we may be in better shape than you think."

"Even if we succeed in mapping the device, we have no idea where they ended up," said Sol dejectedly. " The good news is that I don't think you can go very far in a single jump. They would not be in the Middle Ages, for example. Also, I think that the location on the screen helps us to narrow down the time and place of the jump. Eddie touched the lower right quadrant of the device when they disappeared. I saw it".

"Exactly, that gives us some hope. I saw him touch the screen as well. Narrowing it down to at least a couple centuries can be helpful," said Vernon as he placed another pebble on the screen. It disappeared. He listened.... nothing.

"We may even be able to do a little better than that," said Sol, deep in thought.

Sol and Vernon were in the barn. It was getting close to midnight. The pile of pebbles had been reduced to a mere handful, with four digit numbers emblazoned on them in yellow magic marker.

Vernon said, "Let's finish this pile and turn in."

Sol said, "We have to get going and find them."

Vernon placed another pebble on the screen. It disappeared. There was a very distinctive "pop" in a far corner of the barn. "I got it!" exclaimed Vernon. "We are within 20 feet of 'home'. Good enough" He began working controls on the device. He turned toward Sol, "Go make sure that that is our pebble."

Sol went to the corner of the barn, "Yes. It is pebble number 1445!"

Vernon said, "That is our 'home'. No matter where we go, we can get to that corner of the barn." He punched some keys on the back of the device. "It is permanently marked."

"Thank God!" said Sol, "Now we can start looking for them."

Sol went back into the trailer and got a duffle bag. In it he placed some power bars, a Swiss army knife, a flashlight, some gold coins and a pistol. He went back to the barn where Vernon was working. He sat in front of a computer screen and the time machine. "I remember the pattern on the screen when Eddie touched it," said Vernon.

"Of course," said Sol. Vernon remembered everything, down to the last detail.

"The pattern on the CKD looks random, but it really isn't," said Vernon.

"I know," said Sol. "Given enough time, I suppose we could get good at predicting where we end up."

Vernon continued, "Our here and now is very close to some specific times and places in history. I think I can get us to within 100 years and a few hundred miles from where they landed. Actually, there is a limit to how far back you can go and how far away. It's like your spaghetti metaphor. If you want to get to noodles far away from where your noodle is, you have to make several 'jumps.'

If your noodle is in the middle of the plate, it might not be touching any noodles toward the edge. You can get to the edge of the plate by going from noodle to noodle. That can work to our advantage, if they don't keep traveling through time and move farther away. That is unlikely, because it will really take effort to move a great distance or to go very far back in time."

"Makes sense; I hadn't thought of those issues since forming the original theory. Do you have an idea of where they are?" asked Sol.

"I'm not sure," said Vernon. "We need go there and find out. But, if I had to guess, it would be the end of the 18th century. Once we land there, we will know that we are within 1000 miles of their location and plus or minus 100 years from their time."

"We'll never run into them. The odds are too high," said Sol.

"Yeah, but we can leave messages. Maybe we will get lucky," said Vernon.

"Leave messages," snorted Sol, "As you said, it's like putting their pictures on milk cartons throughout the ages. Not a great strategy, but the best we can come up with, I suppose. I am worried that we might change history."

"You saw *Back to the Future* too many times," chided Vernon. "We have already told the people we are going to speak to. We aren't going to 'change' anything. Anything we do in the past has already happened."

Vernon looked into the bag Sol had packed, "We'll need some other stuff. Warmer clothes, maybe a hunting knife and water. We don't want to have to come running home because we are hungry, thirsty or cold. Plus, I need to complete a set of notes so we can take them with us. The notes will take some time."

"I have some pictures of them on the hard drive," said Sol. "We should print some so that we can show them to people."

"We should print lots of them, so we can leave them with people," said Vernon. "The gold coins were a good idea. We may need money."

Chapter 5
August 25, 1776

A Traitor in Washington's Camp

Outside of the tent, Lieutenant Collins was listening so intently, he did not hear Simmons come upon him. "Lieutenant, what are you doing down there?" he asked. Collins panicked—there was too much to explain. He cocked the gun under his belly as he rose. Surprisingly, Simmons was just staring at him with a puzzled look. His weapon was not at the ready. In fact, he didn't seem to suspect anything. Collins got up and pointed the gun at Simmons. "I don't want to hurt you, private," Collins said. "Let's just take a little walk away from all of these tents."

"You're a spy!" exclaimed Simmons.

"Quick as ever, Billy. You have a wonderful grasp of the obvious. Think of me as an English subject, loyal to my king. A very well-paid English subject," said the lieutenant.

At that moment, Simmons lunged at him. The gun went off. Simmons fell. "Idiot!" said Collins. "I was just going to tie you up and get away." There was commotion in the camp; he ran off into the woods.

They all ran outside. Eddie got there first; he was the fastest. He saw Private Simmons lying on the ground, bleeding from his upper thigh. Eddie took off his T shirt and pressed it against the wound. Simmons sat up, "He'll get away!"

"Lie still!" said Eddie. "You're bleeding." At that moment he was really glad his mother made him take that Red Cross course, although he was pretty put out about giving up a Saturday afternoon when he took the class. Seconds later, Angie got there with Washington and some others. She saw the blood and promptly passed out.

"What's happened?" demanded Washington.

"Collins is a spy. He shot me," Simmons said, wincing in pain.

Some men carried Simmons to the surgeon's tent, with Eddie walking along, putting pressure on the wounded leg. A large sergeant carried Angie back to Washington's tent.

Lieutenant Collins made his way to the East River. He cut across orchards and forest and made his way about a mile upriver of Washington's camp. He had hidden a boat there. He decided to travel away from the camp by water for a little ways and wait for the excitement to blow over.

Was what those children said true? Washington certainly believed it. They were dressed like nothing he'd ever seen. The boy wore a garment that was decorated like an artist's canvas, or printed like a lithograph in a book. It had a drawing of a bull, looking red and angry. The boy said they were from Chicago; it was a strange strange word that was written on his shirt and the word "Bulls". And the shoes! What strange multi-colored ornaments they were. They were not made of leather. It was impossible to say what they were made of. Again printing, like on the shirt. They had the word "Nike," whatever that was. Maybe it was in a foreign tongue, like the long word "Chicago" on the boy's shirt. The girl said they were from the future, then she proceeded to tell about the coming battles. Washington believed her; he really believed her. He is a smart man, maybe he was right to believe her. If the children were from the future, they would know about every battle plan the Americans would have. If he could capture those children, the British would know about the battle plans even before the Americans knew. Those children had enough information to put an end the rebellion. What would THAT be worth to General Clinton?

He found his boat in some bushes. He paddled away, thinking about his future good fortune. Perhaps he should not be in such a hurry to escape to the British lines. He decided to stay nearby, just going upriver far enough to avoid any rebel patrols.

***

Eddie went back to the tent Angie had been taken to. General Washington was not to be seen. He had the search for Collins and preparation for tomorrow's battle to deal with. Two children were pretty far down the list of his priorities. When Eddie entered the tent, Angie was sitting up. She was looking a little green, but seemed ok.

Angie's revelations to General Washington shocked Eddie. After he made sure that she was alright, he said, "I don't think we should be telling people about the future, Angie, what if we change something?"

Angie was starting to come around; she admonished him, "Do

you think we're going to disappear, like in *Back to the Future*? Look at your school ID and see if you are fading." She laughed. "If we're here now, it means that we always were part of this history. We can't change anything."

He knew she was feeling better because her sarcasm had returned. "I don't know if you can be so sure," Eddie said. He shrugged, the cat was out of the bag anyway, so he gave up on arguing. They had told the general a great deal about the future. If they were going to disappear, they would be gone by now. "All I know is that we have to get home."

"Quite frankly, I kind of like it here," said Angie. "We could stay. The air and water is clean. We could meet all of the Founding Fathers. This is a very exciting time to be alive."

"Are you out of your mind?" yelled Eddie. "Forget the fact that there is no TV, movies or internet. There is no running water. You have to dig a hole to go to the bathroom. Not to mention that we're in the middle of a war."

"Funny," said Angie. "Even with the war coming, I feel safer here than I do in our own time. The war will happen in very specific places so we can avoid it. Also, there is no pressure to succeed, no pollution, weapons of mass destruction or reality TV. Everything is so lush and green. Not to mention that we get to watch, in person, the birth of our nation."

"That's crazy talk. You'll change your tune when you run out of Cheetos," Eddie said. He looked at his bloody clothes and changed the subject. "I wish I had a change of clothes," he said.

"I wouldn't mind wearing something a little more contemporary," Angie said.

As if on cue, a woman entered the tent holding a bundle. She was a young woman in a long blue dress, with brown hair and brown eyes. She nodded a greeting and said, "I was told that you two may be in need of fresh clothes." She looked at Eddie, "No doubt that you need them, young man." She dropped the bundle on a cot and left the tent. Apparently, General Washington thought it best that they blend in with the rest of the people in the 18th century. There was a pair of trousers and a white shirt that fit Eddie pretty well. Angie received a long dress that was a greenish color. It also fit pretty well.

After a few minutes the woman entered the tent to see how Eddie and Angie were doing. There was some difficulty in finding shoes that fit, so they still wore their Nikes. Other than that, they looked like Colonial children. She nodded approvingly at her handiwork, gathered up the old clothes and left the tent.

Chapter 6
August 26, 1776

Eddie and Angie Leave Camp

The next morning, Angie wanted to see how Simmons was doing. She and Eddie found the surgeon's tent. When they entered, they saw the doctor, who had a serious look on his face, dabbing Simmons's forehead with a damp towel. The doctor looked up at them and said, "Fever."

"Of course he has a fever," Angie exclaimed. "You don't sterilize anything." The doctor just looked at her quizzically. She reached into her backpack and pulled out a bottle of pills. "I get ear infections," she said. "My mother stocks up on these for me." She brandished the pills for the doctor to see. He just stared at her, not comprehending what she was talking about.

"It's bacteria. You have to kill it. Give him these pills and clean that wound," she said with authority. "Wash the wound with alcohol—kill the bacteria."

"It's bad humors," said the doctor. "We're going to have to bleed him."

"That's crazy," cried Angie. "He's already bled a great deal. You're going to kill him... Eddie, tell him."

Eddie leaned in toward the doctor and said, "We're from the future. We know the secret of disease. Those pills will clean up the humors without bleeding. Ask the General." He continued, "They work when you clean the wound with alcohol. Clean his wound with whiskey and cut away the dead tissue. Make sure you wash your hands in the whiskey before you touch his leg—and wash them EVERY time. In our time, we learned how to truly get rid of bad humors."

He said this with so much authority, the doctor began to follow his instructions. Angie gave Simmons one of her pills and a glass of water. Eddie said, "You have to give him one of these twice each day, or he will DIE!"

Angie whispered to Eddie, "Humors?! Tell him about the bacteria."

Eddie whispered back, "He won't get it, Angie. We can't change his way of thinking, but he might accept that we know a better way to deal with humors, but by the time you explain bacteria to him and then convince him that the concept is valid, Simmons will be dead. We just need to tell General Washington to make sure the doctor follows our instructions."

"Tell Washington. Ironic, since some quack will bleed him the night he dies," murmured Angie. She patted Simmons's shoulder and made eye contact and smiled reassuringly. "You will get better," she sighed to him. She stood there for a minute, just looking at him, transfixed. Then she turned to the doctor and said, "Make sure he takes those pills."

"And you want to stay here in the 18th century?" said Eddie. "You may get killed by a doctor."

"A bit further into the future would be nice," said Angie. "But I still prefer it to the 21st century."

"We got bigger problems," Eddie said. "General Clinton is already on Long Island and we are about to be in the middle of a war. We need to find a boat and get off of the island. You said it yourself—August 27th, right?"

"We can't leave them. Maybe we can help," said Angie.

"Help what? You gonna pick up a musket and defend your country? You said yourself that the Americans get their butts handed to them, and we can't change anything."

"We can't travel alone. What if we get lost?" protested Angie.

"We'll figure it out. We can always ask for help. We're two lost children—people will help us. We can't stay here; we could easily become collateral damage."

The doctor was looking at them, listening. "You're about to get really busy," said Eddie, looking over at him.

"Eddie, that's terrible," said Angie.

"It's the truth," said Eddie. "We need to get moving."

"We could cross the East River to Manhattan," said Angie. "That's what Washington will do. We absolutely need to talk to him after the battle. He knows something about us, I am sure of it."

Angie bent close to Simmons, "Goodbye Private Simmons." She kissed him on the cheek and stared at him for a minute. She turned toward the doctor and said, "Give him the pills and clean the wound. General Washington's orders." She picked up her backpack and she and Eddie left the tent.

"Let's just make our way along the shore. Maybe we'll get lucky," Eddie said.

Eddie and Angie made their way down to the river. "Can we stop a minute? I'm tired," Angie complained.

"Jeez, Angie," said Eddie. "We've been walking for 10 minutes. How do you let yourself get like this? You really need to lay off of the Doritos and exercise more."

"You're always so critical of me," Angie protested.

"And you are critical of almost everyone and everything," Eddie countered. "Besides, you SHOULD take better care of yourself. It's not just about looks; you could get diabetes or something. Let's go along the shore, maybe we will find ourselves a boat."

"Eddie, we can't steal someone's boat. What if they need it?" she said, not liking this course of action at all.

"You said to cross the East River; how did you think we would do that? Don't worry, we'll leave it on the other shore. They'll find it. Besides, once the British start shooting, everyone around here will have a lot more to worry about than a lousy boat."

They stepped into a clearing that was slightly elevated. Eddie pointed. "Look! There's the river." He began running down the hill toward the water.

"Waaaaait," Angie moaned.

In a couple of minutes Eddie was standing on the shoreline. A few minutes later an out of breath Angie joined him. "Don't ever do that again. What if we get separated?"

"Lighten up, Angie," he said. "It's not like I was out of your sight. You really gotta take better care of yourself." His eyes scanned the shoreline. "There!" he exclaimed.

About 50 yards upriver from them, partially hidden near a tree and some bushes that extended into the water, was a small rowboat. "Come on, Angie," cried Eddie, running toward the boat. Angie gave a resigned sigh and trudged along after him.

An attempt had been made to hide the boat. Eddie cleared away brush and prepared to launch the boat. Angie approached. He looked up and saw a startled look of fear on her face. "Eddie!" he heard her scream. Then everything went black.

***

General George Washington was in the surgeon's tent, looking in on an already improving Simmons. "Yes doctor, I know it is unusual, but keep doing what they told you. These children...um.... know things. Where are they?"

"Gone," said the doctor.

There was a look of disappointment on Washington's face. "Where?"

"Dunno," said the doctor. "The young man was concerned about the upcoming battle. He wanted to leave. He convinced the young lady and they left camp."

"Wisely so, I suppose," said the General. "The British are on the island. They came over right after the storm on the 21st... just as the girl observed. Still, I hoped to speak with that little girl before the battle. I have some information that I should have shared with her. I thought I'd have time."

"I believe they were going to cross the river," said the doctor.

"She says that's what we should do. She may have a point," said the General.

He looked down at Simmons. "Private, it looks like you might not be doing much fighting for a while," he said. "I may have a little mission for you once you are able to walk." He put his hand on Simmons' head, "Doctor, I believe that the fever has broken."

Chapter 7
August 26-27, 1776

General Clinton's Camp

Eddie awoke. It was evening. He went to scratch his nose and noticed that his hands were tied. He was seated next to Angie on the floor of a tent. Angie was looking at him. She whispered, "Sorry, I tried to warn you but Collins moved so fast."

"Collins?" whispered Eddie.

"Yeah," whispered Angie. "He's working for the British. Simmons caught him doing something and that is why he got shot. I think that was his boat we were trying take. He hit you over the head and grabbed me; now we are with the British in General Clinton's tent."

Eddie looked over and saw Collins talking to a man in a British uniform. He was not overly tall. His narrow shoulders and the beginnings of a middle-aged paunch belied the boyish look he had. His eyes were a soft brown, but had an edge to them. He had an aristocratic bearing and an air of authority that would be present even without the resplendent red uniform that he wore. This was General Clinton.

He spoke to Collins, "So you would have me believe that these children are from the future. That they know the strategies and outcomes of the battles. It's preposterous."

"Washington believes it, sir," countered Collins. "They told him you would win the battle. They knew of other engagements."

"Hardly evidence of any foresight," sniffed Clinton. "We will rout that rabble and we will finish them when their backs are to the river and they can't escape. I don't need a fortune teller to tell me that."

"Look at their shoes," said Collins. "Have you ever seen anything like those?"

"Yes, yes, yes.... their shoes are ridiculous looking. Clearly that means that they have traveled through time to confound us."

"They told Washington that the rebels win the war."

"Well then, there you have it. The Rebel army—the one that

breaks and runs at the sight of bayonets, the undisciplined mob will defeat His Majesty's finest troops. How could I doubt the psychic ability of these two?" he said sarcastically. "These are daft little insane children with insane shoes. And you are as daft as they are. Get out of my sight."

Collins hastily left the tent. General Clinton walked over to where the children were tied up. "So, what am I to do with you. You have seen the camp and know our strengths. I believe I will keep you here until after the battle. Then you can go back to wherever it is you came from."

"Fort Pitt," said Eddie.

Angie rolled her eyes. The General looked at her and said, "Let's say I humor you and assume you are from the future and you know about the battle. What could you tell me?"

Angie said, "You are going to outflank Washington. Jamaica Pass is not defended. You will split your forces, with the larger portion going through the pass. A small force will keep the Americans occupied at their strongly defended position. While the bulk of your force circles around behind them."

General Clinton stared at the girl in amazement, "Yes, that was the plan, but General Howe turned it down. The plan is too 'German,' cleaver tactics that are wasted on the ignorant rebels."

"He'll change his mind," said Angie.

"I see," Clinton snorted a laugh. He turned his attention to a map on a nearby table, and spoke quietly to one of his officers.

"How do you know this stuff?" whispered Eddie.

"You don't know because it wasn't on the test. You learned about Bunker Hill, not Long Island. Uncle Sol says our educational system has dialed down its expectations to having the students sit still and stay off of drugs. He says they used to teach Latin in high school, now they teach remedial English in college. The little bit of effort you put in actually makes you stand out. I actually like knowing stuff," Angie whispered. "Clinton wins, but misses the chance to wipe out the Continental army. He waits, and Washington escapes with his army."

"He could have wiped out Washington's army?" Eddie whispered.

"Easily," said Angie. "It was like Dunkirk, the Germans hesitated and the English escaped. The same thing happens here."

"What's Dunkirk?"

"You'll find out when they test you on it."

"So you're saying that Clinton wins, but doesn't press his advantage and Washington gets away?"

"Yeah, so we can't let them know that."

Just then a soldier entered the tent and handed a dispatch to the General. He read it and stared wide-eyed at Angie. "It would seem that we are going through Jamaica Pass," he said.

"Nice going, Angie," Eddie whispered to her.

"It doesn't matter," said Angie. "This is what happens. We haven't betrayed Washington. It was going to happen anyway."

"Not that, you moron," whispered Eddie. "They were going to let us go. You had to show off and now we are vital to the British war effort. Nice going."

General Clinton looked down at the children. "I think we should spend some time getting to know one another," he said with a smile.

He turned to one of his staff, "Get Collins in here."

Collins came into the tent. "Yes sir," he said to General Clinton.

"Collins, there may be something to that fanciful tale you told us earlier. So I am going to have you stay here and keep an eye on these children. I wish to question them once I have dispatched Washington and the rebel army." He turned to one of his staff, "We move within the hour."

Eddie stood up. "Be careful. It's a trap."

"What is a trap?" asked Clinton.

"You rout the army, but be careful after the battle when Washington's back is to the river. He will have a little surprise for you."

"What kind of surprise?"

"I am not sure; we didn't cover it in school. All I can say is be cautious after the battle."

"And why would you tell me this?"

"I like England. Actually, most Americans living in my time like England. We're sorry the whole revolution thing happened. England totally wins, but it is a black spot on our history. You can put it away right now, but don't get cocky and make sure that you watch out for Washington's counter attack. Wait for reinforcements."

Angie saw what Eddie was trying to do and figured that it couldn't hurt. She said, "Yeah, remember Bunker Hill. Charging a fortified position is dangerous, don't you think? You guys won at Bunker Hill, but it was costly."

General Clinton knit his brow, "We will discuss this after the battle."

Angie and Eddie looked at each other and smiled. They didn't know if what they said had any effect, or if Clinton would still have hesitated and let the Americans escape if they did not say what they said. But they felt as though they had just helped General Washington and the Americans. It was getting late. Angie knew that General Clinton would move out of camp around midnight. The battle would start tomorrow. Rain and fog on the 28th and 29th would take the British navy out of play and the Americans would escape across the East River.

Chapter 8
Early Morning June 7, 2014 and Other Dates

Sol and Vernon Begin the Search

Vernon and Sol had been working through the evening putting together a package of notes, calculations and instructions that could be left for the children, should the occasion present itself. They now had two duffel bags, crammed with clothes, tradable items, survival gear, food and even some weapons. Sol owned a pair of Smith and Wesson revolvers. One was a hammerless .38, the other was a .44 magnum. Sol, oddly enough, was a Dirty Harry fan. Vernon had a small .38 strapped to his ankle as well. They were not violent men, but having protection at hand seemed like a good idea.

They linked arms and Vernon touched one of the spots that was in the lower right quadrant of the device. There was a "pop" and the barn was empty.

They appeared in a surreal scene. It was night time. There were fires burning all around. There was the sound of screaming and gunfire. A bullet actually hit Sol's duffel. He turned to the right and saw a man in feathers and face paint hurtling towards him with a small ax raised. Before he could react, Vernon touched the screen, there was a loud "pop" and the man with the ax fell on his face after lunging at the strange men who were no longer there.

They were back in the barn. "Oh, thank God, Vernon," said Sol. "Another few seconds and that fellow would have split my head open."

"It *is* an imperfect system," said Vernon.

Sol examined the spot on the duffel where the bullet entered. It had passed through a jar of peanut butter and lodged into a jean jacket. Nothing else was seriously damaged. He set about to cleaning the mess. When he finished cleaning out the duffel. He got an old time tire patch and fixed the hole. He put his index finger in his mouth and licked a dab of peanut butter off of it. "Now what, Vernon?" he asked.

"I guess we try again," said Vernon. "Odds are that we are going to end up in several inappropriate places. We have no choice."

"You're right, we have to keep trying. Besides, I think I would rather have my skull caved in by a savage with an ax than to face Ellen's wrath when she finds out what happened."

They linked arms and Vernon touched a bright spot in the lower right hand corner of the screen. There was a loud "pop" and they were gone.

They were on the deck of a ship. It was very cold outside. Sol said to Vernon, "This ship is tilted toward the bow. Something is not right." There was commotion, people shouting, people running, and boats being lowered into the water. A band was playing on one of the upper decks. Vernon grabbed one of the circular life preservers and showed it to Sol. It said "Titanic."

Vernon touched the spot for home on the screen. There was a loud "pop" and they were back in the barn. "0 for 2," said Sol sadly.

Sol was discouraged. Two attempts not only did not yield any results, both had put him and Vernon into harm's way. "This isn't going very well," he said.

"Eventually we will get somewhere useful," Vernon said. "What concerns me is that my calculations are way off. I figured we could get within 100 years of where they ended up, but clearly the time span is over 100 years. That last stop was in 1912, I still can't figure out how we ended up there. The first stop was somewhere between the mid-18th century and the early 19th century. I need to go over my notes. From what I know so far, the 18th century is still our best bet."

"I will feel better if we give it another try," said Sol. "Third time is a charm." His old exuberance was coming back. "We have valuable information for them. We just need to get it into their hands."

"If I take a day or two, we could provide them with better information," Vernon protested. "I think I am on the verge of being able to come up with a rough estimate of the time and place of our arrival."

"Come on," Sol said, "One more. We can't do any worse, and time is a-wasting." He clapped Vernon on the shoulder.

"The amount of time we spend on this end does not matter," Vernon explained. "Even if we make contact next month, we may arrive at a time that is only days or even minutes after their initial arrival. What matters is when we arrive, not when we leave."

"It's late and you won't be able to accomplish much without some rest; let's try one more. Besides, the amount of time on this end DOES matter. We have to find them before my brother and his wife get back from Greece," Sol insisted.

"Very well," said Vernon. They linked arms and there was a loud "pop" and the barn was empty.

Chapter 9
August 27, 1776

Eddie and Angie Leave General Clinton's Camp

The British army was on the move. Eddie and Angie were alone in the command tent with Collins. It was late.

"You told Washington that the rebels would win the war. You went into great detail," said Collins.

"We can say whatever we want," said Eddie, "Because we know what happens and you don't. What do you care anyway? You're just a mercenary out for a buck."

"I get paid for *good* information. That stuff you told the General was nonsense."

"Was it?" said Eddie. "How would you know? Maybe we were lying to Washington and telling the truth to Clinton. If you think I am wrong, why not switch sides and be on the winning side?"

"The Americans don't pay. The British do."

"We could escape, then you wouldn't get paid."

"Hah! I'd like to see you try," Collins pulled his pistol halfway out of his belt and gave them a menacing look.

"Well, if you'd like to see me try, I'll have to oblige you." Eddie stood up and showed Collins that his hands were no longer bound. He looked at each hand and made a surprised look. "Can't shoot us, Collins. The General wouldn't like that."

Collins began to move toward Eddie. He didn't get very far. In front of Eddie, on the desk, was a crystal ink well. It was a heavy glass thing, about the size of a baseball. Eddie picked it up and threw it at Collins with all of his might. It was outside the strike zone because it caught Collins in the center of the forehead. Ink gushed all over and Collins went down, with surprisingly little sound. Eddie went over and untied Angie. "They didn't tie the ropes very tight," he said. "After all, we're just kids."

"How are we going to get out?" she said. "There are still sentries and family members in the camp."

"They bring their family members to war?" Eddie asked incredulously as he cut a small hole in the back of the tent. "There is one more row of tents behind this one. If we can dash across to them and get between them, we can sneak out through the woods." He cut a slit large enough for them to go through. Angie gathered up her back pack and the disc. "I'll hold it open and you just run to the other side. I'll be right behind you."

Eddie cut the tent and peered through the hole. It was clear. Angie shot across to the other side and hid between two tents. Then it was Eddie's turn. He ran out. "Halt!" a voice yelled. Eddie made it to where Angie was hiding, but a sentry had seen him. The sentry appeared between the tents, his weapon pointing at Eddie. He did not see Angie, who lay flat on the ground.

"Don't shoot me sir," Eddie said with a little quiver in his voice. "I am just waiting for General Clinton."

"Then why did you sneak out of the back of his tent?" The sentry asked with his bayoneted gun pointing ominously at Eddie.

"It was hot in there, I wanted to get some air," Eddie explained. The sentry wasn't buying it. Eddie had palmed a large, smooth rock. It was a little ovoid for his tastes, but it would have to do. He stood up and fired the rock at the sentry's head. The sentry ducked, then he smiled and raised his musket. Then Angie did the most amazing thing. She dashed out from between the tents and tackled the sentry around the legs, taking him completely by surprise. He went down hard. The gun discharged. Before the sentry could get up, Eddie beaned him with a second rock. The sentry was unconscious, but his shot had alarmed the entire camp.

"Crap!" said Eddie. "That will bring everyone who is left in camp." He grabbed Angie by the hand and the two children ran off into the woods in the dark. They could hear shouts and commotion in the camp. When the sentry comes to, soldiers will be out looking for them. Angie fell and got up breathing hard. "We'll never outrun them," she panted.

"You're right 'WE' will never outrun them," Eddie said derisively. Angie began to cry. Eddie softened, "Come on Angie, you're smart. Think of something."

She sniffed and looked around. Looking up, she pointed to a tree. "Can you help me get to that first branch?" She asked. "Once we get there, it is pretty easy to go a lot higher."

"Not a bad idea," Eddie agreed.

He boosted her up to the branch. It was a struggle; he grunted and panted. "You gotta give up the Doritos," he said. He pushed her up; she fell. The shouts were getting closer. "You have to help," he said with a harsh whisper. He wrapped his arms around her upper thighs and pushed up with a great grunt.

"I got the branch," she said. Eddie let go of her ankles and pushed her feet up. Angie struggled, but made it on top of the first branch and began climbing. Eddie jumped up, grabbed the branch and pulled himself up. The two made their way up the tree until they felt comfortable that they would not be seen from the ground. Beneath them, men ran through the woods, searching.

"That was close," said Eddie. "But I don't think they will see us up here."

"Unless they look," Angela said sarcastically.

"I like our chances. It's dark out and they would really have to expect us to be in this particular tree. We can't be seen unless someone is directly below us. If we go up higher, it will be really difficult to see us from the ground. Have faith, sis. Freedom is within reach."

"Then what?" she said dejectedly. She reached into her pack and retrieved a Twix bar. She ate it slowly, in a sullen mood.

"My God!" said Eddie in a harsh whisper. "Are you trying to turn yourself into a useless blob?"

"I'm hungry," she said. "We haven't eaten since breakfast at Washington's camp." Angie frowned and took another bite of her Twix bar.

"Aren't you going to offer me any?" he asked.

Angie frowned and handed over the other half of the bar. "I thought you didn't eat stuff like that," she said.

"It's not really food, but it is the closest thing we have right now," Eddie conceded as he took a bite. "Don't pull out the Doritos though, you'll wake the whole camp."

The activity below them went on for a few hours. Eventually, people went back into the camp and it became quiet again. "We still have another couple of hours of darkness," whispered Eddie. "Maybe we can climb down then and get away."

"And do what, wander around in the woods in the dark?" protested Angie.

"We can't stay here. In the morning they start shooting at each other. Besides there is a compass and a light in the iPhone. Maybe we can find a road that goes east, away from the fighting."

"Ultimately we have to go northwest, up to Long Island Sound. We can cross it and get away from Long Island and into Connecticut. But you're right, we have to first go east to get away from the fighting."

"Why would we have to cross? We would be just as lost in Connecticut as we are here," Eddie pointed out.

"This is British territory," Angie said patiently.

"So what. We're civilian children. We can get along fine with the British," Eddie said.

"Yeah," said Angie. "Until one of King George's loyal followers finds out that General Clinton is looking for us."

"Oh, yeah, you're right. But who's fault is that?" said Eddie.

"Yeah, yeah, I know—shouldda kept my mouth shut. My bad," said Angie. She changed the subject. "We can cover our shoes with mud, and with these outfits we can pass for Colonial children. We'll have to come up with something better than your stupid Fort Pitt story."

"We can work on it on the way. I haven't heard anything in a while, let's take advantage of the darkness and get out of here. As far as Fort Pitt goes, I was thinking on my feet," said Eddie as he helped her down from the low branch.

"You were on your feet, but you really weren't thinking. When we get home, ask Dad to drive you 400 miles to go shopping. I would like to hear what he says."

"They have to get supplies somewhere."

"Yeah, a freight company—18th century UPS. They don't just pop over to New York and pick up some flour and molasses. Also, there are settlements that are much closer than Long Island."

"Flour and molasses?" Eddie mocked.

"Or whatever they need in Fort Pitt," she said.

They made their way to a road. Eddie took out the iPhone, turned it on and tapped the compass ap. Angie looked at the screen and pointed up the road. "This road goes northeast. We should take it for a while and then find a crossroad that goes west," she said, powering down the phone to save battery power. "Put it in your pack," said Eddie. "It'll be safer there."

Chapter 10
Summer, 1765

Sol and Vernon Begin a New Adventure

"Third time's a charm," said Sol with a grin. They had landed in a pleasant pastoral area with rolling hills, trees and comfortable, balmy weather.

"Beautiful day," said Vernon. "But my body thinks it's 3 AM."

"Let's get a sense of where and when we are, then we can rest under those trees over there."

They were on top of a hill, which afforded a view of quite some distance. Sol reached into his duffel, pulled out a pair of binoculars, and started looking through them. Vernon did the same. They were in a fairly isolated place.

There was a tree nearby and some bushes. The spot provided some protection from being seen. Vernon had a rolled up blanket in his duffel. He spread it on the ground. Sol laid down, head resting on the duffel. Vernon took up a spot next to him. Sol sat up, pulled the .38 revolver out of his ankle holster, and placed the weapon under the duffel with his hand touching the revolver. He began to read some notes that he had in his other hand. "You never know what or who will come by," he said. Vernon pulled out the notes and the device, reviewing the notes and looking at the device. It wasn't long before they both fell asleep.

Sol awoke to a pebble hitting him on the head. He opened his eyes to see a man in a green frock coat, a green tricorne hat, with an ostrich plume stuck in the side and flowing back. He was brandishing two flintlock pistols. "Good afternoon to you, sir," he said with a flourish. Sol's hand was still on the pistol beneath his duffel, but the man was too close. Sol could get to the gun, but the man could still hit him before Sol could take aim, even with those primitive weapons.

The man continued to speak, "I am Sir Henry, the guardian of these parts; protector of all I survey. You two are trespassers."

There was a green bandana covering the lower half of the man's face, like those worn by outlaws in old Western movies. All they could see was his eyes, which peered out through a slit between the bandanna and his hat. Vernon began to stir. The man went on with his speech, obviously one he had given many times. He was enjoying himself, like someone acting in an amateur play production. Sol thought that it would have been funny, it it wasn't for the pistol the man had pointed at him. The bandit continued, "Watching over the lands is tedious and EXPENSIVE work. I need to feed my horse. I need powder for my pistols, food, supplies, oh my, the list goes on. Fortunately, my many charges support me in my efforts. By your choice to stay here, you have elected to be one of my charges."

Vernon sat up. The man straightened his arm and pulled the hammer of the pistol back. "No sudden moves, my friend," he said.

The CKD was on Vernon's chest while he was sleeping. He had fallen asleep studying it. When he sat up, it caught the outlaw's eye.

"What have you got there, my friend?" he asked. "Some kind of fancy clock?" He moved astride Vernon and lifted the strap of the CKD with one of his pistols. He placed it around his neck. "I'll just take this and those bags and I will be on my way."

Since he had been focusing on Vernon, Sol took the opportunity to grab the .38 revolver. He pointed the gun and fired twice. Sol was a terrible shot. He didn't hit anything, but he did manage to startle the outlaw, who dropped the cocked weapon. It fired, fortunately missing Vernon. The man turned and ran to his horse. Sol fired two more times, with similar ineptitude. The outlaw got on his horse and galloped away, with Sol firing a final shot. He got lucky with the last shot and hit the man's shoulder. Unfortunately, the bandit managed to stay on the horse and he and the time machine galloped away.

"Crap!" cried Sol. "We gotta find him."

"Yeah, and hope he doesn't touch the screen," said Vernon. He grew thoughtful, "I gotta make it harder to trigger the mechanism. It needs a safety switch or something."

"We'll do that; IF WE EVER GET THE THING BACK. CRAP!" exclaimed Sol.

"My guess is that we are in the 18th century, judging by the clothes and weapons. That was an American accent, not British, Irish or Scottish. Getting stuck here would not be the worst thing in the world. Not so bad here. No terrorists, no pollution and lots of open space. We can do alright. With our knowledge, you and I can do pretty well here."

"Yes," Sol said patiently, "Except for the fact that my niece and nephew are lost."

"On the bright side, this is where and when we thought the kids would be—give or take 50 years." said Vernon.

"We are in the right ballpark, but even if we are off by a day we will not find them," said Sol. "We need to get our machine back."

"I still don't understand how we ended up in 1912 that one time," said Vernon

"My guess is that you missed the point you thought you were hitting. I think your calculations and assumptions about the machine's patterns are correct. You must have hit the wrong spot," Sol said. He paused and looked around, "I really don't want to be stranded here. We need to find that guy and the machine."

"Shouldn't be too hard. He is a dandy and a show off. Plus, I don't imagine many people live around here, so he should stand out," said Vernon.

"You're right. It's just that if anything happens to those two children, I will never forgive myself."

"They are smart and resourceful. And, this is an exciting time and place to live. With their knowledge, they will do well."

"Be serious. We have to find them and get them home," said Sol. "We have to find that guy. I winged him, so it will make him easier to find. We will need a base of operations. There must be an inn or a town nearby. I have Krugerrands, we can buy goods and services, and most of all a place to stay." He emptied the spent shells, reloaded the gun and placed it back into the ankle holster. "Heading east increases our chances of finding civilization," he said. "Let's go."

"Winged him?" Vernon asked in an astonished tone. "I can't believe it. You are such a bad shot that watching you shoot reminds me of that scene in *Cat Ballou*, where Lee Marvin misses the barn. Yet you actually hit something."

"Someone," Sol corrected "Even a broken clock is right twice a day. Besides, Lee Marvin did hit the weather vane on top of the barn." They picked up their gear and headed east.

Chapter 11
August 27, 1776

Collins Begins Pursuit

Back in General Clinton's camp, one of the camp women was cleaning and dressing Collins' wound. She was a short, plump woman with a pleasant face. He was a mess. The ink had stained his left cheek and forehead. The ink well had split the skin over his forehead, so dried blood mingled with the ink, staining his face red and black. The skin of his left upper eyelid was darkened—it was like he had a reverse black eye.

She had a bucket of hot water, some whiskey and some rags. She dabbed at the cut. He squirmed and winced in pain, swearing at her. "Watch your language!" she said, "Or I'll leave you to clean it yourself. Good luck with that."

"Drat, woman!" he shouted. "Do you have to be so blasted rough?" He swore again.

"I warned you about your language," she admonished. He pouted and muttered an apology.

The woman did the best she could. Her scrubbing made the ink stain lighter and got rid of the dried blood. She bandaged his forehead. Collins was not a handsome man to begin with and when she had finished her ministrations, he still looked frightening and grotesque. He put on his hat; it didn't help his looks much.

"If it's the last thing I do, I'm going to get those two," Collins growled. "Sure, I want them to talk to General Clinton, but if they don't come quietly..." He fondled the handle of his pistol. In a way, he hoped that they resisted.

He paused and thought for a minute. Then he said, "They would have had to go east, to get away from the fighting. That means they followed the road going up the coast." He said the words aloud, but was not really addressing the woman. "They're on foot, so they won't get far, perhaps to the nearest town—maybe even Jamaica." The woman gathered her bucket and rags and hastened out of the tent. Collins did not thank her, but took the whiskey and took a long drink.

He put a second pistol in his belt and picked up a small canvas sack that he had filled with lead shot, making a sap. He slapped the sack into his palm. "I'll find 'em," he said to no one in particular, and took another long drink of whiskey.

Collins took a horse from camp and made his way up the road toward Jamaica. Just beyond the pass there was a tavern. He would start his search there. The tavern was a two story frame building, a bit larger than the average house. It had sleeping rooms upstairs and a dining area below. Collins tied his horse up outside of the building and went in.

Even though it was mid-morning, the inside was dimly lit. There was a plump barmaid behind the bar and a man seated at a stool, resting his head on the bar. Not much business this morning so close to the fighting, just the one drunk napping at the bar.

Collins approached the bar. The barmaid greeted him, "Mornin' sir, what is your pleasure?"

"I'm here on the King's business," Collins said with authority.

"King's soldiers were here last night—wouldn't let anyone leave. Some kind o' big mission," she said. "They kept everyone in the tavern until it was time for them to leave—some kind o' big secret attack."

"Yes, I am with that army unit. I am on a special mission to find two children. A girl, about 9 or 10; a chubby thing with red hair. The boy is about 12, slender with long dark hair," Collins said. Eddie was small for his age and that was Collins' best guess.

"No sir, no children in here," said the barmaid.

The drunk at the bar sat up and shook his head, "Nope, no kids in here," he said. "What's the King want with a couple of children?"

Collins said, "Not that it's any of your business, but those children know Washington's plans."

"Oh, well, no wonder. The fate of the Empire rests on the shoulders of two little kiddies," the man said as he gestured widely. Collins fumed. The man said, "Tell the King to get someone else to look for them. My God you are an ugly bugger. Those kiddies are gonna have nightmares after they get a look at you. Whatcha all painted up for? Going on the warpath?"

Collins walked over and struck the man with lead-filled canvas sack, breaking his cheek. "Drunken scum," he said as he turned to leave the tavern. He strode toward the door to leave. When he reached for the door, everything went black.

Chapter 12
August 27, 1776

The Battle of Long Island

Brooklyn in 1776 was nothing like it is now. It was heavily wooded and rugged terrain. The Americans had about 3,000 troops on a bluff of heavily wooded hills. There were another 9,000 in fortified positions at Brooklyn Heights. The terrain was as much of a barrier to the British as the troops that guarded it. There were breaks in the natural barrier, called passes. East of the American position was a pass that was not well guarded, Jamaica Pass. Only five soldiers manned that post. General Clinton grew up on Long Island and knew the lay of the land. His attack on the Americans was simple, direct and effective. It was hard to believe that General Howe originally did not approve of the plan. Clinton scouted the area thoroughly before the battle and saw the weakness in the American lines. The smaller part of Clinton's force engaged the Americans on the bluff, a feint, while a larger force under Clinton marched on the American left flank to Jamaica Pass, and were able to pass through it facing negligible resistance. The Americans on the bluff were very pleased with themselves in the early part of the battle because they were "holding their own" against British regulars. They had no way of knowing that fight they were in was merely a diversion, and that disaster awaited them when the bulk of Clinton's force would attack them from behind.

The British were able to get behind the Americans and rout them. Hessian mercenaries bayoneted Americans as they tried to surrender. At the time, it was the largest battle ever fought in North America. It dwarfed the Battle of Bunker Hill.

General Washington sat atop a horse at other fortifications located at Brooklyn Heights. He looked through a telescope and watched the battle unfold before him. It was mid-morning and the British were sweeping over his men. They were within two miles of the fortification at Brooklyn. Thousands of men were on the run, their lines having collapsed. General Stirling had moved, with his force of 1,600 men, to help hold the Gowanus Pass. Stirling had no idea what an overwhelming force he was facing. His men stood and fought, for so long that it made escape all but impossible. Part of his force counterattacked General Cornwallis (later to become famous for surrendering at Yorktown) —hitting the British with withering fire. Stirling's men were late to try to retreat, and most of them were killed or captured. Washington watched this from his vantage point at Brooklyn Heights and said, "Good God, what brave fellows I must this day lose."

Through the day and night, his defeated soldiers made their way back to the Brooklyn fortifications. He had the British navy in the river at his back and he had an overwhelming force in front of him. He thought back to his conversation with the strange children. They had predicted this. Then he remembered what else they told him.

Even if they had not been outflanked, the Americans would have lost the battle. It was foolish to try to hold an island against the greatest naval power in the world. The British had over 20,000 troops on the island, as well as absolute naval control of the waterways. The Americans had only about 10,000 and lost around 1,000 men, killed or captured. General Howe reported the number to be around 3,000, exaggerating his victory. The remaining 9,000 Americans, along with stragglers who managed to retreat from the battle, holed up in fortifications at Brooklyn Heights, with the East River at their backs. They were trapped.

General Clinton, if he had pressed the attack, could have annihilated the Continental army and possibly ended the war right there. He did not. Historians tell us that General Howe ordered the halt because of the losses the British army suffered by attacking Americans in their fortified positions on Bunker (actually Breed's) Hill. The British won that battle, but lost over 200 soldiers killed and over 800 wounded. Howe worried about a similar disaster on Long Island. However, some of members of General Clinton's staff said it was Clinton who hesitated and failed to destroy the American army because a little boy warned him off.

Chapter 13
August 27, 1776

Eddie and Angie on the Move

Eddie and Angie were on a reasonably straight thoroughfare that went north and east. Angie guessed that it would eventually follow the Atlantic coast of Long Island. Angie said, "This will take us away from the fighting. We should take it east for a while, but take the next turnoff that goes north. We have to come up with a story, in case we run into someone."

There was plenty of mud available; it had been a rainy couple of days. They had muddied their shoes enough so that at a casual glance, they just looked like dark shoes. Other than Angie's brightly colored backpack, they looked like they belonged.

"We're from New York and are visiting relatives on Long Island. We wandered away from their farm and got lost," Eddie suggested.

"Yeah, but what is the name of our relative?" Angie asked. "This is pretty rural; not a lot of people live around here. They probably know each other. If we can't give a name or if the name we give doesn't make sense, they will never buy the story."

"Have you got a better idea?" asked Eddie.

"I'm thinking," said Angie. "We have to be anonymous and lost. We can't have connection to anyone on Long Island. Maybe a tragedy separated us from our parents."

"Yeah, but what are we doing on Long Island, with no parents?"

"Maybe we're not from Long Island. We're from Connecticut. There have been some storms lately. We can say we were in a boat and it capsized during a storm," Angie suggested.

"What were we doing in a boat during a storm?" Eddie asked.

Angie thought a minute, then looked to her left. The sun was just beginning to peek over the horizon. It was still dark, but visibility was improving. She dashed into the field on her left. It was full of short, stubby trees. "An orchard!" she cried. Eddie looked and ran after her.

She reached a tree and swung her backpack at a low-hanging branch. Several apples fell to the ground. Angie picked them up, sat under the tree and began eating. "I'm starving," she said. Eddie knocked some apples down and joined her.

"I remember reading about the British soldiers being impressed with the wealth of the colonies when they saw the farms on Long Island. They saw it as an idyllic place, with orchards. To the average soldier, the colonists looked incredibly wealthy and were ungrateful and cheap to not want to support the Empire with taxes," Angie said.

"How do you know all of this stuff?" asked Eddie. "I mean you know Clinton's strategy—heck, you even know where the hole in the Americans' line is. And now you know what the average British soldier thought about the people on Long Island." He took a bite of his apple.

"You don't know because you only study for tests and to please Mom and your teachers. So you know about Bunker Hill, maybe Saratoga, and Yorktown." Angie said thoughtfully. "But you have so many other things: your sports, your friends, school activities... the world is your oyster. Education is not your priority, so you don't study to learn; you study to gain praise. I don't have friends, I hate sports, Mom thinks I am a loser, but I have reading. I love knowing things. Education is my biggest priority." She paused, took a bite of her apple, and continued, "I mean this war was amazing. I still can't believe that the Americans pulled it off. About one-third of them wanted nothing to do with the war and another third remained loyal to the king. The army didn't know how to fight—they'd panic and run from British bayonets. They were perpetually short of gunpowder and other supplies. They never got paid. But they hung on long enough until the French and Spanish turned it into a world war."

"You could have more friends. You need to take better care of yourself and to go out and get involved with other people," said Eddie. "Heck, you might even make more friends if you weren't so cocky. You're critical of everyone and everything; that's not a good strategy for making friends. No one is perfect and you need to cut people some slack. It's not enough for you to know more about the war than I do; you have to make a statement about how ignorant I am and how bad the school system is."

"You should talk about arrogance. You are such a show off and you are always mean to me," Angie countered.

"You seem to be making yourself miserable. I am just trying to get you to snap out of it. You are in horrible physical condition, you have no friends and now you are getting rotten grades. Yet you act all superior. I mean, I know you're smart; why not just apply yourself and get ahead?" Eddie said.

Angie said, "Most people are boring and caught up in their own issues. How many people do you know who are as interesting as Uncle Sol? If I ever meet someone as interesting as a book, I'll hang out with them. My best friend has to have been Great Grandpa. He was really cool. We used to watch old movies together; he knew lots of stuff about the actors and the history of his day. Maybe that is why I like big band music and Cary Grant. As far as school goes, I just get irritated with the self-righteous bureaucrats who run it and I could care less about scoring points and meeting their standards. It seems to be more about finding which slot a student belongs than it is about learning." She took another bite of her apple and continued, "I look at your friends and am glad that I keep my own company."

"What do you mean by that?"

"Oh PULLLLLEEESE. Look at Amy Andrews. You are so hung up on her; and I will give you that she's pretty. But give me a break. She is as dumb as a post, shallow and a little nasty. She watches the Kardashians for God's sake. I've even seen you watch the Kardashians; my guess is that it will give you something to talk about with her. Because otherwise," she paused and jabbed her finger into her head several times, "nobody home." She sighed. "Mom thinks that I'M the one not living up to my potential. You never challenge yourself. And those guys from your team that you hang out with, they're all morons."

"The guys from the team are fun to be with," protested Eddie.

"Yeah, like Ted Knight," said Angie. "The kid wears his hat backwards—there's a look that might come back in the next decade or so. His dad owns a software company and they're Presbyterians who live in the suburbs, but he talks like he's from the ghetto—what's that all about? He calls women 'bitches,' 'know what I'm sayin'," she said, with a mocking Ted-like accent for emphasis. "He blasts hip hop music in his Range Rover. Should I go on? I'll take my social life over yours any day of the week thank you very much."

"Ted is a really good friend. You just notice the superficial stuff about him. He talks funny and you can't understand him half the time, but he is a great ball player and will do anything for a friend. You could be more tolerant. No one is perfect, but they all have something to offer if you give them a chance before judging them. Did you know that Ted was a very talented artist? No—because he has a way of socializing that you do not approve of." They heard gunfire in the distance. "It's starting," said Eddie.

The sounds of battle were close. The fighting was just north of them. Eddie and Angie continued on the same road that Clinton had taken to get to Jamaica Pass. They had not reached the pass yet; it was a good thing, because they would have run into the main body of troops.

They heard a horse and rider coming from the west. Eddie got behind a tree and lay prone, hidden by the tall grass and the tree. He motioned for Angie to do the same thing. She hid along with him. "Good God! It's Collins," she whispered.

Eddie snickered quietly, "I wonder how his head is feeling."

They gave Collins time to get far ahead of them, then they gathered up some apples and started to move eastward, away from the war. Their route would eventually take them past Jamaica Pass, but Clinton's men would be long gone—chasing down rebels. They figured that was where Collins was going since he was with the British.

"So what is our story?" Eddie asked. "So far, it's that we were on the Long Island Sound during a storm and the boat capsized. Why were we out on the water in a storm?"

Angie paused and thought a minute, "We had to get away... from... um... our father! Yes! That's it. He beat us terribly. Some days I could hardly walk, the pain was so bad."

"Great story, wrong delivery," said Eddie. "Don't give any details. Don't even say the word 'beat'. To some of the folks around here, that's just good discipline. Children should be beaten—it keeps them in line. There is no DCFS[1] here. Tell the story with your eyes, not your words. You are a traumatized CHILD. You can't even talk about what happened to you. You avert your eyes, you sob, you sigh and you tremble a little. If pressed, you say, 'my father did UNSPEAKABLE things'. You saw it happening with your sister until she killed herself. If I am asked, I will act really protective around you. I will use the word 'unspeakable' as well and talk about our dead sister."

"Wow, that's really good! What was our dead sister's name?" asked Angie.

"Good point," said Eddie. "How does Emily sound?"

"Good as any," said Angie. "How long has she been dead?"

"Six months," said Eddie. "She died on a cold day in February. Six months should be about how long our father could control himself."

---

1 DCFS is the Department of Children and Family Services.

"That is a pretty smart way to do it," said Angie with admiration in her voice.

"Details are what make most stories fall apart. Most of the time you don't need them. Since we are kids, we can be too shy and too frightened to say much. No one will question that," he explained. "Besides, their imaginations will come up with more horrific details than we could ever describe."

They made their way past Jamaica Pass. A little further up the road there was a fork. Angie took the iPhone out of the pack, turned it on, looked at the compass and said, "This branch goes north and west. It will take us closer to the Long Island Sound. From there we can get a ride to Connecticut." She powered it down and put it back in the pack.

"Then what?" said Eddie. "We are still in the 18th freakin' century and no idea how to get home."

"We have the device. We can always try to get to another time and place," Angie offered. "Besides, I can think of worse things than not getting home. Look at this countryside—it's beautiful!" Angie continued, taking a deep breath. "Smell that air; clean, fresh, and no hydrocarbons. Uncle Sol and Vernon will look for us. Maybe they know more about using the device. Maybe they can even figure out how to track this device. It just seems to me that we should try to stay here for a while."

"Except for one thing—we're in the middle of a WAR! You surprise me," said Eddie. "You're usually such a Debbie Downer. Now a war is just a minor inconvenience to you. What got into you?"

"As far as the war goes, as I've already told you, it will be easy enough to avoid," Angie said. "Besides, we have a way out of here. It's in my backpack. We simply have to figure out how to use the device. Plus, Vernon is like off the charts smart. He may already have an idea of where and when we are. That's why we should stay here a bit and see if he can find us. And, quite frankly, if we are permanently stuck here in the 18th century, I am fine with it."

"Fine with it? Are you kidding?" Eddie asked incredulously. "This is a primitive Hell hole with people trying to kill each other."

"Funny you should say that," said Angie. "That is my view of the 21st century."

They walked up the road for about an hour, the sounds of the war becoming more distant as they went. It really was beautiful country: there were dense woods, orchards and the occasional farmhouse. There had been a lot of rain over the last week and everything was lush and green. It was a pastoral paradise, save for the sounds of the war some 10 miles away. The dirt road had ruts with puddles of water in them, but it was passable. They each walked on one side of the road, where it was more level. They saw a farmhouse about 50 yards off the road.

"We could try there and get some help. Do you think you can sell our story?" Eddie asked.

"I would rather keep going. There may still be people looking for us, especially that Lieutenant Collins. From his point of view, I bet it's not about the reward anymore, especially after you humiliated him," Angie said.

"Did you see the look on his face when he went down?" he asked, laughing. "I bet they can't get that ink off his face. He's going to look like a Rorschach test."

"Exactly," said Angie. "He's going to want to redeem himself with the British and get even with us. Even if Clinton forgets about us, Collins won't. We're on an island, so there are not that many places we can go; he knows that. We have to find help and shelter. It's going to rain again in two days—that's when Washington makes his escape. But that farmhouse is a little too close. It will be one of the first places Collins goes."

"Do you know Washington's shoe size and what he did last Saturday night?"

"Twelve, I think and last Saturday he was checking on his defenses." Angie didn't really know the shoe size and Saturday was just a good guess, but she wanted to mess with Eddie a little. "I just remember what I read and I read a lot. David McCullough wrote a wonderful book about the events of 1776; I was just lucky enough to have read it."

"McCullough wrote about Washington's shoe size?" Eddie asked. Angie just grinned at him. He paused, she began to speak and he held up a hand to shush her. "Hear that?" he said.

The sound was indistinct at first, but gradually became clearer. It was singing. As it got closer, they noticed that the singing was in a rich, deep, beautiful deep voice.

> "O soul, are you weary and troubled?
> No light in the darkness you see?
> There's a light for a look at the Savior,
> And life more abundant and free!

"Turn your eyes upon Jesus,
Look full in His wonderful face,
And the things of earth will grow strangely dim,
In the light of His glory and grace."

They looked behind them, and coming over the hill was a wagon drawn by two horses. Driving the wagon was one the biggest men either of them had ever seen. He may have been 6'6", it was hard to tell from the distance. He had big broad shoulders and could have been on a linebacker in the NFL. Heck, Eddie thought, he could have been a defensive end. He very nearly took up the entire seat of the wagon. He was a little soft through the middle, but his arms were solid, muscular and as big as tree trunks; they were barely contained by his white cotton shirt. The shirt was open to the middle of his chest, which was hairless and glistening with sweat. It was getting very warm out. He wore a brown flop hat and tan pants that were tucked into buckskin-fringed boots. The boots were like moccasins, but came up to his mid-calf. Homemade, Angie thought. Who could manufacture shoes for this giant? She wondered if there were any Colonial "Big and Tall" shops. He had a round face that was not quite jowly. He was more than a few pounds overweight, but under the softness was a solid, powerful man. As he drew closer, Angie saw kindness in his brown eyes. As he came nearer, he continued singing.

"Through death into life everlasting
He passed, and we follow Him there;
Over us sin no more hath dominion—
For more than conquerors we are!
"Turn your eyes upon Jesus,
Look full in His wonderful face,
And the things of earth will grow strangely dim,
In the light of His glory and grace."

He stopped the wagon just short of the children, who stared at him in amazement. "You have a beautiful voice, sir," Angie complimented.

"Never mind my voice," the man said. "What in Heaven's name are you two doing out here in the middle of a war?" Eddie pointed toward the farmhouse. "Don't give me that, the widow Smith does not have any children," the man said.

"We're sorry, sir," Angie said with a little tremble in her voice.

She had learned Eddie's lessons very well. "We're just scared and lost."

The man tilted his head back a little, knit his brows and looked askance at her. "That doesn't explain how you have come to be here with a war going on," he said.

"Our boat capsized and we were dumped into the Sound during the storm the other night," Eddie said, hoping that was the term the locals gave to the body of water to their north. "It was horrible; I was sure that we were going to drown." He guessed that the man was religious, judging from the hymn he was singing, and continued, "The good Lord must have been watching over us. We made it to shore and have been wandering the island, trying to find food and shelter."

"We live in Connecticut," Angie said vaguely, looking down at the ground. "We had to get away from our father...he...he...." She began to sob. Eddie looked at her admiringly; she was really good. "After my sister killed herself, after the unspeakable things he did, I knew that I was next, he was..." Her voice trailed off and she continued to sob.

"She doesn't like to talk about it," said Eddie. "It was really bad at home. We had to get away."

"Oh you poor child. You have been through a terrible ordeal," the man said. He stepped down from the wagon. "I guess that me and the Missus will have to look after you two." He bent down and lifted Angie into the wagon as if she weighed nothing. He turned toward Eddie. Eddie held up his hand, indicating for the man to hold off a minute, and climbed aboard the wagon. Both children thanked the man from the back of the wagon because there clearly would be no room on the seat in front.

Chapter 14
August 27, 1776

Collins Regroups

Collins woke up on the floor of the tavern with the plump barmaid bending over him, dabbing his face with a damp cloth. "You're finally commin' around. You been out for a while. shouldn'a struck Old Ethan," she said. "He's tough and ornery."

Collins sat up. He put his hands to his side and noticed that his pistols were gone. "Aye, and your purse is gone and he took your horse; called it 'recompensatory damages'. Old Ethan was a lawyer before he took to drinkin.'" She s squinted at him as she dabbed his face, "What did happen to your face, anyway? You look like a painted Indian." She went on, in spite of a lack of response from Collins, "He's a tough old bird, always brawlin'. He's not someone I'd want to get on the wrong side of, that's for sure. He broke that chair over your head." She pointed at the damaged piece of furniture. "He paid me for the damages out of your purse; he knows I won't serve him if he breaks up my place."

Collins got up on shaky legs. He could hear the sound of gunfire in the distance. His head hurt and he felt weak in the knees. He opened the door and left the tavern, with the barmaid still talking behind him. Eight miles! He had to walk it; "Old Ethan" had stolen his horse. He was going to have to walk back to camp to get new weapons and another horse. By the time he had a mount and was back here, it would be late afternoon.

Had Collins not spent the last hour unconscious on the tavern floor, he would have run into Eddie and Angie when he walked past the crossroads east of Jamaica Pass. As it was, they were already on the road going north and out of sight.

It was mid-afternoon when Collins made it back to the British camp. He was tired, his head and body hurt, and he was angry. Those children had brought all of this misery upon him, and he was determined to find them in spite of his fatigue and pain. He would get a new horse, new weapons and head east along the coast. He would catch them if it were the last thing he ever did—especially that cocky boy.

He got to his tent and decided to rest for a few minutes. His head and upper back were throbbing and he was a little dizzy. He was exhausted; other than the time he spent unconscious on the tavern floor and in Clinton's tent, he had been up all night. He just wanted to take a few minutes and rest. He fought the urge to lay down, but pain and fatigue triumphed over anger and determination. He fell asleep.

Chapter 15
August 27, 1776

Eddie and Angie with Angus

The big man's name was Angus Van Auken. He did most of the talking, to the relief of Angie and Eddie. "I was in Jamaica on business. I had no idea that the British were going to start this ruckus when I got there," he said. "I hope it doesn't spill over onto this road before we get to Musketa Cove."

"It won't," said Angie. Angus turned around to look at her. Angie said, "Uh, I heard that Washington is at Brooklyn Heights; the British will concentrate there."

"It's sinful," said Angus. "Men killin' each other over what? A few cents tax? Our Lord commanded us to love each other. Nothing in this world is worth disobeying his commandments. He let them hang him on a cross. He died to prove to us that no matter what happens to you here, it does not matter because we were given the gift of eternal life. He forgave those who tortured and killed him. He rose on the third day, proof of his promise of eternal life. If you have eternal life with our Lord, what can be worth fighting for if it endangers that gift? The men fighting and dying over pennies are spitting on our Lord's gift. The British are no better; they place a mortal King above God's law and our Lord Jesus Christ—sinful. There is never reason to do violence to any man."

Angie and Eddie said nothing to this. It made sense. If you were truly a Christian, that should be your attitude. Both of them really admired his faith. They found it ironic that men on both sides of the conflict considered themselves Christians and wondered what they would say to Angus' words.

Angus lived on Musketa Cove, a settlement that was on the western end of Long Island Sound. Today it is called Glen Cove. It was perfect—close to Connecticut and far from the battle. They would be on the road for a few more hours with the roads as rough as they were. Angie and Eddie were famished; the apples they had eaten a few hours earlier were inadequate as the first meal they had had in over 24 hours. They were in their second day of 'not much food.'

"I hope you're hungry," Angus said looking back at them. "My missus is a wonderful cook and dinner will be waiting when we get home. Of course you will stay with us, until you can find family to take you. And if you can't find family—well, there is plenty of room at our place. Musketa Cove even has a schoolhouse."

It was late in the afternoon when they pulled up in front of Angus' house. It was a large, two-story brick house that Angie believed would be called a "saltbox." There were five windows across the second floor and two on either side of the door. Nice digs, she thought to herself. Whatever Angus did, he was successful at it.

A little wisp of a woman with blue eyes and auburn, shoulder-length hair came out to greet them. She wore a white cap, common headwear for women of the day, and a dark blue full-length dress. She was a delicate woman with small hands. She was pretty, her features were almost angelic. She was very light-skinned, but you would not call her pale. An 18th century poet may have used the word "alabaster" when describing her. This was Mrs. Van Auken. Angie was astonished. She could practically fit into one of Angus' pockets. Next to her was another woman, with skin as dark as mahogany. Similarly dressed with her dark hair tied back under her white cap. She was a couple of inches taller than Mrs. Van Auken, with a round face and what seemed to be a perpetual smile. She was bigger and rounder than the blonde woman, but not overweight. She was young, maybe 17.

"Hallo!" she said. "Angus, dear, who is that you have with you?"

"These children have escaped an evil fate... it is up to us to help them," Angus said solemnly. "This is my wife, Annie; and that there is Sadie with her. This is Eddie and Angie. They are from Connecticut."

"Of course," Annie said. Addressing Angie and Eddie, "You two must be hungry. Dinner will be ready shortly. Sadie, will you take the children upstairs and help them to wash up, please?"

Angus stepped off the wagon, swept his wife up in hug, and spun her around. They lingered in the hug for a moment and Angus turned around and gestured toward Eddie and Angie. "Go on with Sadie, she will help you to get settled." They followed her into the house, leaving Angus and his wife alone.

They stepped up to the small portico and through the oak doorway into the house. It was a nice, bright and comfortable house. To the left was a parlor and to the right was a dining room. There was a doorway straight ahead to the left, which Angie assumed went to a kitchen. In front of them was a stairway, with a smooth banister, made of dark maple. The steps were maple as well, the wood between the steps and the supports for the banister were white. A long rug was attached to the middle of the stairs and went from the floor to the top of the stairway. It was blue-grey and had an oriental design. "Angus does very well for himself," Angie thought.

Sadie motioned with her arm, indicating that they should go upstairs. At the top of the stairs was a hallway with several doors opened to it. Sadie led them to the first door and told Angie, "You go in there, little miss, and I will be along shortly." She led Eddie to a room further down and across the hall.

The room Angie went into looked like it belonged to a little girl. There was a rag doll on the bed and the room was done in pinks and pastels. There was a cherry wood dresser and a single bed with a cherry wood headboard and footboard. The floor was wooden, but had rugs on either side of the bed and at the foot of the bed. Next to the window, between the bed and the dresser was a pedestal and chair. On the pedestal was a pitcher and basin for washing. Angie sat on the chair. After a few minutes, Sadie returned with a bucket of warm water. She filled the basin and the pitcher and placed a couple of washcloths on the pedestal.

Angie looked at her and asked, "Are you a slave?" Then she caught herself and said, "I am terribly sorry. That was rude of me. I am new around here."

Sadie laughed and said, "No, little miss. I am not a slave. I was one and Mr. Angus inherited me. But Mr. Angus says that it is wrong for one human being to own another. It is a sin against God and to own slaves is like being a pagan king of Babylon. There were six of us and he set us all free. I wanted to stay here, so did Lucias—you'll meet him. I like it here, the Van Aukens are nice folks. They let me stay and I help out." She pointed toward the closet, "Mr. Angus says if you want clean clothes, Miss Rebecca's things might fit." Sadie looked down and wiped a tear from the corner of her eye. "It's alright to wear the clothes, Mr. Angus says." She quickly moved out of the room.

Angie really wanted a shower. That was not going to happen. Even baths were rare in Colonial America. You used a basin of water and some cloths and washed as best you could. She was grateful for that, it was a hot and dusty day. She took off the clothes she was wearing and began to wash.

Sadie paid a visit to Eddie in his room and filled the basin and pitcher. She told him that someone would come along with some clean clothes for him. Eddie also wanted a shower, but figured that washing from the basin was as good as it was going to get. When Sadie left, he took of his clothes and began to wash his body.

Angie cleaned herself as best she could, using the two cloths and the basin. It wasn't a shower, but it was refreshing and she was grateful for it. Eddie cleaned up in his room. When he was finished, Sadie knocked on the door. She had clothes with her, and they looked like they might fit. She laid them on the bed with no explanation and left the room. Eddie changed into the clothes. The bed looked inviting, so he decided to lay down while he waited for Angie.

When Angie finished cleaning, she went into the closet and found a clean dress. She missed her jeans. She found a plain, dark green dress and tried it on. It was similar to the dress she had received in Washington's camp. It fit well enough. There were shoes and undergarments in the closet as well. She got dressed, and looked at herself in the mirror in her new era-appropriate apparel. "Not bad," she said to herself. She even put on the little white dusting cap to complete the Colonial look.

She went out into the hallway looking for Eddie. She looked into the door of an open room and found him sound asleep. She went over to him and gently shook him. He woke up. "Sorry, must have dozed off," he said.

"We should go downstairs for dinner," Angie said.

"Those are the most beautiful words I ever heard in my life," said Eddie.

"Me too. I'm starved."

"I'm so hungry my stomach thinks my throat is cut, nyuck, nyuck, nyuck," said Eddie.

Angie just looked at him strangely. "The Three Stooges," Eddie explained. "Uncle Sol played some of their videos for me once."

She shook her head. "Of all the great comedy from that era, you choose to quote the Three Stooges, unbelievable. If you're going to get into vintage comedy, you really ought to look into the Marx Brothers, or at least Laurel and Hardy."

"See what I mean," said Eddie. "Instead of appreciating the joke, you need to correct me and tell me about something better. People don't appreciate that."

Angie said nothing. They headed down the stairs.

When they got down the stairs, Angus, and his wife were seated at the table. Sadie was serving them. Eddie and Angie entered the room and Mrs. Van Auken looked up and appeared a little startled when she saw Angie. She smiled and motioned for the two children to sit down. Angus just stared at Angie for a moment, then smiled and said nothing.

On the large round table was a feast. There was a roast beef, boiled potatoes, green beans, sliced tomatoes and cucumbers. Eddie sat next to Angus and Angie sat next to his wife. There were two other places set. The children hungrily began filling their plates. Eddie took a forkful of meat and was about to take a bite when Angus laid a big beefy hand on his shoulder indicating that he should stop. "As soon as Sadie and Lucius join us we can say grace."

Sadie sat down and a black man that they had not seen before took the seat next to her. Angie noticed that Sadie looked up and smiled at him, then shyly looked away. Lucius nodded to her and sat down. It surprised Eddie and Angie that the two African Americans were welcome at the table. The Van Aukens were very progressive for their time. Sadie and Lucius weren't servants, although they did work around the house. They were more like family — they helped out like family members do. It was not forced labor. She noticed the chemistry between Lucius and Sadie. They stole glances at each other, but looked away if the other made eye contact. They were very shy around each other. Angie thought that they would make an attractive couple. Both were in their late teens, maybe 20, but not older. Lucius was solidly built and was maybe an inch taller than Sadie. His skin was not quite as dark. He had an infectious smile.

Angus took Eddie's hand and his wife's hand. He said, "Join hands," and everyone at the table did so. Angus began the prayer:

> "Dear Lord, thank you for this food.
> Bless the hands that prepared it.
> Bless it to our use and us to your service,
> And make us ever mindful of the needs of others.
> Through Christ our Lord we pray. Amen."

"Amen!" Eddie said zealously, and dug into his roast beef, it was the best food he ever had in his life. Angie was so intent on eating that she did not hear Mrs. Van Auken speaking to her.

"I understand that you children are from Connecticut."

Sadie nudged her. Angie looked up and noticed that she was being spoken to. "Yeth," she said through a mouthful of potatoes. She swallowed and remembered herself. "I don't like to talk about it, Ma'am." She stopped eating, looked down and slumped her shoulders, showing a defeated body language.

"I'm sorry dear," Mrs. Van Auken said. She sighed and said, "That dress was our Rebecca's favorite. It looks wonderful on you."

"Thank you Ma'am," Angie said. "I really appreciate you and Mr. Van Auken taking us in."

"Think nothing of it. The Lord commands us to care for each other," Angus said. "You are welcome to stay as long as you like. If you have family that you can stay with, we will see that you get there—war permitting."

"We have an uncle in Manhattan that we can stay with," said Angie, prompting an open-mouthed, wide-eyed look from Eddie.

"That may put you close to the fighting," said Angus. "You'd best stay here and wait until the fools come to their senses."

"Thank you, sir," said Eddie. "That is a good idea."

"Manhattan should be ok—er—safe," said Angie, realizing that the term "ok" didn't become popular until Martin Van Buren ran for office. Van Buren was known as "Old Kinderhook", which was shortened to "ok" during his campaign for president. Martin Van Buren is "ok" with me. Ok meant "oll korrect"; it was a cute pun. She continued, "Washington will have to retreat and New York will be relatively safe, but under British control."

"How do you know so much about the war?" asked Lucius.

"Um, er... we were actually in Washington's camp for a while. We were picked up by a Colonial army patrol shortly after we landed on the island," said Angie. "We escaped and then we were picked up by the British. We were in both camps and it looks like the British are going to easily win the battle. Washington will have to retreat."

"Retreat where?" asked Lucius. "He's surrounded by water."

"Then the war will be over," said Angie. "There won't be fighting in New York."

"It's sinful," said Angus, "for both sides to involve a couple of children into their disregard of God's law. Sinful!"

"Enough talk of war," said Mrs. Van Auken. "You will not be traveling in the near future, so you two will join us for Wednesday service tomorrow. What denomination are you?"

"Uh...we don't go to church," said Eddie. "Our father says it is just a bunch of lies to control the people."

"The heathen adds blasphemy to his sins," fumed Angus, "and he denies his children the gift of eternal life. You will come to service tomorrow. He may be doomed to the fires of Hell, but there is time to save the two of you. Is this uncle of yours a man of God?"

"Oh my, yes," said Eddie. "He even gave us a Bible, but our father took it. He said he wouldn't have us reading all those fairy tales and nonsense." Angie thought that Eddie was laying it on a little thick, but she understood what he was doing. The more Mr. Van Auken disliked their "father," the less likely it was for him to try to reunite them with the family in Connecticut.

Angie was enjoying the meal. She liked the Van Aukens and she liked that they were so religious. She liked that the whole family ate together. She was finally beginning to feel sated. She could not believe how hungry she had been, and had never enjoyed a meal as much as this one. Even the vegetables tasted good and she was surprised to find herself enjoying them. She normally hated vegetables and avoided them. She felt obligated to eat them here because she didn't want to leave anything on her plate; it might be considered rude. She relaxed and enjoyed the food and the company at the table.

Angie decided that she should contribute to the conversation. She complimented Mrs. Van Auken on the meal and thanked her again. She thanked Angus for his kind hospitality and for the clothes. She said, "I look forward to going to church with you Mr. Van Auken. I have never been to church." This was not a lie. Her parents were not particularly religious. They weren't atheists nor did they have anything against religion. They just didn't care for church and found it to be a waste of a perfectly good Sunday morning. Church simply did not fit into their busy schedule.

When dinner was finished, Sadie and Lucius cleared the plates, stealing glances all the while. Angie helped. Lucius sat down and Sadie went into the kitchen and came back with a pie. The crust was a golden brown dome that glistened a little. She set it on the table with some small plates. Angie's eyes got wide.

"Apple pie from our tree," Sadie said as she began cutting the pie, putting pieces on plates and distributing them to the diners. She presented Lucius' pie as if she were handing him the Academy Award. Angie noticed.

The children ate their pie. They felt full, satisfied and safe. Angie thought to herself that getting stuck here would not be so bad. She would miss her parents, some of the technology, junk food and Uncle Sol. Although, who knew? Uncle Sol could show up. She really wished that they had running water and that she could take a shower. Eddie, on the other hand, was feeling homesick. He saw life here as miserable and primitive; although the food wasn't bad.

He wanted to see his friends. He wanted to play baseball. He really wanted to see Amy. This was much worse than being stuck in Greece for the summer.

The meal was finished and Eddie and Angie helped Sadie clear the remaining dishes and clean up. They went into the kitchen and Angie said, "That Lucius is a good looking man, isn't he?"

Sadie gave a shy smile and looked away. "I believe he is," she said. "And smart, too. He reads and writes."

"I think he likes you," said Angie.

"I like him too. We're good friends," said Sadie.

"I think it's more than that."

"Oh, no, I don't think so. He's just polite—a real gentleman."

"A real gentleman with a thing for you."

"What kind of thing does he have for me?"

Angie realized that she had to watch her use of slang. "I mean he LIKES you—more than as a friend," Angie said.

Sadie grew thoughtful for a moment and said, "You really think so?"

Just then Eddie came into the kitchen with more dishes. He said, "Sadie, that was the best meal I think that I have ever had. This is the last of the dishes."

"Thank you," said Sadie. "Now you two go on out to the dining room and let me finish up. Go visit with Mr. and Mrs. Van Auken." She gently pushed them toward the door.

"Thanks a lot, Eddie," Angie said. "I was just telling her about Lucius."

"What about Lucius?" Eddie asked.

"What about Lucius? Are you blind?" said Angie. "He likes her, and I think she likes him. Neither of them knows how the other one feels."

"How do you know *that*?" asked Eddie.

"The extent of your cluelessness knows no bounds," said Angie.

They emerged into the dining room and Angus stood up. "Come children, let's take the evening air," he said. He motioned with his arm toward the doorway leading into the front hall.

They stepped outside. It was a truly beautiful scene. Angie felt like she could literally taste the air. There was no pollution, no greenhouse gasses, no acid rain and the simple act of breathing was invigorating. The Van Auken's house was on a hill; it was part of a working farm. Down the hill and to the west he could see some rooftops; clearly the town of Musketa Cove. You could see the water of Long Island Sound; it was maybe a mile away. Much of the land was cleared and crops were planted amid the stumps of trees that had been removed. The land was partially ringed by trees. There had been a lot of rain lately, and pathways leading around and through the property were a little muddy. Angus owned a good sized piece of property. There were two other buildings to the east of the house. One was a barn and the other was a one-story residence of some sort. Eddie wondered if that was where Lucius stayed. He saw two other men entering the building.

"It's like a little slice of heaven," said Angus, looking out toward the bay. "I have much to be grateful for." He looked at Eddie, "I see that the clothes I had Lucius get for you fit well enough."

"Yes, sir. Thank you so much. It is very generous of you," said Eddie.

"Your name is Angus, that's Scottish, isn't it?" asked Angie.

"Yes, my mother was Scotch-Irish. She had red hair and green eyes, like you. My father was Dutch. His family had been on the island for over 100 years," Angus explained. "My little girl, Rebecca, had red hair like yours. You kind of favor her. She passed last year. Died of fever." Angus wiped a little tear from the corner of his eye.

Death of loved ones was a regular occurrence in Colonial America. That didn't make it any less painful. Angie was overcome with several emotions at the same time. Sadness for the Van Auken's loss of their child, gratitude for their extreme kindness, and guilt for having deceived such nice people. She wanted to share the truth with him, but did not see that as an option.

"You two are welcome to stay as long as you like. We tried for a long time to have children. Rebecca was our little miracle, but she is gone. I do not think there will be others. The Lord has blessed me with material things. The farm was doing well, so I invested with a man who was wanting to get into shipping. For now, he is located just outside of Freeport. I was on my way back from there when I came across you two. We now own four ships, with good, hardworking, and honest captains and crews. We have done well. I am certain that the Lord would want me to share my good fortune," said Angus. "I have to admit, that the sea is not for me, but I am blessed with a partner who loves it and who takes care of much of the day to day business."

Angus was unaware that his partner, Charles Langley, had gotten into a little smuggling, war profiteering and even some privateering. He had taken steps to move their operation to New England now that the British were out of Boston. Charles loved Angus like a brother, but was a little more devoted to making a profit than he was to the Lord. Angus invested in Langley's business when he was first starting out, and Charles remained grateful. He happily shared the profits with Angus, but was careful not to let him know how the money was made.

"We would love to stay here," said Eddie. "But just for a short time. We really should get back to our uncle in New York. He will protect us from our father."

"I just want to thank you for everything," said Angie. "You literally have saved our lives. Eddie, we don't have to be in such a hurry to leave, do we?"

"Yes, I think our Uncle GEORGE, will want to see us," Eddie said pointedly. He wondered what was up. Angie was the one who came up with the idea of contacting George Washington again. Now she was dragging her feet. It was almost as if she did not want to go home.

"We can discuss it in the morning," said Angus. "For now, let's enjoy this evening that the Lord has provided."

"Amen," said Angie. It was beautiful here. She even felt better physically. At home she spent most of her time feeling tired and unhappy; here she felt pretty good.

Chapter 16
Summer 1765

Sol and Vernon Find an Inn

Sol and Vernon began heading east. Sol had brought a compass. The countryside was pleasant, with rolling hills and trees. They eventually came to a dirt road, which headed north and east. They followed it for about an hour.

"This is terrible," said Sol. "We have no way back. We have no way to find the children. We have to find that guy."

"We'll find him," said Vernon. "He's a show off. He talks like he's acting in bad community theater. Look at that outfit; it's like he thinks he's an 18th century version of the Green Lantern."

"Except that the Green Lantern is not a villain. I get what you mean though; costumed and flamboyant. He would fit in at Comic-Con"

"That should make him easy to find."

"We know his approximate size and I would recognize his voice anywhere," said Sol. "Plus, he has a wounded shoulder."

"I still can't believe that you actually hit him," said Vernon.

The road came to the top of a hill and from that vantage they could see a town about a quarter of a mile ahead at the bottom of the hill. It was not a large town. There were a few houses, a general store and an inn. They walked down to the town and first went into the inn.

Inside there were a dozen or so wooden tables and six people seated in various places around the room. All of them were men. A group of three were seated near a window and having a lively conversation: a short, stout man in his fifties was regaling two younger, thinner men with what appeared to be a very funny story. They had mugs and plates of eggs and bread in front of them. The stout man took a long drink from his mug and continued his story.

Sol scanned the dining room. None of the voices of the three matched his assailant. One man sat alone on the other side of the room. He was sipping from a mug, deep in contemplation. He was not very tall, and had blonde hair. At another table was a very tall man with sandy colored hair; it wasn't him, thought Sol. The robber had dark hair. Two other men sat in a corner near the back of the place. They were having a quiet conversation. Sol looked at them. Both had dark hair and were the right height. Sol walked over to introduce himself. Vernon stayed near the door.

"Hello," he said, offering his hand to shake. "My name is Sol Fitzgerald and I am new in town." He shook each man's hand and clapped him on the shoulder. Neither had been wounded. Sol learned their names were Aaron Cooper and John Knowles. One was a merchant who owned one of the shops in town, and the other owned a plantation a few miles outside of town.

"No one in this tavern is our robber," said Sol.

The proprietor came out into the dining room. He was a short, heavyset bald man with huge grey muttonchops covering his jowls. He was nearly as wide as he was tall. He wore a tan shirt and a white apron. "Hullo," he said. "Can I help you gentlemen?"

"Yes sir," said Sol. "We would like a private room."

"Certainly, that will cost you..." the man said.

Sol cut him off, "We are not from around here and do not have local currency. I can pay you in gold."

The man nodded, "That would be acceptable."

Sol took six of the Krugerrands and handed them to the man. "This should be more than enough to pay for the room for one week." The man examined the coins and nodded appreciatively. "He should be appreciative," thought Sol. "I just paid $8,000 for a room."

The man took them to the room upstairs. He filled a basin from a pitcher, and began to go into his instruction speech. Sol interrupted him, "Do you know of a bandit around here who wears green? He talks funny, like he is acting in a bad play."

"Oh, you mean Sir Henry the Pirate," the old man said with a chuckle. "I fancy you hadn't met him or you wouldn't have these nice gold coins." He jingled them in his hand.

"Pirate?" said Vernon.

"Well he really isn't a pirate...I mean he don't have no ship or nuthin' like that. But he will rob ya—I guess that's what makes him a pirate. Least that's what folks here call him. He leaves the locals alone; only robs strangers. Why do you ask?" the man said.

"He robbed us this morning," Sol said.

"He didn't do a very good job; you still got your gold."

"I shot him, but he got away with something that is very valuable to us."

"You shot Henry...by Jove you are a dangerous man. No one ever gets the drop on Henry. He's been robbin' people around here for years. Always makes a clean getaway. He's a bit of a legend, you know."

"We need to find him," said Vernon.

"Good luck with that," the man said. "He's a slippery one, that Henry."

"There are six more gold coins in it for you if you help us catch him," said Sol.

The man's eyes got wide and he thought a minute. "I will see what I can find out," he said, and left.

"He knows more than he's saying," said Vernon.

"A man who robs strangers would do well to get information from the man who ran the inn," Sol agreed. "I doubt he will take our deal to pay him for information about the robber. He may make arrangements for his robber friend to get all of our gold. I'd even be willing to wager that our friend shows up at this inn."

"Knowing that gives us an advantage," said Vernon.

"Yes," said Sol, "and we have a lot more firepower than he does."

"Until he finds out what a terrible shot you are," said Vernon.

Chapter 17
August 28, 1776

Collins Continues Pursuit

It was morning when Collins woke up. His head felt a little better, although he still had a low-grade headache. He felt rested and was beginning to feel a little more like himself.

He got up, and made his way to the town of Jamaica. He stopped at a general store, another tavern and knocked on the doors of several houses. No sign of the children. His head was beginning to hurt, but not as bad as on the previous day.

Sitting on the porch of a small, shabby house near the edge of town were two men. They were as unkempt as the house. One man was tall, thin, with sunken brown eyes, a large hooked nose and black hair. His clothes were old, dirty and had holes in them. He smoked a pipe. When he smiled a greeting, his brown teeth showed. His companion was fat and bald, with long stringy brown hair around his ears and the back of his head. He had a big bulbous red nose, round flushed cheeks and several teeth missing. His brown threadbare jacket had several stains on it and his hat was pushed back high on his head. They were passing a jug of whiskey back and forth.

"A little early in the day, don't you think?" Collins said as he approached the two men.

"What's it to ya?" snarled the fat man.

"Nothing to me if a couple of drunken sots waste their day... or their lives for that matter," Collins said haughtily.

"Then I guess we won't be offering you a drink," said the thin man.

"Is there a reason you're inneruptin' our conversation with your insults?" inquired the fat man. "If I was as ugly as you, I'd be slow to offer insult to someone else. What happened to ya anyway; fall face first in some tar?" He laughed. "A fella who looks like you should have a drink, no matter what time of day it is—help him forget how gawdawful ugly he is." He laughed again. "Maybe we should offer him a drink, Nate." He poked his friend in the ribs and took a long drink from the jug.

"No, thank you," said Collins. "I am here on the King's business."

"Ohhhh, the King," said Nate, pretending to be impressed. "Shouldn't drink if you work for the King." He took the jug from his friend and had a big swig. He wiped his mouth and passed the jug back. "Jonathan, show some respect. We are talking to the King's agent." He belched.

"I am looking for two children," an exasperated Collins said.

"Why didn't you say so?" Nate said with mock seriousness, leaning in. "Did they steal the King's whirlygig?" Nate laughed and Jonathan, who had been taking a pull on the jug, did a classic spit-take, spraying whiskey on Collins' pants. Collins looked at the stain on his pants. He put his hand on one of the pistols, but managed to control his anger.

"These 'children' know Washington's plans are vital to his majesty's war effort. The boy is slender, dark hair and perhaps 12 years old. The girl is...well...'plump', about 10 years old and has red hair. Have you seen them?"

"How do you know that we isn't patriots who would jump you and slit your throat to save Washington's prize spies—aged 10 and 12?" Nate said, laughing.

"In your condition, you couldn't slit a sheaf of paper," Collins said, pulling a pistol. "I think I would have no trouble stopping you."

"Take it easy," said Jonathan. "We isn't patriots. For that matter, we isn't Tories neither. What we isn't is damn fools who are willing to die by taking sides in this nonsense."

"A wise choice. Washington and the Continentals are being swept from the island as we speak. Now, have... you... seen... these... children?" Collins said through clenched teeth, forcing self-control.

"You know, now that you mention it," Nate said. "Two children came through here a couple of hours ago—tall, dark-haired boy and a fat red-haired girl. They was terrified. They said that this ugly bugger, painted up like an Indian was after 'em. They were going to Freeport to try to get to a boat to get away." He took a pull off of the jug, "Isn't that right Jonathan?"

"Yes, yes, they was white with fear—trembling. Begged us not to tell anyone about them. We wasn't gonna tell you, but since it is for His Majesty, well, we have to do the right thing. Freeport is where they be."

Collins turned on his horse and headed east without thanking the men. "Never saw a horse with two rumps before. One in the usual place, and one sittin' on top," said Jonathan once Collins was out of earshot. "I hope he enjoys Freeport," said Nate, laughing and taking another long, slow drink of whiskey.

It was afternoon when Collins arrived in Freeport, which was about 15 miles from Jamaica, on the Atlantic side of Long Island. It was just beginning to rain. He spent a few hours going door to door to ask about the children. No one had seen them.

He could go further up the coast on the Atlantic side of the island, they could have gone that way—maybe; but maybe not. Assuming they knew that Long Island would be held by the British, it would make sense that they would want to get off of the island.

It would be much easier to cross the Sound to Connecticut than it would be to try to get a boat on the Atlantic side and sail down the coast with all the British warships in the area. He doubted that they would find a ship to take them north to Boston because they would know of the British plan to isolate New England from the rest of the colonies. If they wanted to get to Long Island Sound, they would have to take a road that goes north. That would mean that they probably would have taken the road that was just west of that first tavern. But the children were not from Long Island; they might not know to do that. If they were not hiding in Freeport, they were traveling, he was sure of it. It made sense to try at least one more town up the coast. He headed up the coast to Amityville. He was beginning to suspect that the two drunks had lied to him. He would not go further up the coast than Amityville.

Collins rode out of Freeport, up the coast to Amityville, which was about 10 miles away. By then it was raining hard, making travel miserable. There was no sign of the children in Amityville. He found an inn and decided to stay the night. He would start fresh in the morning.

Chapter 18
Summer 1765

Sol and Vernon Spend a Quiet Evening at the Inn

Sol and Vernon went downstairs for some food. They picked a corner table and sat next to each other. Their backs were to the wall and they looked out over the dining area. The barmaid came and they ordered. After about 15 minutes, she came back with two huge plates and two huge mugs. They had a thick beef stew, which they ate with huge slabs of coarse brown bread and mugs of ale. Sol looked around at the other patrons, ruling them out one at a time.

"This is really good," said Vernon.

Sol nodded agreement. "Sir Henry isn't here," he said.

"If you're right about the arrangement with the innkeeper, he'll show," Vernon said. "Maybe later tonight, when the place is a bit noisier and full of drinkers."

The innkeeper came over to the table. "You gentlemen enjoying your meal?" he asked.

"The food is wonderful," said Vernon

The innkeeper patted his large stomach and said, "Ah, my wife is a difficult woman, but an amazing cook." He paused and cleared his throat. "I hate to bring this up, but our arrangement does not include meals."

Sol reached into his pocket and pulled out another coin. He handed it to the innkeeper. "I trust that this should be sufficient to cover our food and drink while we are here," he said.

The innkeeper greedily snatched the coin. "Don't rush back up to your room. You should stay down here and have a dram or two. Saturday night, there will be music and merriment," he said. "Another coin should cover your bar tab." He held out his hand in anticipation.

Sol dug out another coin and handed it to him.

"Strange looking coin," the innkeeper said reading the words on it. "'South Afrika', is that where you're from? I didn't know any white folks lived in Africa."

"We have business there," said Sol. "With people who are more honest and less greedy than you."

"My friend is joking," interjected Vernon said, putting a hand on Sol's shoulder. "He can be off-putting sometimes, but he means well. We love your wonderful establishment and your fare is second to none. We consider it a bargain." Then he whispered in Sol's ear, "Stay on his good side, let him think we are stupid and happy."

The innkeeper smiled and thanked Vernon for the compliment. "Business, eh? Slave traders?" he asked. Sol smiled at him and said nothing.

"Ivory," said Vernon, not wanting to carry that stigma.

The innkeeper cleared the plates and left.

"It looks like we should stay and enjoy the party," said Sol. "I paid enough for it."

"Oh, what do you care?" said Vernon. "You'll never spend half of what you made on those glasses in your lifetime."

"I know. It's just that I can't stand venal and greedy men," explained Sol.

"You don't have to stand him, just put him at ease and watch him," said Vernon.

"If we are going to a party, I need to go upstairs and get something," said Sol.

Sol went up to the room and retrieved his harmonica. As he was leaving the room, he thought of something. He opened his duffel and retrieved the hammerless .38, which had placed there earlier. He opted not to use the ankle holster and put it instead into his front pants pocket.

Sol went back downstairs and joined Vernon. They sat in the back corner of the tavern, nursing their mugs of ale, watching each patron as he came in. The place was filling up. They wanted to stay sharp, so they did not order a second mug when they finished their meal. The innkeeper came by to see if they wanted anything else. They ordered tea, which the owner brought with some tasty little cakes his wife had baked. Sol felt for the man and his marriage, but the woman could cook. They sipped their tea, nibbled their cakes and waited.

"You know something, Vernon?" asked Sol.

"What is that?"

"We still do not know when or where we are. I mean, clearly we are in 18th century America. It seems to be before the Revolution.

Most likely it is the period between the French and Indian War and the Revolution. My guess is that we are in the Mid-Atlantic region, maybe the South. But we do not have an exact date or location," said Sol.

"It's summer," said Vernon. "Pinpointing the time isn't vital. I agree with you; it is sometime between 1764 and 1775. That's the right ballpark. If the opportunity presents itself, we should leave an envelope."

"Yeah, then maybe Eddie and Angie can come and save us," said Sol. "We could add a note: 'Help, we're trapped in the mid-18th century'."

Just then some men carrying musical instruments came into the tavern. One had a violin, another had a flute, a third one had what looked like a guitar, but it had 10 strings and a teardrop shape. They sat on the opposite side of the room from Sol and Vernon. Sol watched the men closely. Two of them were the right height.

The guitar player (Sol called it a guitar because he could not remember the proper name of the instrument, which was actually an English guitar, a now extinct 10-string version of a Renaissance cittern with a flat back and a tear-drop shape, tuned to an open C chord) went over to the innkeeper and got several mugs of ale. They chatted a bit while the innkeeper poured. The "guitar" player took the drinks over to his mates just as a fourth musician came, holding what looked like a pair of sticks.

Sol watched the men with great interest. The men sat with their drinks for a few minutes before they picked up their instruments and began to play. The music was lively and the two men began to enjoy themselves. The tavern began to fill up. The two men began to relax and Vernon ordered another two ales. It was turning into a party. A couple of men even got up and danced a jig.

Sol had been watching the band intently. The music was lively, and he was starting to enjoy himself. He turned to Vernon and said, "Shall we show these guys a little John Mayall?"

Vernon grinned. "Room to Move?" he said.

"Of course," said Sol. "I've got my harp."

"Maybe that guy will let me borrow his bones," said Vernon. The fellow with the two sticks, called bones, was the percussion section of the band. The bones were held like a pair of chopsticks and could provide a rapid clicking rhythm not unlike castanets.

The two men walked over to the band just as it was finishing up a tune. Sol stepped up when the tune ended and said to the guitar player, "Mind if we join in and play a little song?"

The guitar player said, "Sure mate, what have you got in mind?"

"It's a little song that is popular where we come from," said Sol.

Vernon went over to the man with the bones and asked to borrow them for the number. The man handed the instruments over.

Sol exploded into the harmonica intro to John Mayall's "Room to Move." Vernon kept beat with the bones. The guitar player watched them and picked up the tune. He was keeping up; Sol was impressed. The man was a very talented musician, he was learning a whole new genre of music in a matter of minutes. The instrumental went on for a few minutes, then Vernon began to sing in a deep voice that filled the room:

> "May seem peculiar
> How I think of you
> If you want me, darlin'
> Here's what you must do
>
> "You gotta give me
> 'Cause I can't give the best
> Unless I got room to move"

Sol and the guitar player went into another musical interlude, with Vernon playing the bones. All of the patrons in the tavern had stopped what they were doing and watched the performance. The guitar player kept up well. The two jig dancers got up and started dancing. Vernon sang the next verse:

> "If you want me darlin'
> Take me how you can
> I'll be circulatin'
> 'Cause that's the way I am
>
> "You gotta give me
> 'Cause I can't give the best
> Unless I got room to move"

Sol was good—at least as good as John Mayall, thought Vernon. Canadian or not, that Nigel Mack was a very good teacher, and Sol was a good student. Nigel taught the blues but from there Sol learned R & B, rock and soul. Vernon kept the beat. The tavern came alive with their music. They finished and everyone in the place cheered. Sol clapped the guitar player on the shoulder by way of congratulations. He winced in pain. Sol grabbed the shoulder, increasing the pressure and pain. He leaned in, pulling his pistol and shoving the barrel under the man's chin. "Hello Sir Henry," Sol said.

Chapter 19
August 28, 1776

Eddie and Angie on the Farm

Angie and Eddie had each been given their own rooms. They were exhausted and slept until it was almost noon. In the morning, each child made use of the pitcher and basin to clean up. They each got dressed and ran into each other in the upstairs hallway.

"Morning," said Eddie. Angie just nodded a greeting. They went downstairs. On the dining room table were biscuits, apples and pears. Angie sat down and buttered a biscuit for herself. Eddie took a pear and bit into it.

Sadie entered the room, "Well sleepyheads, it's about time you got up. We'll have lunch in about an hour. Mr. Angus says you can join him outside after you've eaten."

Mrs. Van Auken came into the room and sat down. "I trust you slept well," she said. "Poor things, you must have been exhausted."

"It was a tough couple of days, especially after falling into the Sound," said Eddie. "We can't thank you and Mr. Van Auken enough for taking us in."

"It's the Christian thing to do," said Mrs. Van Auken. "I trust you will do the same for someone when you are older and have the chance."

Angie nodded with her mouth full. She was eating her fourth biscuit. Sadie came in with some tea and poured them each a cup. "Lemon or milk?" she asked. Eddie shook his head. Angie swallowed her bite of biscuit and said, "No, this is fine."

"Angus says you have family in Manhattan," said Mrs. Van Auken.

"Yes Ma'am," said Eddie. "Our mother's brother. He will protect us from our father. He was always suspicious about what happened to mom..." his voice trailed off and he wiped an imaginary tear from the corner of his eye. Eddie continued, choked up, "He was always partial to our sister Emily."

"Where is Emily now?" asked Mrs. Van Auken.

"She's not with us any longer...she's with the Lord... our father... I can't," Eddie sobbed. "That is why we had to get away, to protect Angie."

"There, there now, dear. I am sorry I brought it up. We won't speak of it again," Mrs. Van Auken said.

Eddie gave a sidelong glance to Angie and smiled. Angie was beginning to feel bad. These were the absolute best people she had ever known and she and Eddie were conning them. There really was no other word for it. This was a scam. The tears that came from her eyes were real. Mrs. Van Auken handed her a hankie. Angie dabbed her tears and said nothing. It was too late to tell the truth now. She doubted the Van Aukens would believe her, and she was afraid of how they would react if she changed her story now.

Eddie finished his pear and said to Angie, "Come on, let's go outside and see what Mr. Van Auken is up to. It will make you feel better." Angie just nodded. She wanted to get away from Mrs. Van Auken and this awkward conversation.

When they got outside Angie said, "We shouldn't be lying to these nice people."

"I know," said Eddie. "But we are stuck with the story now. I hadn't figured that we would be spending a lot of time with any local people. We should get out of here anyway. Collins will eventually find us if we stay. You mentioned that we should talk to General Washington on Manhattan."

"I just have the feeling that he knows something about our situation. He might even know who we really are. But I really like it here. Staying would not be so bad; but we would have to come clean to the Van Aukens." Angie said.

"We can't stay here, and we certainly can't come clean, Angie," Eddie said. "It's not safe. It is only a matter of time before Collins finds us."

"You're right, unfortunately," said Angie.

"You yourself said that Washington escapes and his headquarters is on Manhattan Island for a while. There will be a lull in the fighting and we may get to spend some time with him," Eddie said. "I worry that it is a dangerous place to go. Is it worth it? I mean, what makes you so sure that Washington has anything to offer us?"

"I don't know. It's just a feeling," She paused. "I like it here, but you're right, we can't stay here. It is not safe and we can't continue to lie to these people. It's just that I feel so guilty," she sighed. "Under other circumstances, however, I would be very happy here."

"Hullo!" They heard Angus holler. He was back toward the

edge of the property, chopping wood. They went back to where he was.

They walked several hundred feet to the edge of the cleared land where there were two fallen trees. One was cut into logs and Angus was splitting the logs with a wedge and sledgehammer. Angus was a big, powerful man and it seldom took him more than one swing to split a log.

They approached him and he handed the sledgehammer to Eddie. "Want to give it a try, son?" he asked. Eddie shrugged and took the hammer. The wedge was in the middle of a log that was about two feet wide and about 18 inches tall. Eddie swung the hammer and hit the wedge with a glancing blow. The wedge shot out of the log. Angie laughed; Angus silenced her with a look.

"Takes some getting used to," he said as he picked up the wedge and tapped it back into the center of the log. "Now don't worry about how hard you hit it. Concentrate on hitting it square. Power comes later. Hit it square on the head." Eddie choked up on the hammer a bit and hit the wedge dead center. It went in another couple of inches. Eddie hit it again, a little harder this time, but still squarely. It went further in. Eddie hit it a third time; this time with real power and the wedge was buried in the log. It split, but did not come completely apart.

"That's very good," said Angus. He put a hand on each side of the split log and tore it apart with his bare hands. "A little practice and you'll be really good at this. It's important work, winter will be here before you know it," he said.

They split logs for about an hour. Angie even took a turn. She could hit the wedge squarely, but was not able to make it go into the log very far. After about 10 swings, Angus stepped in and finished splitting the log with a single blow. About that time, Sadie stepped out from in front of the house and called them for lunch.

Angus pointed to a bucket and said to Eddie, "Take that bucket there and feed the pigs, then we can go in and eat." He set up another log and split it with a single stroke. He split a few more logs before heading toward the house.

There was a barn about 50 yards away with a pigpen protruding from it. The pen had the wall of the barn as one of its sides. The sun was out today, but the inside of the pen was still muddy from all of the rain earlier in the week. Eddie was about 30 paces ahead of Angie; he just moved faster. He opened the gate a crack and squeezed into the pen, bucket in hand. When Angie arrived, she opened the gate wide and a little pig dashed through the opening. Angie chased after it, but it was hopeless. "Good grief, Angie," Eddie shouted as he ran out of the pen to catch the errant pig.

Angie was already after the pig, but it was hopeless. The pig was much faster than she could ever hope to be. The pig stopped to smell something in a nearby bush. Angie took the opportunity to sneak up on it; when she got close she leapt at it and actually managed to grab it by the legs. Unfortunately, she had gone face first into a mud puddle. The mud made the pig very slippery and it slid out of her grip. Eddie was already upon them and tried to leap and grab the pig, but with no luck. He too ended up face first in the mud. Just then, Lucius came up and whistled. The pig ran over to him. Lucius slipped a rope around the pig's neck and led him back to the pen. Eddie and Angie looked at Lucius and then at each other. Eddie shrugged. Lucius turned toward the two laughing, and said, "You two go on in and get cleaned up. I will feed these guys."

The two got up, futilely trying to brush the mud off their bodies with their hands. They slowly waddled back to the house.

Lunch was sliced roast beef from yesterday, made into sandwiches. Sadie brought plates out to the two children who ate their lunches on the porch, not wanting to bring their muddy selves into Mrs. Van Auken's pristine home. There were sliced tomatoes and cucumbers, and pitchers of water. They were all very thirsty after working in the hot sun. They ate, and drank and were satisfied, albeit a little embarrassed.

Angus told them that they would work for a few more hours and then they would have to come in early and clean up so they could go to the church. Supper would be early today. He looked them over and said with a chuckle, "We may need a little extra time for you two to get clean." Eddie and Angie were covered from head to toe with mud. After lunch they went back out into the field and split more logs, stopping to brush mud off of their bodies every few minutes as it dried. Their skills improved. Eddie got to point where he could split a log in six or seven strokes. Angie actually was able to split one.

After they cleaned up and ate dinner, Angus went to the barn and came back with a buggy drawn by a pair of horses. It was covered and there was plenty of room for everyone.

They rode the buggy toward town and Mrs. Van Auken turned to them and said, "Angus is giving the sermon today. He's a deacon, and the pastor is not feeling well." She looked at her husband proudly. A light rain was beginning to fall.

The church was a plain, white wooden structure with a steeple and a bell. They parked the buggy on the side of the building and went in. Angus excused himself and the rest of the group sat in the third row, taking up most of it. Mrs. Van Auken sat on the aisle, then Sadie, Lucius, Eddie and Angie. Sadie and Lucius sat with the Van Aukens. It was unusual, but if any one in the congregation had an objection to the African Americans sitting in their church, they kept it to themselves. Angus had helped most of the people in the congregation at one time or another. The others were afraid to cross him. Not that he was violent, but he could give a very sharp rebuke that would make the recipient feel small and un Christian. Angus felt that all men were brothers and no one would dare say otherwise to him.

The service was beautiful, Angie thought. She loved the singing. Angus stood at the pulpit and sang along with the choir. With his big, deep, beautiful voice, the choir sounded like his backup singers. When the singing stopped, he stepped up to give the sermon. Thunder could be heard in the background.

Angus gave a rather lengthy sermon about peace and loving your fellow man. He had a few bad things to say about the patriots and the British fighting and "defying God's law." He was a good speaker and it was clear that he was passionate about the subject. The man was an absolute pacifist.

The service ended and they left the church and waited for Angus outside. The rain was steady and a little heavier. "This is the rainstorm that enables Washington to make his escape," Angie thought. She looked up at the sky and enjoyed the drops hitting her face. Then she climbed into the buggy. Angus was one of the last people out of the church. He tolerated the rain to linger and talk to several of the parishioners. He joined them when the crowd had sufficiently thinned. They all got into the buggy and headed home.

Chapter 20
August 29 & 30, 1776

Collins Continues Pursuit

In the morning he arose, went downstairs and to eat breakfast. Breakfast was served by a small man with brown hair, small hands and a pinched face. He was obsequious and reminded Collins of a mouse. Collins asked him if he had seen two children and gave the descriptions for Eddie and Angie. The man said that he had not seen anyone like that; he said he would ask the other patrons. He bowed and left the table—too polite to ask Collins about his face, which still had ink stains on it. The man came back in a few minutes and said that none of the patrons had seen anyone like that. He offered to keep an eye out, should Collins decide to come back.

Collins finished his breakfast and went to every dwelling and business in the town, asking about the two children. It was still raining, and in a short time he was soaked to the skin. No one had seen them. Collins began to think that the two drunks had sent him on a wild goose chase. If the children had come this way on foot, they could not have been very far ahead of him. They would not have gotten any farther than Amityville.

He headed back west and by late afternoon he was passing through Jamaica. It was raining hard. There was no sign of the two drunks. Lucky for them, Collins thought. He would have harmed or possibly killed them, he was so angry. He traveled past the inn, approached the crossroads and headed northwest. After traveling a little way on the north road, just outside of Manahasset, he saw a house about 50 feet off the road. The resident would have a clear view of the road, maybe he would have seen the children. Not to mention that it would be good to get in out of the rain.

He rode his horse up to the house. It was about 5 o'clock in the afternoon; the rain was increasing. He approached the front door and knocked. The tiny, slightly bent old woman answered the door. She wore a flowered housedress and a dusting cap. She had wire rimmed glasses and pure white hair that was tied in a bun.

"Yes," she said. "Can I help you, young man?" She looked at him more closely and said, "Oh my Lord! Whatever happened to you?"

"It's nothing Ma'am, just wounds suffered in the King's service. My name is Ezra Collins," Collins said. "I was wondering if I could prevail upon you for some information." Collins was an abrupt and impatient man, but he did possess a modicum of self-awareness, and knew that was his tendency. He forced himself to be polite and patient.

"Of course, of course," she said. "I am Agnes Smith."

Collins said, "Pleased to meet you, madam."

She said, "First you must come in and let me get you a change of clothes. My Albert's clothes should fit you. Stay and have some tea, you'll catch your death out there."

"Ma'am, there is some urgency," protested Collins, but not too sternly. The rain was picking up.

"Nonsense! You young people never have time for pleasantries. I have been alone in this house for 30 years, since my Albert died. We shall have tea, you will dry off and I will answer your questions," the woman said.

She motioned for him to enter, then told him to wait in the entryway. She left the room and emerged with an armload of clothes. She motioned to a room off the entryway and told him that he could change there. Collins emerged drier and feeling somewhat refreshed.

She led him into a parlor with high windows that had a view of the road. The place smelled of lavender and was spotless. He sat in a floral, high-backed chair and she left the room. She returned in a few minutes with a plate of cookies, and left again.

Collins took a bite of a shortbread cookie and looked out over the road. This was a blasted waste of time. He could still make Oyster Bay and resume his search there. It would be late, for sure, but not too late. He hoped that he could get on his way with some useful information. He would wait and have tea with the old woman, because maybe she saw something. Maybe she could point him in the right direction and he would get hold of those blasted children.

After about 15 minutes, the woman returned with a tray containing a teapot, cream, sugar and two cups. She filled the two cups, asking Collins, "Cream or sugar?"

"Thank you Ma'am, no," said Collins.

She presented him with a cup, took one for herself and sat down in a chair opposite him. The house was spotless and was appointed with expensive furniture. They sat either side of a beautifully carved mantle. The floor was wooden and covered with an ornate area rug. Very nice, Collins thought to himself as he took the room in. She noticed Collins looking at the luxurious items in the room.

"My Albert passed away nearly 30 years ago. It will be exactly 30 years in November," she said, and then she paused and thought a minute. "No, this is '76, so it would be 31 years in November. He died so young; barely in his forties." She paused, took a sip of her tea and continued, "My but he was handsome—and successful. The man had the golden touch. Every venture he tried made money. Even with him gone, I want for nothing. We were very well off. Oh, but I miss him. Now I am alone—not that I didn't have suitors, but after Albert, well, what was the point?"

Collins was getting antsy during this monologue. He wanted to ask about the children. He looked for an opportunity to get a word in, but was having difficulty because the woman never stopped talking. Also, he was not feeling like himself. His head had begun throbbing again, the upper part of his back hurt and he was exhausted. He missed the opportunity to break in when she took a sip of her tea. He wished she had offered him something a little stronger than tea.

"Fever, it was," she continued. "We had an excellent physician from Freeport come and bleed him, but to no avail. He lingered for three days and then he was gone. I thought I would never recover. I still miss him terribly." She took another sip of tea.

Collins took the opportunity and said, "What about the children?"

"Children, oh my no," she said. "Not for want of trying, but the Lord saw fit to deny us the pleasure of children. It is my greatest regret. I would not be so alone now if we had children. Oh, people come by and visit and I have help taking care of the place. You know, I am getting on in years and can't do it by myself. Jinny helps with the cooking and cleaning and Thomas helps with the farm. I suppose they will inherit this place. I don't have any family. I appreciate you coming to visit me; it does get lonely. What did you say your name was again?"

"Collins, Ma'am," he said. "I was wondering...."

But she cut him off. "Mr. Collins, whatever has happened to your face? You look like a painted Indian."

"I was hit by an ink well," Collins explained. "But I would really like to know about the children."

"No children here," she said. "My Albert and I never had any children. It's sad, really. Your sons and daughters can comfort you in your old age. You are still young enough to raise children. Are you married?"

"No, Ma'am," Collins said. "I am looking for two children." He was getting impatient with her, but she so reminded him of his Aunt Elizabeth, he just let her speak. Besides he was tired and in pain; it was as if the will was sapped out of him. Then there was the rain, so he suffered through her incessant yakking.

"Well, Mr. Collins, you should get yourself a wife first, don't you think? If you want children, you should be married. I don't have no children, I am very sorry about that," she said. "But it must have been the Lord's will; it must have been his will to take my Albert. So sad, we were so in love. I am getting up there in years; so I guess I will be seeing him soon. You should find a young lady and have some children. You will regret it if you don't. You know, I was just about to have my dinner. Ham and potatoes—there is plenty. Won't you join me?"

It occurred to Collins that he was very hungry. He had not eaten since leaving Amityville. This conversation was getting nowhere, but his head hurt, he was tired and he was hungry. He simply did not have the energy to force the issue of the two children with her. It was getting late. Plus, there was still the chance that she had seen something, he would just have to find the right opening. He said, "It would be lovely, Ma'am. I would love to have dinner with you."

She led him into the dining room and left. She returned in a few minutes with two plates. The one she placed in front of him was piled high with ham, potatoes and green beans. The food on her plate may have been enough to sustain a small bird.

Collins ate in silence while Mrs. Smith talked incessantly. She talked about Albert. She talked about Albert's business acumen. She talked about Thomas and how he helps her out. She talked about Jinny, and how Jinny prepared the food before she left and how Jinny was a treasure and how she could never get along without Jinny. She talked about the weather. She talked about the British invading the island. Collins wondered how she could have the energy to talk so much with so little sustenance.

Dinner lasted well over an hour, and Collins could see the sun beginning to descend below the tree line across the road. He felt a little better and his head was throbbing a little less now that he had eaten. But the day was wasted. Mrs. Smith cleared the plates and came back into the dining room with two slices of pie. She went back into the kitchen and after a few minutes, emerged with a fresh pot of tea.

She sat down and took a bite of pie and Collins took the opportunity to speak, "Ma'am, I am in the service of His Majesty. I need to find two children, one is a chubby red-haired girl about 10 years old and the other is a thin boy about the age of 12. Have you seen them?"

The woman swallowed her bite of pie and put her fork down. "Do you know Angus Van Auken?" she asked. Collins shook his head no. "He has a wonderful singing voice. It is deep and loud and my how it carries. He always sings spirituals. Angus is a real man of God. Everyone goes to church, but let me tell you they forget what they heard during the week. But not Angus—he lives like Jesus is looking over his shoulder and telling him what to do. Let me see, was it yesterday, or was it the day before? My memory is not what it was. He travels between Freeport and Musketa Cove. He lives in Musketa Cove, but has business interests in Freeport. You can hear him coming for miles because he sings. I will often come outside and listen. He will smile and wave. I saw him yesterday; or was it the day before?" she paused and looked pensive.

Collins said, "Ma'am, I am sure that this Angus is a wonderful man and a superb singer, but I am really wanting to know if you've seen these two children."

"I'm getting to that," she said. "I heard his singing yesterday, or was it the day before? Anyway, when I heard him, I went to the window to listen. Beautiful voice that man has. Anyway, there were two children in the road ahead of him and he stopped to pick them up."

"A red-haired girl and a dark haired boy?" Collins asked.

"I believe so," said Mrs. Smith.

Collins got up to go. "Thank you for your kind hospitality," he said.

"Oh nonsense," said Mrs. Smith. "It's pouring outside, it's getting dark and you have nearly a half-day's ride to get to Musketa Cove. Angus' place is not too far from the water, a little way outside of town. His farm is more than 15 miles away. You should spend the night and get a fresh start in the morning."

Collins was watching the rain hammer away at the window. He considered what she had said and accepted her offer. It would be a miserable ride and he would still have to find somewhere to stay when he got to Musketa Cove. Nothing was going to happen until tomorrow anyway. He would leave tomorrow morning with a new sense of purpose.

Collins woke up at dawn the next morning. It was still raining hard. He decided to endure the weather and go to Musketa Cove. He wanted to be there when the weather cleared. He figured that the children would still be with this Angus Van Auken, but such might not be the case in another day, especially after the weather cleared.

He went downstairs and Mrs. Smith was already up, drinking tea and eating biscuits that she had just baked. When he entered the dining room she said, "Sit, have some tea and biscuits. You should stay here until the weather clears."

"I thank you for the breakfast," Collins said, "but I must get going as soon as I eat."

"Nonsense, you'll catch your death," she said.

"King's work, Ma'am. I have to get going," he said.

"Well at least let's get you properly attired. Albert had a wonderful, large hooded cloak. It will protect you from the rain and the cold. Yes, cold. I know it is August, but the winds have kicked up and there is a chill in the air."

Collins accepted the cloak and went on his way, pocketing a few biscuits for the trip. She told him to keep the clothes she gave him yesterday as well, since she had no use for them. It was raining hard and it was slow going, but he would make Musketa Cove well before nightfall. He was grateful for the cloak. By mid afternoon he was there, and it had stopped raining. He found a tavern and entered.

The proprietor greeted him and Collins asked, "Do you know Angus Van Auken?"

The proprietor said, "Everyone around here knows Angus. Good man, he's a deacon at the church, you know. He has a place a few miles outside of town, near the water." Collins thanked the man, gave him a few coins and got directions to the property.

Chapter 21
Summer, 1765

In Pursuit of Sir Henry

Sol had backed Sir Henry up against a wall, squeezing his shoulder and forcing the gun under the man's chin. "You have something that belongs to me," Sol said.

It is not certain whether the man did not believe that Sol would shoot or if he simply did not recognize Sol's gun as a weapon; but he kneed Sol in the groin and pushed him down to the floor. Before Sol could get up, the man was out the door, leaving his "guitar" behind. Vernon gave chase, but the room was very crowded and Vernon doesn't move very quickly. By the time he got outside, the man was nowhere to be seen.

Sol got up slowly. He stepped up to the violin player and demanded, "Who was that man?" The violin player just looked at him in stunned silence and shook his head.

"I know who he is," said a voice behind Sol. Sol turned around and was facing a very tall, broad-shouldered man, who was a little taller than Sol himself.

"What was that fight about?" asked the man.

Sol said, "That was Sir Henry, the Pirate. He robbed us this morning."

The man laughed and nodded. "That explains a lot," he said. "That man is actually Silas Smoot. As lazy and indolent a human being as you will ever know. The man does nothing but play music in taverns; and he rarely does that. He drinks; he gambles; he chases women, and yet, he never seems to be lacking funds. He says he has an inheritance, but I never believed him."

Just then, the innkeeper came up and said, "What do you mean—causing a disturbance in my place?"

"Easy, Toby," the tall man said. "You know, I always thought that you and Silas were as "thick as thieves". It turns out that that may literally be the case, since he is Henry the Pirate and you are very likely his source of information about travelers. Would you like to leave us be or would you like me to broach the subject with my friend, the Magistrate?" The innkeeper turned and left without saying a word.

Sol looked at the tall man and said, "You look very familiar to me."

"Yes, I saw you this morning," said the man.

"No..." Sol said shaking his head, "that's not it."

"It will come to you," said the man.

"We have to find this Silas," said Sol.

"Oh, he is easy enough to find," said the tall man.

"Unless he decides to leave town," said Sol. "It is VITAL that I get back what he stole from me. It is a very unusual object, an heirloom, you might say."

"We can go to his place now," said the tall man. "Do you have horses?"

Sol and Vernon shook their heads no.

"My place is nearby. Wait here and I will return with some horses," said the man. "It's not far, it will take me less than an hour."

The man left and Sol said to Vernon, "If I were Silas, I would skip town as soon as possible."

"Yes," said Vernon, "But traveling at night is tough in the 18th century. He also has to decide what to take with him and pack. He might even stay put hoping that we won't figure out who he is."

"Of course he knows we'll figure out who he is. The man is a local character. It is just a matter of us going around the bar and asking, 'by the way, who was that guitar player?' No, the man knows his cover is blown and either we or the Magistrate will come knocking soon."

"Cittern player, but I get your point," said Vernon.

They went upstairs to the room, gathered their belongings and packed their duffels. They went downstairs, ordered another ale and waited for the tall man to return.

Chapter 22
August 30, 1776

The Limits of Non-Violence

A little while after lunch, Angie was out on the edge of the Van Auken farm, near a wooded area. It was nice to be outside again. It had rained all night and into the morning. It finally stopped about mid-morning. Angie thought that by now, General Washington was safe with his army on the other side of the East River. Everything smelled so fresh after the storm. Angus had gone into town on some business, but said he would be back long before lunch.

It had been raining since they left church on Wednesday. It rained all day Thursday and they spent the day making candles. Angie found making candles to be both boring and interesting at the same time. Interesting because it was new and she had never seen it done before. Boring because it was repetitive. There was a big pot of hot fat, it was either beef tarrow or lard. There were strings or equal length tied to sticks. You dipped the strings into the fat and lifted them out. The hot fat would cling to the strings; you then took the strings out of the pot and let them hang to cool. You repeated the action with a second set of strings, and a third, a fourth and so on. When the first set of strings had cooled and hardened, you repeated the process. With each dip the candle became a little thicker. They must have made a hundred candles; it was tedious but it helped the rainy day pass.

Eddie had been getting bored and restless, sitting inside and doing the tedious work. It was his habit to pick on Angie under such circumstances. He teased her about being fat and slow when she struggled with a rack of candles. Angus stood up immediately and took him aside. He told him that Angie was his family and he should show her love and respect because they were all that each other had. No bond was greater than the bond of family. He talked to Eddie, away from the others, for quite a while. When they came back, Eddie gave an extremely sincere apology to Angie.

Ever since the "talk," Eddie had been extremely nice and attentive to her. It was a little bit cool outside in the morning, but it was a nice day. Angie went outside alone. She tried to walk on grassy areas because all of the bare ground was muddy. At the edge of the line of trees were some wild flowers; she went over to pick them.

Lucius had been teaching Eddie to ride. Angie wasn't interested in that, so she was off on her own. When Eddie finished his lesson, he looked over at her to wave, but she went into the trees and out of sight.

Angie had seen a rabbit and was quietly following it into the trees. She was very close to it, holding her breath when suddenly someone grabbed her from behind and covered her mouth.

"Say a word and I will break your neck." It was Collins. She felt sudden panic. Her heart was racing as he put her arms behind her and bound them with a cord. She could feel the cold steel of the pistol against her cheek. "Don't think I won't use this; I only need one of you," Collins said. "Now, call your brother over here, like a good girl."

She forced herself to breathe slower, trying to calm down. She then looked at him defiantly and shook her head. Collins bound her ankles and said, "Oh, I think we can make you cry out. It's alright for you to cry out, now that I have you secure." He dug his fingers into the sides of her neck. She felt her arms going numb. She yelled, "Stop!"

Eddie heard the yell coming from where Angie had gone into the woods. "Angie?" he said and walked toward the woods. He drew close to the woods and Collins leaped out and grabbed him by both arms. Eddie and Angie had another uncle, their mother's brother, a marine sergeant who trained men in hand to hand combat. He always told Eddie that in a fight people always want to hit the opponent in the face, but if you really want to disable your opponent, take out his knee. He even practiced some kicks with Eddie, who was very athletic and mastered some effective moves. Eddie lifted up his right leg and kicked sharply down and across, hitting the middle part of Collins' right knee joint, just like his uncle had shown him. He heard a pop; his uncle had told him that that was the sound a ligament makes when it gives. Collins screamed and let go, and Eddie ran away, yelling for help.

As this was going on, Angus was riding his wagon up toward the house. He saw Eddie running toward him and Collins hobbling in pursuit. Eddie saw Angus, so he turned toward Collins and screamed, "Dad, DON'T, please, we're sorry! DAD, please leave me alone!" Angus ran past Eddie, toward Collins.

Collins was chasing Eddie, with difficulty. He said, "I am His Majesty's agent. These two are wanted by the Crown," as he began to draw his pistol. He never got a chance to reach the weapon. Angus picked him up by the back of the neck and hit him so hard in the face that Eddie swore he heard bone crack. Angus held him above the ground and kept hitting him, until the man's face was a bloody pulp. He then threw the unconscious Collins to the ground.

Eddie watched in amazement. Angus was the gentlest, most non-violent person he had ever known. Looking down at Collins, he was really glad that he was on Angus' good side.

"We best get you two out of here," Angus said. "Where is your sister?" He looked down at the unconscious Collins and bowed his head to say a little prayer. "I must atone for that," he said to himself.

"I heard her crying out in the woods. He must have caught her there," Eddie said. He and Angus headed toward the woods, where they found Angie tied up and lying in some leaves. "You ok, Ange?" Eddie asked. Angie sat up and nodded, though it was clear that she had been crying.

Chapter 23
August 30, 1776

Collins' Night in Musketa Cove

When Collins awoke, he couldn't breathe through his nose. His face was covered in dried blood and his nose was broken. He tried to touch his nose and found that his hands were tied to a chair; his feet were bound as well. His right knee was throbbing. When his eyes came back into focus, he noticed the giant who had attacked him, sitting across from him, just looking at him.

"What is the meaning of this?" Collins demanded, although the broken nose gave his voice a muffled quality.

"I do apologize to you, sir. I let my temper get the better of me," Angus said sincerely. "It was wrong of me to attack you. But I cannot allow you to harm those children anymore. I used a bit too much force, but it was right to protect them. Once they are safely away, you will be free to go—but without your weapons."

"I am on the King's business. Those children are wanted by the Crown. By hindering me, you are committing treason," sputtered Collins.

"Treason, is it?" said Angus. "And what exactly do you have on your person that tells me that you are an agent of the King? I searched you and I didn't find any such thing."

"I am a captain in His Majesty's army. I serve under General Clinton. Those two children have information that is vital to General Clinton and the army," protested Collins. Of course, Collins was lying about being a captain—he was just a paid informant who was actually a lieutenant in the American army.

"And yet you have no uniform, no insignia and no written orders," said Angus.

"I am in disguise; this is a secret mission," said Collins.

"Disguised as what? A painted Indian? Or a brutal and evil father?" asked Angus. "The story I find much more believable is the one about the father who so harmed and frightened his children that they left by sea during a storm to get away from him. It is not for me to judge you but the book of Luke, Chapter 17, Verse 2 says,

'It were better for him that a millstone were hanged about his neck, and he cast into the sea, than that he should offend one of these little ones.' I know you are not a Godly man, but there is still time for you to obtain His forgiveness."

"I am in His Majesty's army. I am not their father, you idiot!" screamed Collins.

Angus said, "No matter. It was clear you meant those children harm. It is also clear that you cannot prove that you are who you say you are. So the sensible thing is to keep you here, make you as comfortable as possible and send you on your way tomorrow." Angus stood up and Collins winced, fearful that he might get hit again. It was fruitless and he said nothing more, not wanting to make the big man angry.

As evening approached, Angus untied Collins. Collins took the opportunity to reset his broken nose, which he did with a short, sharp yelp. Mrs. Van Auken came into the room with some hot soup and bread for Collins to eat. Angus had Collins' pistol and his sack of lead shot. "You may eat," he said, "But no funny business." Collins gratefully ate the soup and asked for seconds.

"We have a room prepared for you," Angus said. "I trust you will not try to escape. Although with that knee, you would have a hard time. The room is on the second floor."

Collins' knee had swollen to twice its normal size. It throbbed. His face throbbed. His head throbbed. He could barely see out of his left eye because it was nearly swollen shut. He could not breathe through his nose. He felt defeated.

Sadie led him to an upstairs bedroom, with Angus following behind with the pistol and the sack of lead shot. Collins ascended the stairs with some difficulty; he could barely bend his right knee. They made it to the top of the stairs and Sadie motioned to an open door with her hand. Collins entered it. They closed the door behind him and he heard the click of a lock.

It wasn't quite dark yet. There were no candles or lanterns in the room; clearly they were not going to trust him with fire. There was a window, but Angus was right, escape from the second floor in his present condition was impossible. He lay down on the bed and fell asleep.

Chapter 24
August 30, 1776

Eddie and Angie Escape Again

Earlier, after Angus had laid out Collins and found Angie, he called for Lucius. He told the children and Lucius to go into the house and wait for him. He then picked up Collins by the back of the collar and dragged him to the house where Lucius helped tie him to a kitchen chair.

Angus then went rummaging through the house for money, giving everything he could find to Lucius. "These children are your charges," he said. "You are to get them safely to their uncle in Manhattan. There is more than enough money there to rent a boat, get a horse and wagon in Connecticut and for food and lodging. I will keep that miscreant here until you are safely away."

Lucius and the children packed a few things, and Angie retrieved her backpack. Angus provided bedrolls and some food. Angus had a friend with a boat that was docked in nearby Hempstead Bay, so they sought him out. His name was Benjamin Cooper and he had a 30' shallop, a boat that with both oars and a sail. He was about 5' 8"; his skin as brown as a pecan and covered in deep wrinkles. He had thick white hair that came down over his ears and a broad smile that showed perfect teeth, which was probably a rarity, Eddie thought. He could not tell if the man was 50 or 70. There was a twinkle in his eye and he was very spry and energetic, belying his wrinkles and white hair. His two sons were with him. They were two muscular men with sandy brown hair and skin as dark as their father's.

Their names were Seth and Samuel, and they were a little taller than their father. Eddie saw a strong family resemblance. Darken the hair and smooth out the wrinkles from Benjamin, and you had Seth and Samuel. All three men were muscular with big calloused hands and thick fingers. Mr. Cooper would not take payment for the trip. Angus had helped him rebuild his house after a fire and he absolutely refused to take Angus' money.

They had expected him to take them straight across Long Island

Sound and drop them off in Connecticut, but Benjamin insisted on taking them to Manhattan Island. If the favor was for Angus, and if Angus wanted the children in New York, he would deliver them. Lucius and the children were afraid of British patrols on the water, but the man hoisted a Union Jack and said that they simply would wave and smile at the British sailors.

Angie pointed out that Manhattan was now a war zone and that the British Navy would be unlikely to let anyone through—friend or foe. The British may buy the 'Loyalist fishermen' story, but the little boat definitely would be boarded and its passengers interviewed. They may even know about the two children General Clinton wanted (she, of course, did not mention General Clinton). The weather was better now and it was likely that there were British ships in the East River. They compromised and Benjamin agreed to take them ashore outside of New Rochelle, which was about 15 miles away. Their hope was that no British patrols would go that far east.

They had a favorable wind and it was not necessary to use the oars. The water was a little rough because of the wind, but overall the trip was pleasant and the children relaxed and enjoyed the nice summer day on the water.

With the favorable wind, the shallop reached New Rochelle in just over three hours. When they reached shore, Benjamin turned toward his two sons and said, "I want you boys to accompany Lucius and the children to Manhattan." Lucius started to protest, saying that they had done so much already. Benjamin said, "It is clear to me that the safety of you and these two children are of prime importance to Angus. I know Angus treats you like family Lucius. He's a good man, but there are a lot of people who are not as good as Angus—Hell, no one is as good as Angus. And an African traveling alone with two white children is like to attract trouble. If my boys go with you, no one will think anything of it. It's only another 15 miles and you and the boys will be back tomorrow. I will wait here and take you back."

"You mean that people will think I am a slave and won't bother us," said Lucius defensively.

"Let 'em think what they want. It's better than what they might think if you don't travel with the boys," said Benjamin. "What do you care more about, your feelings or their safety?"

Lucius nodded, "I get your point."

It was about 3:30 in the afternoon and there was still plenty of daylight left. They walked into the Village of New Rochelle. Seth told them about the small village. About 600 people lived there; many of them were French. Many French Protestants left France following Louis XIV's revocation of the Edict of Nantes, which had protected them from religious persecution. They settled in the area, their new home was named after La Rochelle, the port from which they had departed France.

There was a blacksmith in town and it turned out that Seth knew him. His name was Henri La Tour. He had a heavy French accent. Many in the town still spoke French. In fact, until the late 1730s town meetings were conducted in French. Seth and Lucius took Henri aside and negotiated renting a horse and wagon from him. Lucius paid the man with the money Angus had given and they told him they would leave with the wagon early in the morning. The man pointed out an inn where they could stay the night.

When they arrived at the inn, the proprietor told them that there was only one room with one bed available. Angie said, "Cool, we have bedrolls, it will be like a sleepover." Seth gave her a puzzled look and told the innkeeper that they would take the room. Lucius paid the man, prompting a puzzled look from him.

The innkeeper was a gaunt, dour looking man about 5'10" tall. He was balding, very thin and had sunken eyes with dark circles under them. Angie thought he looked a little like a corpse. He took them upstairs and showed them the room. They left their belongings and headed downstairs for some food. The food was not very good—overcooked chicken, cold potatoes and hard bread; but they ate it and were glad to have it. The men had mugs of ale and the children drank water. Eddie took a bite of his chicken and said, "No wonder the guy is so thin."

Angie said to Lucius, "You have a crush on Sadie, don't you?" Lucius gave her that puzzled look again. "You're in love with her," she clarified. Lucas gave her a sheepish look. She continued, "Don't be shy; I think she has a crush on you too." She paused, "I mean she loves you too."

"How can you be sure of that? You're just a little kid; what would you know? It doesn't matter anyway," said Lucius. "I can't have a wife. I have nothing to give her. I pretty much depend on Mr. Angus. A man has to make his own way if he wants a wife." Seth and Samuel nodded agreement.

"Tell her how you feel," said Seth. "I know the cards are stacked against you because of your race. But you are a smart and determined man. Maybe you could work for Langley; I hear he is doing very well. Come back for her when you're successful." Samuel nodded agreement. It was clear that of the two brothers, Seth was the talkative one.

"You gotta tell her," Angie said, agreeing with Seth. "I'm not kidding; you'd make her the happiest person in the world. She doesn't care what you HAVE, she cares about YOU. Trust me, a woman knows these things."

"No," said Lucius. "I need to be my own man."

"He's right," said Seth. "It's a quandary."

Angie thought for a minute and said, "You know, I have just the thing. How would you like to be rich?"

"YOU are gonna make ME rich?" Lucius said, laughing. "I would surely like to see that."

"You have been living with Angus long enough, to know that you should have a little faith," said Angie with a sly look. "I want to show you something when we get upstairs."

They finished their meal and headed upstairs. In the room, Angie went to her backpack. She took the story about Blackbeard's treasure out of it and went over to Lucius. She looked over at Seth and Samuel and said, "You two may want to look at this also. There is plenty for all of you." She handed the news story to Lucius. He read it.

"Where did you get this? How are these pictures possible? What is this?" Lucius said, very confused.

Eddie said, "Are you sure that telling them everything is alright?"

Angie nodded and said, "Still think your school ID is going to fade?" Then to Lucius she said, "Lucius, after we tell you what we are going to tell you, you HAVE to explain to Angus and tell him how sorry we are for deceiving him."

Lucius asked, "How did you deceive him?"

Angie said, "It's a very long story. But the truth is so unbelievable that we had to come up with a plausible story for two people our age to be wandering around Long Island without parents. We never thought we would spend any length of time with anyone, especially someone as nice as Angus and his wife."

Eddie said, "Are you sure you want to tell them this?"

Angie said, "Don't worry, we won't change the future." Then to the others, "After we tell you, you'll understand why we kept quiet about the truth. We are not from Connecticut; we are from Elm Grove, which is a little town just outside of a very big city called Chicago. It's about 800 miles west of here and is part of the United States of America. Three days ago we were living in June of the year

2014. That is the newspaper from the morning we left."

Eddie grew thoughtful for a moment and finally said, "Angie, show them the iPhone."

Angie turned on the iPhone and tapped on Angry Birds, just like she did for General Washington. She started a game and showed it to the three men. They actually laughed when they saw the birds being launched by giant slingshots and hitting the pigs.

Eddie said, "Could you even imagine something like that being built now?" The three men shook their heads.

"Then who was that man who was after you?" asked Lucius.

"He was a British spy who wanted to bring us to General Clinton to help him with the British war effort," said Eddie. "He overhears us talking to Washington, kidnapped us and took us to General Clinton. We escaped and he has been after us ever since."

"Please make sure that you explain to Angus and tell us how sorry we are. Collins is still a very bad man. He's a traitor and he shot a young soldier in camp and almost killed him," said Angie. "We were just trying to stay hidden and made up a more believable story than the truth. By the time we got to know you, Sadie and the Van Aukens, it was too hard to change the story. Please, please, please tell him we're sorry." She touched his knee with an imploring look.

She took a breath and said, "I really want to help you and Sadie get together. The article is about the treasure found in North Carolina in 2014. It's there right now. Blackbeard has been dead for almost 60 years. You can find that treasure. The only thing I ask is that you leave some for the Duke University crew to find in 2014. Please don't take all of the treasure," said Angie. "This newspaper article tells you EXACTLY where to find it. It has a map and everything. Lucius, you can get rich and marry Sadie! And there is plenty for you two, Samuel and Seth."

"Hard to believe," said Eddie. "But can you come up with any other explanation?"

The three men shook their heads. They had a million questions for Angie and Eddie. Lucius wanted to know about slavery and the future of his race. Eddie told him about the Civil War, the Emancipation Proclamation, segregation and the struggle for civil rights in the 1960s. "We even have a black president," Eddie said.

Angie said, "Don't be too proud of that one. He really is not one of the great presidents."

"Are you kidding me, Angie? I am trying to make Lucius feel good about the future. I know you do not like Obama, but consider

Lucius' feelings. What are you worried that he is going to go into the future and vote for him? Besides I like Obama," Eddie said. "He really cares about everyday people." Then to Lucius he said, "His election really shows how things will change. And, in spite of what my sister says, he does get elected twice. And EVERY president has critics." He looked pointedly at Angie. She became quiet and looked away.

Seth and Samuel were curious about how the Americans won the war. After Washington's defeat on Long Island, it did not seem like the Continental Army could possibly stand and hold its own against the British.

Angie said, "The key is the French. The colonies send Benjamin Franklin to France to ask for aid. He is a big sensation there. The French love him. John Adams goes too. He is a hard worker, but the French don't like him that much; he's kind of a pill. In 1777, the Colonists win a big victory at Saratoga and capture General Burgoyne, seven members of Parliament and Burgoyne's entire army. It is such a stunning victory that the British abandon their plan to separate New England from the rest of the colonies. They have to change their entire strategy. It also starts the French thinking that the Colonists are for real. The French wanted to mess with the British — they hate the British after having lost the Seven Years War — or the French and Indian War, as you know it. They didn't want to back a loser and weren't sure that the Colonists could be taken seriously until the Battle of Saratoga. When France and Spain enter the war, it becomes a world war. The British have to devote resources all over the globe, making the war in America only one of many theaters of war. They could no longer focus their efforts solely on defeating the Colonists. Also, France has a navy, which negates one of the huge advantages the British had over the Colonists. The other factor is that the Continental Army gets much better at fighting, and the United States of America wins its freedom."

"So what kind of government do we end up with?" asked Lucius.

"We get a democracy," said Eddie. "There are three branches of government, so that the power is shared. There is the Executive, that is the president and the cabinet departments. The president is elected every four years and can only serve two terms. There is the legislative branch, it consists of two houses, the Senate, which has two members from every state. They are elected every six years. The other branch is the House of Representatives; their members are elected every two years. The number of House members is proportionate to the population of each state. That way the large states only have an advantage in one of the houses of congress. Congress writes the laws, but the president has to approve them. Then there is the Judiciary, they can rule laws unconstitutional. The members of the Supreme Court are appointed by the president and approved by congress."

"You sound like a civics textbook," Angie said. "The truth is that we end up with a weird sort of oligarchy—rule by the wealthy. Big corporations can literally buy elections. People vote, but a rich corporation can anonymously raise money and buy advertising— unlimited money can be spent—and no one is held accountable. Super Pacs can work in secret; they are buying candidates and elections and where all the money is coming from is kept secret. If a congressional representative does not 'play ball' the corporation can spend a fortune to cause him or her to lose his or her seat. If he or she cooperates with the corporation, he or she gets financial help in getting elected. The news media, also owned by big corporations, keep us distracted with arguments about nonsense like gay marriage and flag burning."

Eddie said, "Angie, gay marriage is important to some people. It isn't nonsense."

"I don't mean that it isn't important. Maybe 'nonsense' is too strong a word; but the focus on it is disproportionate. It is the perfect distraction. Important enough for people to care about and debate, but it crowds out information about GMOs, the banks, and the way corporations have purchased our Congress."

Seth interrupted her, "Why do people argue about gay marriage? What's wrong with gay marriage? Don't you want your marriage to be happy?"

Angie answered, "It is kind of complicated in our day. Forget I said 'gay marriage'. It is hard to explain. Let's just say there are issues that we are kept focused on so that we don't pay attention to how the country is being run and the fact that the rich and powerful have purchased our government. The corporations not only control the media, they influence the agencies in the Executive branch that regulate them. Executives from drug companies actually work for the FDA—the agency that regulates the drug companies. They influence the decision of the government agency in favor of the corporations. And taxes, you think the tea tax was bad. In our day, Americans in our day spend more than half of their earnings in taxes."

"Oh for God sake," said an exasperated Eddie. "You sound like one of those Tea Party people. Sure we pay a lot in taxes, but we get a lot too. We have beautiful national parks. We have free education. Students can get help from the government to get through college. We have health care. We have wonderful roads. We have Social Security, so people get money from the government when they retire. If they are disabled, they get help from the government. And taxes are high, but it is an income tax. So if the government pays a company to fix a road and the company pays employees, the government gets a lot of the money back in taxes. Those workers pay someone for goods and services and the government gets some of that money. It makes the economy thrive. As far as the corruption you talk about, Winston Churchill said, 'If you live in a democracy, you get what you deserve.' Super Pacs can buy advertising, but it is up to people to think for themselves."

"Winston Churchill? Eddie, I'm impressed," said Angie. "Was that on a test?"

Eddie shook his head and said, "Mr. Ruminski said it in class. I thought it was a cool quote."

Seth said, "Sounds like things haven't changed much. Political discussions in the tavern often come to blows. People don't always agree. It sounds like you live in a very complicated society."

Angie said, "You have no idea."

Seth said, "To tell you the truth, I hope that I have a gay marriage. In fact, I can't believe that people in your time are against it."

Not wanting to get into a long discussion about the 21st century meaning of "gay," Angie simply said, "Me either." Eddie just laughed. Seth looked confused.

Lucius felt bad that he had triggered this political argument, he decided to change the topic and said, "Sounds like some very good things were invented in your day."

"There are machines that fly; they can take people across the country in a few hours. They travel at over 600 miles per hour," Eddie said.

"And movies—wonderful movies. They can record everything that happens in a stage play and you can watch it," Angie said, taking out the iPhone. Eddie frowned, thinking that she had co-opted it from him. "Watch this." She moved around the room, taking a little video. Then she played it back for the three men. They looked at it in amazement. "You can use a similar device to record a story—you can have men riding horses outside, conversations inside and you can fool around with the recording and make it look like you are in outer space or anywhere. The stories are so real, it's like you are there."

"People don't ride horses to get from place to place. Horse riding is more of a hobby. They have machines that travel over hard, smooth roads. The machines can go several times faster than the fastest horse," said Eddie.

"We have indoor plumbing, something I really miss," said Angie with a sigh. "You can turn of a faucet and fill a tub with hot water and take a bath—anytime you want."

"That device Angie has is actually a telephone. You can punch in a number of a friend's telephone and actually talk to him through the device, even if he is hundreds of miles away," said Eddie.

They talked for hours before finally drifting off to sleep. Angie lay awake for a while, thinking about home. Maybe it wasn't so bad. Then she finally fell asleep too.

Chapter 25
August 31, 1776

Collins is Set Free

In the morning Angus went upstairs and opened Collins' door. "Come on downstairs and get some breakfast," Angus told him. "Then we will send you on your way."

Collins got up slowly. He hurt all over and he had trouble bending his knee. He made his way downstairs slowly, leaning heavily on the railing. He looked disheveled as he had slept in his clothes. "We brought your horse in from the edge of the wood. We fed and watered him. He is fresh and ready to go," Angus said.

Collins sat down to a feast of eggs, bacon, potatoes, and biscuits. His injuries did not harm his appetite. Collins did not have anything to say and the other members of the household sat and ate in silence. It was very awkward. When he finished his food, Angus stood up and said, "I will take you to your horse."

Angus took him outside and helped him get on the horse. He gave Collins all of his belongings, except for the pistols. The knee pain the man endured while on the horse was not Angus' problem. Angus looked Collins in the eye and said, "You are not to bother those children, understand me?" Collins looked down at him and nodded. He slowly rode off.

It took Collins all day to get back to the British camp. It was a miserable trip. Every step the horse took made his knee throb. He had trouble breathing. His head hurt. When he got to camp, he did not even report in. He found a tent and a cot and went to sleep.

The next morning, the camp surgeon took a look at him, cleaned his wounds and wrapped his knee. He was then summoned to General Clinton's tent.

Clinton was seated at a large table with maps, flanked by two officers. Collins entered and without looking up Clinton said, "I understand that you managed to lose the two children." He looked up, saw Collins and said, "Good God man! What happened to you?" Collins' eyes were both black, one eye was swollen shut, his nose was broken, his face was covered with cuts and bruises and the ink stain was still present.

"Uh, I was attacked by a very large man who took it upon himself to protect the children from me," Collins said.

"Where are they now?" The General asked.

"The last I saw of them, they were in Musketa Cove, but my guess is that they are in Washington's camp," Collins said. He had deduced the correct location for the wrong reason. Because of the lies they told to the British, Collins was sure that the two were working for Washington and wanted the Americans to win the war. "I have a colleague in the camp. He can tell me what they are up to. It may still be possible to capture them."

"Excuse me if I don't jump for joy at having you back on the trail. You have proven yourself less than competent. In fact, I have decided that you should not be wandering around the country on your own looking for these children," said General Clinton. He turned to an aide and said, "Bring Captain Goodman in here."

The aide left the tent and returned with the most perfect looking human being Collins had ever seen. He had dark hair, grey eyes and perfect Patrician features. He was right around six-feet-tall, with broad shoulders and a narrow waist. His dark hair was tied in a knot in the back; he did not wear a wig. He was not in uniform.

"Captain Aubrey Goodman, this is Ezra Collins," said General Clinton. "Mr. Collins, Captain Goodman is to accompany you on your mission to find these children; although it seems pointless. We should be able to wipe out these rebels and be home by Christmas. But I like to be thorough, so you two are to bring these children to me. Do not harm them, just bring them here. Captain Goodman will be in charge of the mission. I trust him to hold on to them once he has them. You two may go."

Goodman stood at attention and saluted. Clinton returned the salute and he and Collins left the tent. Collins fumed. The last thing he needed was having an officer and a gentleman looking over his shoulder.

Chapter 26
August 31, 1776

Help from George Washington

When they got to the Blacksmith's shop in the morning, Henri was already hard at work. He motioned with his head toward the wagon, horses hitched and ready to go. The group got into the wagon, with Seth driving.

It was lunchtime when they reached the East River. Manhattan was on the other side. They found a man with a boat who was willing to take them across, but he could not accommodate the horse and wagon.

"Where does this uncle of yours live?" asked Lucius.

"Richmond Hill, it's about a mile outside of the city on the other side of the island."

"How do you know all this stuff?" said Eddie.

"Richmond Hill is where Washington set up headquarters on Manhattan. I read it," said Angie.

"Yeah, but you know where to find it," said Eddie.

"I Googled the location. I was curious," said Angie. "It is just south of where Greenwich Village would be in our day. It is close to the opposite side of the island from where we are. I've seen pictures, so I will recognize it when I see it."

The boatman stared at them for a moment with a confused look on his face. He shrugged his shoulders and set about negotiating with the group. For a fee (that Seth thought was outrageous—being in the same business), he agreed to take them downriver and drop them off just outside of town. That way they would only have a short distance on foot.

Seth and Samuel had a discussion about whether or not to continue on. Seth, the younger of the two brothers, wanted to go and find the treasure. Samuel thought that it was a fool's errand. Since they did not have the opportunity to discuss it with their father, they finally decided to return to their father's boat. Lucius and the children could easily make it to Richmond Hill before nightfall, so Seth and Samuel decided to let them continue on, alone. Neither man was going to go on a hunt for pirate treasure, in spite of Angie's efforts to convince them. When it was clear that Seth and Samuel were not coming, Lucius took the opportunity ask them to explain to the Van Aukens that he was going to be gone a little while longer because he was going to "pursue and opportunity". He also told them to tell the Van Aukens that he was going to continue to keep an eye on Eddie and Angie. The members of the party said their goodbyes, and Eddie, Angie and Lucius were on their way to Manhattan Island.

The boat touched shore in what would now be the East Village. Angie figured that this was less than two miles from Richmond Hill. They were fortunate and did not come close to any British ships. They found a path that seemed to be going in the right direction. Angie checked the compass on the iPhone. They were going in the right direction. She powered down the phone and put it back in her backpack. It took them almost an hour to reach the Hudson River. From there they headed south, eventually finding the Richmond Hill estate. This was Washington's headquarters at the start of his long retreat.

When they neared the estate, they were stopped by a sentry who asked them their business. Angie said that she was a friend of General Washington's and wanted to see him. This confused Lucius, who asked, "General Washington is your uncle?"

"Lucius," Eddie said patiently, "The whole 'uncle' story was made up as was the abusive father. For some reason my sister thinks it is important that we talk to General Washington."

"We're really sorry to have lied," said Angie. "Make sure you tell that to Angus."

The sentry came back and said, "General Washington is actually anxious to see you." He led them to the door of the big mansion and opened it. In a room off to the side was General Washington seated at a table with some of his officers. He motioned to the group to come in. As they approached, he said to his men, "Will you gentlemen excuse us for a few minutes?" Lucius, Angie and Eddie each took a seat.

Angie saw the look in his face and said, "It was bad, wasn't it?" Washington just nodded. "It gets better," she said. "You do win. It's just going to suck for a while."

"I actually have known about the outcome of the war for quite some time," the General said. "Back in '65 I met two men who told me about the events that were about to unfold. I was in a tavern near my home. It was a lively place with good food. The proprietor and his wife were reprehensible people, but the food and drink were second to none. A group of musicians frequented the place and on a Saturday night, it was a very pleasant place to be.

"One Saturday night, two men joined the musicians. One sang and the other played this strange little metallic instrument—like a tiny horn. They played a very lively tune, unlike any I have ever heard. They were very good. At the end of the song, however, one of the men accosted one of the other musicians. The musician kicked the man and ran out of the door.

"I went over to see what was going on. It turns out that the man, who was named Sol, had been robbed by the musician and that the musician was a well known bandit in the area, Henry the Pirate. I believe that he fancied himself to be like Henry Morgan. I believed Sol because the musician was a lazy man with no visible means of support—yet he always had money. His name was Silas Smoot."

"OH...MY... GOD....You saw Uncle Sol!" exclaimed Angie. "I knew that you knew something! Did you see Vernon too?"

"Was he a bald man with a beard who looked like Father Christmas?" Washington asked.

"Yes, that was him!" said Angie exuberantly.

Washington continued his story, "Sol and his friend did not have any horses, so I went back to my farm and got some horses so we could track down Silas Smoot. Watching those two try to ride was one of the funniest things I have ever seen. Vernon had trouble getting up on the horse, and fell off when the horse started moving. Sol kept going around in circles. I had to stop and teach them how to ride. Our little adventure is perhaps too long of a story. The point is that Sol and Vernon told me that I might meet two children, a girl with red hair, about the age of 10 and a boy with long dark hair about the age of 16. Although, young man, I would have guessed you to be 12. They told me that they were from the future, as were you two children.

"Your Uncle Sol told me about this war, and back in '65 it seemed like the most preposterous idea in the world. We were all loyal Englishmen. There had been some complaining about taxes, but nothing that would lead to conflict, or so I thought. Yet everything he has told me has come true. He even showed me some money with my picture on it—horrible likeness. I looked like an old woman. It looks like I will have a high price to pay for liberty if that is the image future generations have of me," he laughed, careful not to open his mouth too widely. "He also told me a little bit about the course of the war. I was loath to believe him, but the events leading up to this war were exactly as Sol had predicted. He told me a little bit about some of the battles. I know about the battle coming up in Trenton, but he did not tell me about Long Island. I have you to thank for the information you gave me about the Battle of Long Island, as discouraging as the results were. Your idea to escape in the fog was inspired.

"Sol told me that if I saw you two, to give you something. He said that you were lost, so he presented me with an envelope that was full of papers with writing and figures. He said that the information would help you to get home. I saved the envelope and kept it for years in my top desk drawer in my study at Mount Vernon. To tell the truth, I had forgotten about it completely, until I saw you two. If you go there, Martha will see to it that you get the envelope. There is a lot more I could tell you about my time with Sol and Vernon, it really is quite a story, but as you see, I have my hands full."

In return for the information General Washington had provided, Angie told him all of the information she knew about the American Revolution. They talked for another half hour.

When they had finished their conversation, Washington motioned to an aide who went into another room and returned with a man walking with a crutch. It was Simmons. Angie saw him and cried, "Private Simmons, you're alright!" She ran over and hugged him, almost knocking him down. Simmons was still not too steady on his feet.

Simmons spoke, "I am alright thanks to the two of you. I owe you both my life. You, young man, stopped the bleeding and you, young lady stopped the festering. I just took the last of those pills you gave the doctor for me; they worked like a miracle. I can't thank the two of you enough."

"Private Simmons will see you and your party to Mount Vernon. He is in no condition to fight, but assures me that he can travel," General Washington said. "I hope we can sit down sometime and trade stories, but more than that, I hope you find your way home."

At that, Angie beamed. She was happy to know that Private Simmons was going to be traveling with them.

"One thing that you might want to know," said Eddie. "The British are after us. They think we can tell them things that will help them win the war."

"Well, we should see to it that they do not find you," said General Washington.

They thanked General Washington and left the room. Washington asked Simmons to wait a minute.

Eddie, Angie, and Lucius stepped out of the building. They waited for Simmons, who General Washington had called aside as they were leaving.

When Simmons emerged, Eddie asked, "What did he want?"

"He gave me some money and a pair of pistols. They were his personal property," Simmons said, handing one of the pistols to Lucius. "Told me that I was to keep you safe. There is a small boat tied near here, on the Hudson. We are to take it to New Jersey, go ashore and make our way to Philadelphia. From there, we can go to Mt. Vernon."

They made their way down to the water, and as promised, was a small dory with four oars. The took it across the Hudson. Simmons and Lucius began rowing across the river; Eddie grabbed an oar and indicated that Angie should do the same. The four developed a good steady pace. They had a favorable wind, and the sail helped them. Angie's endurance was improving. They followed the New Jersey shoreline to Staten Island. They followed the north shore of Staten Island to its west shore. From there, they followed the west shore to the Raritan River, which took them to the town of New Brunswick.

New Brunswick was a bustling little town. It was an important hub on the King's Highway, which ran between New York and Philadelphia. Many travelers going between the two cities used New Brunswick as a stopover.

New Brunswick was first called Prigmore's Swamp (1681–1697), then known as Indian's Ferry (1691–1714). In 1714, the settlement was given the name New Brunswick after the city of Braunschweig (called Brunswick in the Low German language), in state of Lower Saxony, in Germany. Braunschweig was an influential and powerful city in the Hanseatic League, later in the Holy Roman Empire, and was an administrative seat for the Duchy (and later Principality) of Hanover. Shortly after the first settlement of New Brunswick in colonial New Jersey, George, Duke of Brunswick-Lüneburg, and Elector of Hanover, of the House of Hanover (also known as the House of Brunswick), became King George I of Great Britain (1660–1727).

The group had gone about 20 miles and were exhausted when they put ashore near New Brunswick. Just outside of town, Angie slapped herself in the forehead and said, "Darn, I forgot to tell him about Benedict Arnold."

It was late in the day and the little party was exhausted. Simmons seemed familiar with the town. An inn, The Sign of the Red

Lion, was on Albany Street just a few hundred feet from the shore. Simmons said that it came highly recommended. Inside, at the far end of an open room, was an older gentleman speaking to a group of a half dozen young men. Angie asked what they were doing and Simmons said that the inn sometimes acted as a classroom. They only had the one room available, but no one complained. They picked up their bedrolls and followed the proprietor up the stairs.

The Trustees of Queen's College, founded in 1766, voted to locate the young college in New Brunswick, selecting the city over Hackensack, in Bergen County, New Jersey. Classes began in 1771 with one instructor, one sophomore, Matthew Leydt, and several freshmen at a tavern called "The Sign of the Red Lion" on the corner of Albany and Neilson Streets (now the grounds of the Johnson & Johnson corporate headquarters). Classes were held through the American Revolution in various taverns and boarding houses, and at a building known as College Hall on George Street. It was the home of Queen's College, which would eventually become Rutgers University. Of course, in 1776 there was not a regular campus as such.

They stowed their gear and went downstairs to eat a quick supper. The meal was a bit better than the food in New Rochelle. When they returned to the room, each picked out a spot on the floor. They gave Angie the bed. She protested, saying that she was their equal, but in the end opted for comfort. With the money that Angus and General Washington had given, they could afford a horse and wagon. Simmons knew where they could buy one and said he could negotiate a fair price. Eddie suggested offering the boat as trade for partial payment.

Before they went to sleep Angie pointedly asked Lucius, "You ARE going to get that treasure in North Carolina, aren't you?"

Lucius said, to Angie's pleasant surprise, "I think that I'd be a fool not to."

Eddie said, "Simmons should go with you."

Angie said, "Yes, Billy. You should go too. There is plenty."

Billy did not know what they were talking about, so Angie grabbed the newspaper article and the map. She beamed as she told the story about Blackbeard and his treasure to Billy.

When she was finished, Billy said to Lucius, "It's a long way, part of it by water. We'll need a boat. Also, if we are successful, traveling with all that money could be dangerous."

Angie said, "The war moves to the South in about two years. It will be even more dangerous then."

Billy said, "I am up for it, if you'll have me."

Lucius said, "Two of us will make it easier; glad to have you."

They were exhausted and slept soundly. When the morning sun came through the window, Eddie woke up first. He sat for a few minutes and nudged Angie. "Hey!" she said. That woke up the others and soon they were on their way downstairs.

Chapter 27
September 1, 1776

Finding Corporal Miller

Goodman had nothing but contempt for Collins. He detested the rebels as being disloyal and ungrateful to their king and country. He hated Collins even more because after Collins chose to be disloyal to the Crown, he opted to be disloyal to his brothers in arms. He did not do it because of conscience or new found loyalty to England. Collins sold them out for money. He was twice a traitor.

The two men traveled by horse to Brooklyn and then north. They crossed the East River just north of the American encampments. "We should be careful that you are not seen, since you were foolish enough to be found out," Goodman said. "They don't know me; I could come up with a story. It would have been wiser for you to give me the name of your contact and let me go on alone. I certainly could cover ground faster." He looked pointedly at Collins' knee.

"I know the contact and I know the children," said Collins. "You need me."

"And the children know YOU," Goodman pointed out. "You can't get within 50 feet of them. You are more of a hindrance than an asset. You should learn that about yourself."

Collins detested Goodman. He was too good for lowly Ezra Collins. Goodman was a member of the English landed gentry. Young for a captain, his money and connections would ensure a life of wealth and ease. The man hadn't said anything to Collins that was not laced with derision and insult.

They walked (Collins with some difficulty) to just outside of where the Americans were camped. "You can't go any further, someone will see you and they will come and arrest you. Give me the name of your contact. I won't leave you here. I am under orders, and as foolish as I think those orders to be, I will not disobey them. I give you my word that I will come back for you. You are to accompany me to find the children. General Clinton could not make it any clearer." Goodman said. "I will not abandon you, my word as a gentleman."

Collins thought for a minute and said, "His name is Jeremy Miller. He is tall, not quite as tall as you, slender and has sandy brown hair and blue eyes. He is a corporal."

"Wait here," said Goodman and began strolling toward the camp. Although Goodman was an aristocrat, he was dressed like a workman in tan trousers and plain shirt. His boots may have been a giveaway, if anyone looked. They were black leather and were expensive. He slung his musket over his shoulder and sauntered toward camp.

He was stopped by a sentry on the perimeter of the camp. The sentry raised his rifle to his shoulder and said, "Halt!"

"Ho there!" Goodman said, with no trace of his British accent. "I hear this is where General Washington is fightin' for liberty. Where do I sign up?" He held up his Brown Bess, "Got ma own gun. Took it off a dead Redcoat. Corporal Miller told me I should come. Is he around here?"

"You know Corporal Miller?" asked the sentry.

"Know 'em, heck we go way back. We went to different schools together," said Goodman, flashing his disarming smile.

"There he is now," said the sentry pointing to a tall, sandy-haired man headed their way.

"Jeremy, so good to see you again," Goodman said as he walked over to him, held his arms wide and embraced the confused Miller. "I am here with Collins," he whispered in the man's ear. "We are looking for the children."

Chapter 28
Summer 1765

Confronting Silas Smoot

George Washington's description of the hilarity that ensued when Sol and Vernon got onto their horses was quite the understatement. Washington's impulse had been to get angry and impatient at losing valuable time, but the two strangers looked so ridiculous that he had to laugh.

First Sol tried to help Vernon onto his horse, since Vernon was so short. Vernon ended up laying across the saddle, but Sol did not stop "helping" him in time and ended up pushing him head first off the horse. On the second try, Vernon managed to straddle the horse, but was facing the rear of the animal. He fell when he tried to correct his bearing. He finally did manage to get upright into the saddle after three more attempts. It looked like he'd made it, but he pulled one side of the reins. The horse began moving in circles. With each turn, Vernon leaned at a slightly sharper angle; he finally fell off. Sol finally managed to get him upright on the horse. By then Washington was having trouble staying on his own horse because he was laughing so hard.

It was then Sol's turn to mount his horse. He got his foot caught in the stirrup and the horse began moving away from him. He fell, with his foot in the stirrup and the horse dragging him. The horse finally stopped and Sol was able to free himself. Sol then decided that a running start was needed. He got up upon the horse and promptly fell off the other side. He managed to get into the saddle on his third attempt and then made Vernon's same mistake with the reins—prompting the horse to move in circles. He almost fell out of the saddle, but Washington came aside, grabbed his shoulder and righted him into the saddle. It was quite a physical feat, because he did it as he was bent over with laughter.

It took about 20 minutes, but Washington was able to get the horses calmed down and show Sol and Vernon enough basics so they could make forward progress at a reasonable rate. Having their duffels laying across the horse in front of each man was not helpful, but they made due.

Finally, they were on their way to the home of Silas Smoot. Smoot lived about five miles outside of town, right near the main road. In the dark, it took them a just under an hour to make the trip.

Smoot's home was a run-down little one story shack. The trio approached the home and dismounted. Vernon, dismounted a little quicker than he had planned. He fell off the horse. Washington suppressed a laugh.

Falling off the horse was a blessing though, because a musket was fired from the house and the shot passed through were Vernon had been sitting. Another shot took off Washington's hat. Sol and Washington dismounted and helped Vernon up. They took shelter behind some trees. Sol returned fire, firing 5 shots towards the house, in rapid succession. He reloaded. Washington stared at him in amazement.

"Sir Henry," Sol shouted into the house. "We have more firepower than you have. It is futile. Soon everyone will know who you are. The sensible thing is to give up."

"I don't think so," Silas shouted back. He fired another shot that hit the tree they were standing behind.

"You should be careful," shouted Silas. "I have a very pretty disc here. Lots of lights. It looks important. I can tell that it is something that you want. If you three don't go away, I am going to put a musket ball through it."

"Crap," whispered Sol. Then he thought for a minute. "Go ahead. If you put a shot into it, it will explode. It will destroy you and your house."

"I don't believe you," said Silas.

"Yes, but are you willing to take that chance?" said Sol. He paused and thought a minute, then said in an almost deferential manner, "Sir Henry, I think I know a solution that will be favorable to both of us."

Sol's offer to negotiate with Silas was met with another musket shot that hit the tree where he was standing. Sol hollered, "Stop shooting, I want to talk to you." His sentence was punctuated by another musket blast.

"He must have several guns in there," remarked Vernon. "Reloads when it's quiet."

"Not a bad shot, either," said Washington.

"That's it," said Sol. He went into the duffel and pulled out the .44 Magnum. It was the "Dirty Harry" gun with the six-inch barrel and all.

"What are you going to do with that?" asked Vernon.

Sol said, "I am going to ask you to put about three bullets, above head height, through his wall. They should pass all the way through the house and out the other side. I would do it, but I don't want to accidentally kill the man. As you have pointed out on occasion, I am not the best shot in the world."

Vernon fired the gun three times. The bullets passed through the house. A shot was returned from inside.

"That was a warning shot," said Sol. "I can put a bullet through your house. You can't hide from it. I can keep shooting until I hit you. You could die during this foolishness, OR you can let me come and talk to you. I have a proposition."

"You can come in, but no guns. Leave your weapons out there," Silas said.

"I will come in, unarmed, but I want your word that you will not harm me. If any harm comes to me, my friends are well armed with guns far superior to yours, as you have seen. They will avenge me," said Sol.

"I promise that you will be safe. Come ahead—just you," Silas said. Sol handed Vernon his revolver and walked toward the shack with his hands up. He entered the shack and saw, by the candle light, Silas pointing a pistol at him.

Sol said, "We outnumber you and we have better weapons. Even if you manage to escape, within a day or two everyone in town will know that you are Sir Henry the Pirate. You will have to flee and become a wanted fugitive."

"That doesn't sound like much of a proposition," said Silas.

"That wasn't the proposition. I was just reviewing your situation with you. Let me tell you what my situation is. I need the item you stole from me today. You were right, it is very important to me; but it is absolutely worthless to you. I am willing to pay you 20 one-ounce gold pieces for the return of the item. That is over a pound of gold," said Sol.

"I'll still be a wanted man," said Silas.

"I understand that you have never harmed anyone, so I don't care what you do and neither does my partner. We will keep quiet," said Sol. "Although I would recommend retiring. It is only a matter of time before that line of work catches up with you."

"You may be fine with letting me go, but I don't think that the self-righteous Major Washington will stand for it."

"Excuse me, who?"

"Major George Washington of the Virginia Militia. He won't

stand for letting a criminal get away."

"THAT is George Washington," said Sol, eyes wide and mouth agape. "I thought he looked familiar, but I had no idea. We never introduced ourselves."

"What is wrong with you? You act like he's the bloody King of England," Silas said.

"As a matter of speaking…" Sol mused. "Let's just say that he is very popular where I come from. Let me go and talk to him. I'll be right back."

"It won't do any good. He won't agree to allowing me to go free," said Silas.

Sol said, "Don't give up yet. Let me talk to him."

He headed out the door, then paused and turned, saying in the most ominous tone he could muster, "Be very careful with that device. It will explode. It will turn you into a corpse and this house into a pile of rubble. Your life is in danger every minute that you are in possession of it."

Sol walked out of the shack and joined his companions. He approached Vernon and Washington. When he told the men of the deal he had proposed to Silas. Washington said, "Do you mean to tell me that you are going to reward this brigand and not bring him to justice? Absolutely not!" It was just as Silas had predicted.

"Look, General Washington…" began Sol.

"I am not a general. I was a major in the Virginia Militia," corrected Washington.

"You are going to be a general. You are going to command the Colonial Army in their fight for independence from Britain," explained Sol.

"Independence from Britain! Are you insane?" said Washington.

Sol told Washington a disbelieving Washington the truth about Vernon and himself. He told them that they were from the future. Washington was loath to believe him, but then Sol showed him his weapons, his iPhone, a flashlight and some other technological goodies. Washington began to believe. Sol told him about what the next 20 years would bring. The war for independence, the constitution, and the presidency. Every few minutes he would yell to the shack, "A few more minutes, Silas; we are discussing the trade."

Washington finally seemed convinced and Sol went on to explain about Eddie and Angie and how they were lost and that he needed the device that Silas had stolen to be able to find them.

Finally, Washington said, "The man is a thief and a liar. I absolutely refuse to keep his secret. For your children's sake, I will allow him a 24-hour head start before I tell anyone or organize an attempt to seize him. But the man must be brought to justice. You absolutely should not reward him with gold for stealing your property. We have him outnumbered; we should go in and bring him to justice."

Sol looked crestfallen. If his bluff did not work, Silas could possibly destroy the disc. He said, "Wait here. I will see if I can sell a 24-hour head start." He yelled to the shack. "Silas, I'm coming back in." He raised his hands and approached the shack.

Once inside, Sol said to Silas, "I can give you the gold and a 24-hour head start. Washington will not say anything for 24 hours. That takes us until tomorrow night, so no one would come after you until the following morning."

"And where am I supposed to go?" said Silas. "No deal. I would be a wanted man for the rest of my life."

Sol said, "I was afraid that you would say that. What if I could guarantee that no one could possibly come after you. I could hide you so thoroughly that even if Washington spent his whole life chasing you, he would never find you."

"Where would that be?" asked Silas.

"Oh, you're gonna like it," said Sol. "I will be right back."

Sol went out again and approached Vernon and Washington. He said, "General Washington, I need a huge favor. Vernon, give him the envelope." Vernon handed the envelope with the information they had accumulated to Washington. Sol continued, "You may run into the two children I told you about. One is a boy about 16 years old, with dark hair and eyes; he's nice looking. About 5' 2' tall. The girl is 10 and just under 5' tall. She is a little heavyset and has red hair and green eyes, and is one of the smartest children you will ever meet. They are my nephew and niece and are from the year 2014. As fantastic as that sounds, look at me and Vernon; look at our weapons and the things we carry. Consider the music at the tavern. You have never seen an instrument like the one I played. It should be clear to you that we are not from around here. We are from the future and these children are from the future. You will know this for sure when the things I told you about the war and the new nation start to happen. Please, if you see these children, give them this envelope. It is a message from me and I may have no other way to contact them. I want your word on that."

Washington said, "I will give them the package."

Sol turned to Vernon, "Let's gather up our things and go talk to Silas." They gathered up their duffels and headed toward the shack.

"Stop right there!" said Silas from the shack. "I didn't give permission for two of you."

"I need him to come and help me to help you escape," said Sol. He and Vernon continued toward the shack without another word.

When they entered, Silas said, "Keep your hands where I can see them."

Sol had his duffel slung across his shoulder and had filled his hands with the gold coins. "I have your money, and Vernon here will help you to get away. I give you my word. No one will come after you." He walked over toward Silas with the money and handed it to him. It was two large handfuls of coin, Silas put down his gun and the disc, greedily grabbed the coins and clutching them to his chest. While Silas was occupied, Sol picked up the disc, linked arms with Vernon and Silas, Vernon touched the screen and there was a loud "pop". The shack was suddenly empty.

Chapter 29
September 1, 1776

On the King's Highway

In the morning Eddie, Angie, Lucius and Simmons awoke, ate breakfast and headed toward a livery where Simmons knew the proprietor. Simmons negotiated with the man and traded their boat and some of the money. He praised Eddie for the idea of trading the boat; it saved them a lot of their funds. Angus and Washington had given them money enough to secure a horse and wagon, but Virginia was a long way, and the group felt it prudent to conserve money. Simmons took the man to the riverside to ensure that the boat was still there—it was. The two men returned and the group took possession of the wagon.

They made a stop to pick up provisions. Simmons said that if there were British agents looking for them, it might be best to stay out of taverns and inns. They bought food, something to cook with, some rope, a large piece of canvas that could be tied to trees and used to shelter against rain, and various other supplies that may have been needed on the trip. They also bought powder and shot for Simmons' musket and the two pistols.

New Brunswick is about 60 miles from Philadelphia. The King's Highway would take them straight there. The King's Highway was a roughly 1,300-mile road laid out from 1650 to 1735 in the American colonies. It was built by order of Charles II of England, who directed his colonial governors to link Charleston, South Carolina, and Boston, Massachusetts. Later, the newly blazed trail was widened and smoothed to the point where horse-drawn wagons or stagecoaches could use the road. Depending on weather and road conditions, it would take them around two days to get to Philadelphia. From Philadelphia it was another 160 miles to Mt. Vernon, which could easily take another four to six days.

The weather was not bad, but recent rainstorms had made the road bumpy and full of ruts. It was slow going. Lucius drove the wagon. Simmons lay down in the back, resting his leg. Eddie and Angie sat in the back, taking in the sights. Eddie, even though he desperately wanted to get home, was starting to relax and enjoy himself a little. Angie was just entranced, she had never felt this peace and joy at home. The countryside was breathtakingly beautiful. The air was clean and fresh and it never ceased to amaze her that act of breathing actually energized her. She put her hands to her waist, surprised at how much weight she had lost in less than a week.

Angie was in no hurry. Eddie was a little impatient, but was still able to enjoy a pleasant, leisurely ride. Collins was out of the picture. There was no war activity here. Things had turned from a desperate run for survival to a pleasant outing. They were on a camping trip—18th century style. No traffic, Angie chuckled to herself thinking that in a traffic jam they would make about the same rate of speed.

If she and Eddie could figure out how to use the machine, they could actually return home within a day or two of when they left. The prospect of going back made her a little sad. Time being spent in the 18th century did not translate to time missing from 21st century Wisconsin. They could spend a year here and still arrive home the day after they left. She was content and in no hurry whatsoever.

Chapter 30
September 1, 1776

Goodman, Miller and Collins

Collins, of course, was not out of the picture. He was seated, leaning against a tree, outside of the Colonial army's encampment. Goodman had been gone for about half an hour. Collins was getting impatient, which was his nature.

Goodman was having a discussion with Corporal Miller. Goodman had a better opinion of Miller than he had of Collins. Miller always was a loyal subject of King George. He felt that the rebellion was foolishness and the idea of the Colonies becoming an independent nation was preposterous. He thought he could serve the Empire best by spying on the Colonial army. Goodman respected that.

Miller was more than happy to provide Goodman with information about the two children. They had been at camp the day before and General Washington had sent them to Virginia, he thought. Miller was also anxious to leave camp. He felt that his close association with Collins had caused some to cast suspicion on him. He had been able to hold suspicion at bay with patriotic rhetoric and by denouncing Collins ("How could I have been so foolish and unsuspecting? I was taken in by that snake!"). He was of the opinion that he was not being of much use in the American camp. It was difficult to get messages out and he felt that he could be of greater service if he simply enlisted with the British army.

Miller told the sentry that Goodman had some gear stowed in a boat on the East River. He said that they were going to retrieve it and return. The two men casually walked away from camp and joined Collins at his tree. Goodman told Miller that he could use him on this mission and that he would help secure an officer's commission for the man once they had accomplished their goal of returning the children to General Clinton's camp.

Without fanfare or greeting, Goodman brusquely said, "Corporal Miller is going to join us. He says the children have a day's head start. They are going to Virginia and taking the King's Highway. We will take the boat back to Brooklyn, resupply and secure transport to New Jersey. They will be traveling slowly and we should overtake them in a day or two. You, Mr. Collins, will need to keep up." Without a word, Collins got up and hobbled along after the two. Things were getting worse; he now had two insufferable Loyalists to deal with.

The trio made it back to their boat on the East River and rowed back to Brooklyn. There Captain Goodman presented a quartermaster with his orders. He left a dispatch for General Clinton, telling him where the children where headed and his plans to overtake them. They were given supplies, money and arrangements were made for them to be taken by boat to New Brunswick.

The boat was a large dory with 10 oarsmen. By early afternoon they were on their way. The water was calm and the 10 sailors set a strong, steady pace and were soon on the Raritan River on their way to New Brunswick. The boat touched shore just outside of town before seven in the evening.

The three men walked into town. Goodman sought out a livery where he could buy some horses, leaving Collins and Miller to wait for him. He returned in about 20 minutes. Collins said, "We should find some place to spend the night and get a fresh start in the morning."

"Nonsense," said Goodman. "We are not on holiday, Collins. We have work to do. The man at the livery told me that they left here early this morning in a wagon. They won't be expecting pursuit and they will be traveling very slowly. There is still two hours of daylight left. We can camp on the road tonight and we should catch up with them by tomorrow afternoon."

Collins dreaded getting on a horse again. He hobbled behind the other two on the way to the livery. Goodman paid the proprietor, the same friend of Simmons who had sold the horse and wagon earlier. Goodman had told him that he was the children's uncle and he had missed them when they came to Manhattan. The fact that the little party was armed was not particularly surprising and he took Captain Goodman at his word. The trio were on their way before 7:30.

Around nine in the evening and it began to get dark. They had made decent time, traveling about 11 miles from New Brunswick. Goodman said, "There is a good place to camp, near that stream."

They dismounted, and Miller set about to making a fire. Goodman had shot a rabbit a mile or two back, when there was still plenty of daylight. The shot was impressive. The rabbit was moving and Goodman was still on his horse. Miller cleaned the rabbit and fixed it onto a spit to cook for their dinner.

Collins set up his bedroll in a soft grassy area covered with leaves. His knee was throbbing, but he went to the stream without complaining and got some water.

When they settled in to eat their dinner, Goodman said, "They probably traveled about 20 miles today. We covered more than half of that distance today. If we get an early start, we should catch up with them late tomorrow morning. We should get to sleep and leave at dawn."

Chapter 31
September 1 & 2, 1776

The Simmons' Farm

It was late in the afternoon and still light outside when the wagon approached a farmhouse about 100 yards off the road. They could have traveled for a few more hours, but Simmons suggested that they stop. Simmons pointed and said, "That is where my aunt and uncle live. We will be able to spend the night there."

Simmons drove to wagon up to the house and a man and woman came out to greet them. They were in their 50s, with blonde hair that had gone mostly grey. Both looked a little squat with their middle age paunch, and both were about the same height and width. She had on a blue dress and white dusting cap, he had on blue pants with a white shirt. Both had round, rosy cheeks and wore glasses. Each had their hair tied back. They were straining to see who was in the wagon, when the man recognized Simmons, he waved, "Hallo Billy. What brings you out here?"

"I got leave to take these two children to Virginia," said Simmons. "Lucius here is helping me," he said turning to the back of the wagon and pointing to Lucius. "And that is Eddie and Angie," he said, changing the direction of his point. "This here is Anna and Andrew Simmons, my aunt and uncle."

Three large men stepped out onto the portico. "Hallo!" said Simmons. "These three are my cousins, Allen, Alexander, and Albert." He pointed to the back of the wagon again, "Lucius, Eddie and Angie," he said. Everyone waved and nodded a greeting.

"You all must be starved," said Andrew. "We were just getting dinner. There is stew and potatoes; not to mention the fact that Anna made some apple pies. The boys can bunk together and you can share two of the bedrooms."

"Oh no, Uncle Andrew," said Simmons. "We will be fine in the barn. No need to put anyone out of his bed. The weather is pleasant and we have bedrolls. A meal would be more than generous."

Eddie said, "Yes, let us stay in the barn. It is like a camping adventure!"

Angie said, "I vote for the barn too; but dinner sounds like a wonderful suggestion."

They went inside. Dinner was satisfying. There was stew and potatoes as well as fresh vegetables from the garden and fresh bread. Angie, once again, found herself enjoying vegetables. After dinner pie and tea was served. Andrew poured himself a glass of whiskey and offered some to Simmons and Lucius; they declined and opted for tea.

They kept conversation light and away from the reason they were going to Virginia. When pressed, Eddie told Andrew that George Washington was a distant relative and offered to let them stay at his home. General Washington assigned Simmons to see them safely there. Everything else he said was pretty much the truth; he just left out a lot of information. The others in the group did not correct him, seeing the wisdom of not discussing time travel. Angie was relieved that he did not create another elaborate lie or go back to the original lie they had told Angus. There was no need to discuss the British or Collins. They were safe from Collins, so there was no point in discussing him with Andrew. They said their goodnights and headed toward the barn.

Eddie woke up just as the first rays of sunlight began to peek over the trees. He could smell breakfast being prepared in the Simmons' house. He woke up Angie. "I smell food," he said.

"What?" she said. "It's still dark out."

"No," Eddie said, pointing through the open barn door. "The sun is starting to come up." They looked out the barn door and saw Alexander Simmons heading toward them. He was the youngest of the brothers and the shortest. He was built like a fireplug. He had a square head and not much of a neck. He was short, about 5'6" tall, but very wide across the shoulders and had arms that hung almost to his knees. He would have reminded Eddie of an ape were it not for the characteristic Simmons' blonde hair.

He saw Eddie and Angie looking at him from the barn. "Breakfast!" he yelled, waving his arm in a beaconing manner. "Tell the others." He turned around and headed back to the house.

Lucius and Billy Simmons began to stir because of all the noise. Billy sat up. "Come on, it's breakfast," Eddie said. Lucius got up and the little group headed toward the house. They sat down to ham, eggs, bread and apples. They ate their fill and were on their way before 8 am.

Chapter 32
Summer 1765

George Washington's Promise

Shortly after Sol entered the shack, George Washington heard a loud "pop". It wasn't a gunshot, more like the sound of a drum. The shack went completely silent. He stood by the tree and listened for about 10 minutes; no sound, no voices no stirring, there was absolute silence. He became concerned about Sol and his friend. He called out, "Sol, are you alright?" There was no answer.

He circled around to the back of the shack. He crept up to the back door and opened it slowly and as silently as he could. It was dark inside, but not completely dark. There were three candles burning at various places in the room. The room was empty.

Sol had wanted to help Silas escape. It looks like he was successful. Washington decided to go home. Tomorrow he would go to the magistrate and inform him of the secret activities of Silas Smoot. He had made no bargain with the man. He was a criminal that needed to come to justice.

He walked back to the horses, mounting one and leading the other two. On the hour-long trip back to Mount Vernon he thought about what Sol had said to him. He and his friend were very unusual and they were in possession of things unlike Washington had ever seen. But the explanation was so fantastic that he could scarcely believe it. The idea that the two men were from nearly 250 years in the future was nearly impossible to believe. Their statement that the colonies would separate from Britain seemed ridiculous. True there had been some protests about taxes, but the idea of armed conflict was absurd.

The promise he had made was easy enough to keep. If he runs into two children from the future, he would give them the small package that Sol had given him. He chuckled at the thought—meeting children from the future. He had better keep an eye out he thought as he laughed to himself. War, revolution, leading an army and leading a country all seemed like pipe dreams. Still, no harm in keeping a little package.

He arrived home, saw to the horses and headed to bed. It was well past midnight. On his way to the bedroom stopped in another room with a desk. He put the package in the top drawer and forgot about it.

Chapter 33
September 2, 1776

Captain Goodman's Surprise

Captain Goodman awoke at dawn. He arose and woke Miller and Collins. They ate a meal of dried meat and biscuits. Goodman did not want to waste any time preparing breakfast. The group was mounted and on their way within a half hour. Collins leg hurt and he was moving slowly. Goodman let him know what a hindrance he was.

They rode about 10 miles, passing a farmhouse about 100 yards from the road. Goodman said, "They cannot be very far ahead of us. Assuming they got an early start, they are probably five or fewer miles ahead of us—no more than 10. In about an hour, Miller and I will ride on ahead. Collins, you stay behind because the children will recognize you. They don't know who Miller and I are. We will be able to ride up right alongside of them without arousing any suspicion. There are two adults with them and, apparently, they are armed. I would rather not get shot because someone recognized Collins."

Collins couldn't possibly resent this man any more than he already did. Goodman was squeezing him out of the mission. Collins was sure that he would try to make sure that he wouldn't get paid.

After riding for another hour, Goodman said, "This is a good place for you to wait for us, Collins. Miller and I will ride ahead and overtake the wagon. We should be back, with the children, in a couple of hours."

When he and Miller were a few hundred yards ahead of Collins, Goodman said, "When we overtake them, act like we are just fellow travelers. Be friendly and chat. When I make my move, pull your pistols. The two adults are armed, but they are not expecting any trouble. Be friendly and watch me. We shall take them by surprise."

They rode together for about an hour before the wagon came into sight. Goodman said to Miller, "Ride on the right side of the wagon, I will ride on the left. Follow my lead." He spurred his horse on to move a little faster, taking him to the left side of the wagon.

Miller also sped up and pulled up alongside on the right.

"Hallo there!" Goodman said as he approached the wagon. "Going to Philadelphia?"

Lucius, who was driving the wagon, turned to the stranger and said, "We are going a little further than that, Virginia."

"You have ways to go," said Goodman. "It's another 30 miles just to get to Philadelphia, I believe."

Lucius said, "Don't I know it. Slow going with these ruts."

At that point, Goodman pulled one of his pistols and shot Lucius. He then drew the other one and pointed it directly at Simmons. Miller pulled a pair of pistols and also pointed them toward the bed of the wagon.

"You shot me!" screamed Lucius.

"Stop complaining. You are not seriously hurt. I just grazed you. If I wanted you dead, you would be dead," said Goodman. It was true, the shot had merely grazed the left shoulder and did not do a great deal of damage. Goodman was a very good shot. He said, "You are harboring fugitives wanted by His Majesty. I have no reason to believe that you have knowledge of this; so I will not treat you as criminals, take you prisoner or do any further harm to you. The children and the wagon are coming with us. I will ask you not to interfere. You two adults, come down from the wagon and sit back-to-back over there, off of the road." The two men did so. Miller kept his pistols trained on the two children in the wagon. Goodman tied the two men together. When he was done, he cleaned and dressed Lucius' wound. When he was finished, he went into the wagon and tied the children's hands and then tied them to each other. He tied his horse to the wagon and turned it around.

"Don't worry," Goodman shouted back to Lucius and Simmons. "You are not tightly bound; I am sure you can get out with an hour's effort. We just need a little head start. I am sure a passing traveler will find you before nightfall. I warn you not to come after us. As of now, you have committed no crime."

Eddie and Angie were silent through the whole ordeal. When they were underway, Eddie whispered, "Crap, we have to find a way to get out of this."

Angie, who had been frightened into silence said, "I don't know what we are going to do. That man just shot Lucius."

"Lucius will be alright," Eddie said. "The man said so. We need a plan."

Goodman heard the voices and said, in a pleasant, almost cheerful voice, "Don't worry about your friends. They can easily free themselves within the hour. The injured one is not seriously hurt. It will not be long before help arrives. Don't worry about yourselves. You will be honored guests of General Clinton. No one wants to harm you. Try to relax and enjoy the ride."

In just over two hours they reached Collins who was sitting under a tree. Angie saw him and whispered to Eddie, "Oh crap! It's Collins."

Eddie said, "You're kidding. He should be in a hospital someplace."

Angie said, "He looks angry. He is going to want to get even with us."

"That's how he always looks. I think we will be safe enough. It seems like this other guy is in charge."

Goodman stopped the wagon and he and Miller dismounted. Collins approached and said, "Took you long enough. Where are the other two?"

"Tied up, back up the road a couple of miles," said Miller.

"What? You can't leave them alive! They will escape and interfere with us," cried Collins.

"You would murder two innocent people? You are a piece of cow dung, aren't you?" said Goodman.

"These children are dangerous. The people protecting them are dangerous. I do not want your casual attitude to interfere with my reward," said Collins.

"Reward! Are you daft? What would you be rewarded for? You let them get away. They bested you at every turn, and you have been nothing but a burden on this trip. My report will reflect that," said Goodman as he turned away from Collins to get back on the wagon. Collins pulled one of his pistols, cocked it and shot Goodman in the back of the head. Angie saw the whole thing and screamed.

Miller stepped up, eyes wide and said, "Are you crazy? He was a British officer. You have no chance of getting your reward now. You murdered him."

"He was killed in action," said Collins. "Who is to say otherwise?"

"I am to say otherwise," said Miller. "This is murder and treason and I will have no part of it."

"Then you should have armed yourself," said Collins as he drew his other pistol and shot Miller in the chest. Angie screamed again.

Chapter 33
June 3, 1925

Silas Smoot's New Home

Vernon, Sol and Silas suddenly appeared on a city sidewalk. It was night time and the pedestrian traffic was light. A couple of drivers did double takes, but anyone who noticed quickly decided that they were seeing things.

"Oh my God! Where are we? What is this strange place?" yelled Silas. He was still clutching two hands full of coins. He began putting them in his vest and pants pockets.

The sight must have been overwhelming to him. There were electric lights, automobiles and very tall buildings. Silas could only stare; he was speachless. He turned slowly around and took it all in.

"Calm down," said Sol, taking Silas' look for fear. "I promised to take you someplace where no one would be able to find you. This is it. You are in the future." Sol looked around himself and noticed that one of the buildings was the Wrigley Building, in Chicago. They were standing on the corner of Michigan and Wacker, on the south side of the Chicago River. The second thing that he noticed was the automobiles. There were a lot of Model T Fords. He scanned the traffic to see if there were any Model A Fords; that would tell him if it was later than 1928. He saw none. The Wrigley Building was built around 1920 (or was it 1921?). The absence of Model A Fords told him that it was between 1920 and 1927.

Sol turned to Silas and said, "It is the 1920s, in the United States in a city called Chicago. It would have been far out on the frontier in your day. It is on Lake Michigan, one of the Great Lakes. It is a time of gangsters, jazz and gin joints. You should feel right at home here. You are in possession of a small fortune and no one can come after you for being Henry the Pirate. My end of the deal is complete."

With that, he locked arms with Vernon, and touched the screen. There was a loud "pop" and the two men were gone, leaving Silas on the corner of Michigan and Wacker, eyes wide and mouth agape.

Silas was dumbfounded. The two strangers had suddenly disappeared and left him alone in the strangest place he had ever seen. It was loud. It was bright. There was constant movement. It was as if the very streets themselves were alive. The streets were full of carriages, most were black and none of them had horses attached. They seemed to be made of metal; they hummed, roared and belched smoke. They made beeping noises at each other. They moved in a procession as if commanded by some invisible conductor, stopping and going randomly, and in unison.

It was nighttime, but there were lights everywhere. There were lights on the vehicles. There were lights lining the streets. There were lights in the windows of the tall buildings. Very tall buildings—he had never seen buildings so tall. They were easily 10 times taller than any house he had ever seen. There were signs made of light. About 100 feet in front of him was a river. He looked up the river and there were lighted bridges every few hundred feet, and buildings as far as he could see. This place made New York look like a country hamlet. It was bright, noisy and full of activity. It was utterly fantastic and beyond anything he could have possibly imagined—and absolutely beautiful.

He had gold in his pockets, he hoped it would buy him a place to stay. Noticing how the other people on the street were dressed, he was glad that he was not in knee breeches. With his dark pants, vest and light shirt, he did not stand out too terribly. He started walking, taking it all in.

He passed a doorway and heard music coming from it. It was unlike any music he had ever heard. It was loud, discordant and full of energy—like the streets he was on. It drew him. He walked to the doorway and a man stopped him and asked him who he was.

"Silas Smoot, from Virginia," he said.

"Who sent you?" the man said.

"A man called Sol; why do you want to know that?" said Silas.

"Sol Lichtenstein? Why didn't you say so? Go on in."

Silas entered into the most amazing scene of his life. The room was full of smoke. Men and women were drinking together—an unbelievable sight. The women we scantily dressed in shimmery gowns that ended well above the knee. Some danced, kicking their naked legs. It embarrassed Silas, and he did not know where to look.

There was a black man playing at the piano. Silas moved over to the piano and just stood and listened. The man was playing the most amazing music. Silas made a point of telling him, and he then nodded his thanks. A waitress came by and asked if he wanted a drink. Silas had money, but he was pretty sure that the coins he possessed were not the usual currency for the area. He did not want to overpay for the drink or launch into a long negotiation, so he waved her on. A few minutes later, a large man came by and told Silas that if he wasn't going to buy drinks, he would have to leave. Silas left.

He went back out onto the street and began walking, taking in all of the sites. Eventually he came to a hotel. He went in, deciding to find out what one of the gold coins would buy him in the way of housing. It was late and he was able to negotiate a week's rent with the desk clerk, who pocketed the coin without writing anything down.

He had no luggage, but a bellhop took him to his room anyway. He was a short blonde haired kid with a limp. The kid opened the room, pointing and announcing things like a tour guide. "There is the bed. You have a desk and chair over there," he said. He turned on the desk light, by way of a demonstration. He turned it off.

Silas walked over to the desk, wide-eyed. He turned on the lamp. He turned off the lamp. He turned on the lamp. He turned off the lamp. He repeated the process several times saying, "This is marvelous! No candles."

"Yeah, amazing," said the kid, rolling his eyes. He pointed toward the bathroom and said, "Your bathroom is in there." He held out his palm, waiting. The tour was over.

Silas ignored the outstretched palm, not knowing its significance. He said, "Bathroom? Do you mean to tell me that there is a room devoted to taking baths?"

"Well, yeah," said the kid, palm still out-stretched.

"Who brings the water way up here?" Silas asked.

"You just turn it on," said the kid, walking in the bathroom and turning on the water, momentarily giving up on waiting for his tip. "And that's your toilet over there."

"Toilet?" said Silas, not understanding.

"Crapper," said the kid.

Silas marveled at the porcelain fixture that had a little pool of water in it. "Am I to understand that that is the privy?"

"Privy?" asked the kid, not understanding. He said, pointing again, "Toilet, you take a dump in it. You poop, you crap, you make do do," frustration in his voice.

Silas looked at the device again, "Am I to understand that I RELIEVE myself in THERE?" he said, pointing. "How to you get rid of the waste? Do YOU come and haul it away?"

"Yes, you relieve yourself in there and NO, I don't haul it away! You flush it," he said, flushing the toilet.

Silas looked at the water swirl and go down. "Amazing," he said.

"Yeah, it's a freakin' miracle," said the kid. "Anything else?" He stood there for a moment with his palm out. Silas looked at the palm and back up at the kid, not understanding. An awkward moment passed and the kid headed toward the door, muttering to himself, "Yeah, like I'm gonna haul your poop away from here—you don't even tip."

Silas ignored him. He stood above the toilet, flushing it. "Amazing," he said.

Chapter 34
September 2, 1776

Collins Takes Charge

Angie was shaking and crying, "OhmygodOhmygodOhmygod...you killed those two men!"

Collins stepped over to her, took her head in both of his hands, and pointed her face toward him. "My God he is ugly," thought Angie. It was beyond ugly; it was like she was staring into the face of evil incarnate. She screamed again.

Collins slapped her then held her head, staring into her eyes, and said, "I need the two of you to stay quiet. I only need one of you alive, so think of that. Be quiet or I will shoot YOU between the eyes and let your brother watch. There is to be no trouble. Is that understood?" Angie sobbed and nodded. She stayed quiet.

Collins reloaded his guns, cleaned out any valuables from the dead men's pockets and dragged the two corpses off the road into some bushes. He tied the horses to the back of the wagon and soon they were on their way.

Eddie said, "Don't worry sir. We will be happy to go and help General Clinton. He will be very pleased indeed with the work you have done. Britain will win the war and you will be a hero."

Angie whispered, "What are you doing? He is a madman. You act like we are going on a summer outing with him."

Eddie whispered, "The operative word is 'madman.' We need to keep him calm and happy. If it dawns on him that we can tell General Clinton about these murders, he will kill us too. He hasn't thought anything out. He just wants to get us back to Clinton. I want to keep him from thinking. I also want to keep him from letting his desire to get even with us outweigh his desire for a reward from the British. You should apologize."

"Apologize, for what?" whispered Angie. "For letting a couple of gristly murders upset me?"

"Just keep him happy. Also, I know the answer to getting home might be in Mt. Vernon, but if we get near the device, we should consider touching it and getting out of here. We are in real danger," whispered Eddie.

"Mr. Collins," began Angie, "I just want to say that we are sorry. We should have stayed with the British camp. We were just frightened, what with the war and all. We will be happy to help General Clinton. In many ways, it will be better for history if the Colonies stay as part of the British Empire. Canada remains as part of the Empire, and they are a fine country with a fine lifestyle. I think you are really on the right side of this conflict."

Collins said nothing in reply, and they continued down the road in silence.

***

Alexander was heading into the house for dinner when he heard a wagon coming down the King's Highway. He turned to see who it was. There was a tall, thin man driving. In the back, he recognized the two children that had spent the night. It was Billy's wagon, no doubt. But Billy was nowhere to be seen. The other fellow was also missing. He rushed into the house.

His father and brothers were already sitting down to dinner. "Billy's been waylaid," he cried. "Someone's driving his wagon. The two children are in it, but Billy is nowhere to be seen!"

He ran out to the porch with his father and brothers. He pointed at the wagon, which had traveled about 50 yards past the house. They went into the house and grabbed some rifles.

The wagon was moving slowly, so it was decided that they could run and catch it without going for horses. They only had about 200 yards to go, so they ran after the wagon, guns in hand. Alexander caught up with the wagon first. He put his gun in the back and climbed in. Collins felt, rather than heard the disturbance and turned around. He reached for a pistol. Alexander was faster, pointing his rifle, "Stop this wagon!" he ordered. The others caught up, brandishing weapons. Collins saw the futility of his situation, put his gun down and stopped the wagon.

Alexander poked his gun into Collins's ribs and said, "What have you done with my cousin?"

Albert entered the wagon and untied the two children. Eddie said, "Two other men jumped us and took the wagon. They tied up Billy and Lucius. They are back that way." He pointed back to the way they came. "Collins here shot those two, stole the wagon and kidnapped us; but Billy and Lucius are safe."

"Come down from there," Andrew ordered Collins. "We have

us a thief and a murderer. I am sure that the magistrate in New Brunswick would like to have a talk with him."

Alexander turned the wagon around and headed toward the house. Allen, Albert and Andrew followed, with their guns trained on Collins, who was in front of them.

When they got to the house, they tied Collin's hands together and sat him down on the porch. They then tied him to a post, looping so many strands of rope around him that he looked like a cocoon. Andrew sat on a stump nearby, pointing his gun at Collins. "Allen, Albert, take some extra horses and go back up the road and fetch your cousin. Alexander and I will stay here and shoot this villain if he moves." He paused a minute, then said, "Take three extra horses, in case you run into those poor souls that this man murdered."

Alexander and the children went inside and had dinner. After dinner, Alexander took his father's place, and watched Collins while Andrew ate. It was after dark when Albert and Allen arrived with Simmons and Lucius. They did not come across the bodies of Goodman and Miller. The four went inside and ate. After dinner, it was decided that Collins was much too dangerous to leave alone, so they would take turns watching him in two hour shifts.

In the morning, Simmons, Lucius, Eddie and Angie ate breakfast and prepared to leave in the wagon. Andrew and Alexander got three horses ready, preparing to take Collins to the magistrate at New Brunswick. They tied his hands and feet. Andrew checked his handiwork and said to Collins, "Won't be very comfortable for you, but I am more concerned with our safety than your comfort. Don't fret, it will only be few hours and you can rest in a nice Gaol—that is until they hang you."

Andrew went over to the wagon with the children and said, "They will need your testimony to convict that man of the murders. I know you need to go to Virginia, but it is important that he receive justice. Can I prevail upon you to accompany me to see the magistrate in New Brunswick?"

"Of course," said Eddie. "Seeing Collins go to jail will be worth it."

"They won't put him in jail," said Angie. "They don't do that. Jail or prison is not a punishment. It is just for awaiting trial or punishment. They do other things for punishment. Collins won't go to jail for murder; they'll hang him."

"Works for me," Eddie said. He turned to Andrew and said, "He's a dangerous man. We'll testify."

It was decided that Lucius and Simmons should stay at the house and rest, both men having been wounded recently. Simmons was getting around, but he was glad to spend a day resting his leg. Allen and Albert were to take extra horses, find the bodies and bring them to the magistrate at New Brunswick. Andrew and Alexander would take Collins and the children to New Brunswick in the wagon. Alexander was armed and would join the tied up Collins and the children in the back of the wagon.

Collins kept his silence; he was miserable. He had not slept. They did not feed him. It was pointless to complain or to try to invoke the King's authority. He had attacked (in their minds) a family member. He had killed two men. He had kidnapped two children. He was just grateful that they allowed him to live. The binding was uncomfortable, but he was exhausted. He fell asleep within minutes of departure.

The wagon arrived in New Brunswick about midday. They approached the courthouse and Andrew dismounted, telling Alexander to wait with Collins and the horses. He came out shortly and said that the magistrate was having lunch in the tavern across the street. He went into the tavern, leaving Collins, Alexander and the children outside.

After a few minutes, he emerged with two men. One was a tall, heavyset, florid man, with puffy red cheeks and a bulbous red nose; the second was thin older man with receding grey hair. The large man was the proprietor of the tavern, but he was also the jailer. The older man was the magistrate.

Jails in colonial times were not used as punishment. Punishments for crimes varied. Criminals were placed in the stocks or pillory for minor offenses. They were branded on the hand for more serious crimes, like theft or manslaughter. They could be flogged for something as minor as public drunkenness. They could be hung for murder. Sentencing people to jail time was not done.

The group approached Collins, laying on his side in the wagon. "His name is Collins. He killed two men on the King's Highway, a few miles past my place. He kidnapped two children and stole a horse and wagon. We have witnesses," said Andrew. "You can find the bodies of the dead men up the King's Highway a little past my place. I have my other two sons looking for them. They will bring the bodies here as evidence. These two children witnessed the crime. I spoke with them and they swear that this man murdered the other two on the road."

"Is that true?" the magistrate asked Eddie, ignoring Angie.

Eddie said, "Oh yes; he shot one in the head and the other in the chest. Then he kidnapped us. Mr. Andrew and Mr. Alexander here saved us."

"Good enough for me," said the magistrate. "Seth, get him down and let's take him to the Gaol. We will schedule a hearing."

The Gaol was in the back of the courthouse. There were several cells. It was not uncommon for a single cell to house five or six prisoners. There were not many prisoners and Collins was locked in the cell with one other man who was seated in a corner, asleep.

The group left the Gaol and stepped into the street. Horses were approaching. It was Albert and Allen with the bodies of the two men on a third horse. "There is your evidence," said Andrew. "The little ones said that fella shot one in the back of the head and the other in the chest. Both were British officers, apparently; on some sort of secret mission." He handed the magistrate a pistol. "Here are the guns I took off of him. Probably the guns he used to kill those two."

"The British are camped not too far from here. We had best notify them about their officers. Andrew and his sons helped unload the bodies onto a wagon.

"We should have someone deliver the bodies to them. Poor devils probably have family in England. This war is a nasty business," said the magistrate.

"Better get a move on," said Andrew. "In this heat they will be ripe before too long."

Chapter 35
June 9, 2014

Sol and Vernon Finally Get Home

Sol and Vernon appeared in the barn with a "pop." "My God, am I glad that's over," said Sol. "I thought we were going be stuck in the 18th century."

"Too bad," said Vernon. "I think that 1765 may have been pretty close to the time they arrived. We may have just missed good chance of making contact. If we actually see them, we can bring them home."

"There is just one thing I can't figure out," said Sol.

"What's that?" asked Vernon.

"We keep coming back to the same place, here in the barn. Why don't we ever run into ourselves?" asked Sol.

"Because the bright spot we touch to get back here gets us to the barn, but the time is always moving forward relative to the time we left. We have been gone about two days, so today is two days after we left for 1765," explained Vernon.

"Oh my God, no!" Exclaimed Sol, running toward the trailer.

Sol opened the trailer door. The place was a mess. The garbage can had been knocked over. There was trash strewn throughout. The dogs, though they were house trained, had made a mess on the floor. Fortunately, it was on the tile floor in the kitchen.

Sam and Dave had been alone in the trailer for two days and did what dogs do when they are hungry and bored. They, had gotten into the garbage, destroyed things, and answered Nature's call. In a way, Sol was grateful for the garbage mess. There were food scraps in the garbage, so the dogs were at least able to find something to eat. They were able to get water out of the toilet, a disgusting proposition, but the dogs never seemed to mind. So the animals were in good shape. The trailer was not, and Sol quickly set about to clean it.

Vernon came and helped him. It was mid afternoon when they

were finished. They took the dogs out into the yard and ran and played with them. When they were thoroughly exhausted, they went inside and got fresh food and water for the dogs. Sol said, "I guess I better call Lucy before we go out again."

Lucy was a neighbor who had a few dozen acres nearby. She raised free range chickens and grew organic vegetables. She and Sol relied on each other to look after things when one or the other had to be away. Sol called her and asked if she would mind taking care of the dogs for a few days. She said that she would be right over.

Ten minutes later, Lucy Lawrence was at the door to the trailer. She was in her early 40s, about 5'8" tall with sandy blonde hair with occasional streaks of silver. She had a light, golden tan complexion with a few freckles across the bridge of her nose. It was the kind of honey colored tan that fair skinned people get when they are out in the sun a lot. She was tall and slender and didn't have an ounce of fat on her. She wore jeans and a t-shirt. Sol looked at her and took her in for a moment. He sighed a little and said, "Thank you so much for taking the dogs. I am going to be gone a lot the next few days."

She crouched down and said, "No problem, I love these two guys. Come on Sam, Come on Dave." She wrestled with them on the floor for a while.

"Can I get you something to eat or drink?" Sol asked. She declined, saying that she had to get back home. Sol grabbed a bag of dog food and some chew toys and headed toward her car. "Come on guys," Lucy said to the dogs as she got up and followed Sol to the car. The dogs ran on ahead to the car; they loved to go for a ride. She opened the back door to her Jeep Wrangler and the dogs jumped into the back seat. Sol put the food and toys on the passenger seat. He touched her arm and said, "Thanks for doing this."

"It's my pleasure, Sol," she said, and kissed him on the cheek. He stood and watched her drive down the long driveway until she was out of sight.

Vernon stepped up behind him and said, "You should do something about that."

"What?" said Sol. "Lucy and I are just friends."

Vernon said, "You and *I* are just friends. You two are something else."

After Lucy had left with Sam and Dave, Sol joined Vernon at the kitchen table to try to learn more about how the CKD worked and if they could get better at pinpointing time and place when traveling.

"It is four dimensional," Vernon finally said. "That makes it tricky to predict. There is an "X", "Y", "Z" and "W" axis. The first three are simply the coordinates—where on the planet. It is a hollow sphere." He wrote a formula down.

"I understand that," said Sol. "I have as much in my original notes."

Vernon nodded and then said, "Yes, but we never looked at it from a practical perspective. We have a fourth axis, that is time. The CKD is scanning all of the time, offering us different coordinates. The machine literally trolls through time and space. Not all of the coordinates are in play all of the time and we get what looks like a two dimensional rendering of possible places to go. The screen is a two dimensional representation of four dimensions. So at any given time, not all possible times and locations are available to us. Notice how our bright 'home' spot is not present all of the time."

Sol nodded and said, "It seems like no matter what you do, the options are entirely random."

"I know," said Vernon. "But there is a pattern. If we forget about space and think only of time, we may be able to pick our year." He wrote some numbers on some paper. He stared at the dots and wrote some more. "You up for a little experiment?" he asked.

Sol nodded, "I will get our traveling supplies."

"No need," said Vernon. "We will come right back. I just want to see if I can hit the date that I want."

"Sounds good," said Sol.

They locked arms and Vernon touched the screen. There was a loud "pop" and they were gone.

Chapter 36
June 4, 1925

Silas Smoot Makes Friends

Silas Smoot had spent a very pleasant evening in 1925. He took a long, hot bath. It seemed to him to be the most indulgent thing he had ever done in his life. He felt pretty good; he had money, and he was staying in room that not only was warm and comfortable, it afforded him more luxury than he had ever experienced. He was living in a world full of wondrous things.

Music was the thing he loved. He played several instruments, including the piano and violin. He could play Mozart. He could hear a song, memorize it and play it. He loved to perform; he sometimes thought he would like to perform in stage plays. He was wonderfully talented, but absolutely unable to make it pay.

He had a hard time making a living playing music, and Silas was always impoverished. He had no other skills, so he had to invent Sir Henry. Toby would never have paid him to perform in his tavern were it not for the arrangement Sir Henry had with him. He was thankful that he had never harmed anyone; he was not a violent man. He was always able to surprise his victims and get away quickly. His relationship with the innkeeper, Toby, had proven to be valuable. Toby not only pointed out strangers and their itineraries, but he also was a good judge of who was timid and who was rich. The innkeeper was also instrumental in spreading the legend of Sir Henry as a man who not only was cagy and clever, but also dangerous and deadly. He spread stories of travelers left to bleed to death on the road and of painful deaths dealt out to those foolish enough to resist. All-in-all it made Sir Henry's career as a highwayman go very easily. All he had to do was wave his pistols and people would give him money—happy to escape with their lives.

It was foolhardy to try to take on the two strangers a couple of days ago without the benefit of the innkeeper's counsel. Was it only two days? It seemed like a lifetime. But they were asleep and looked like easy pickings. He could never have been more incorrect. The incredible amount of firepower they were able to bring to bear was frightening. The tall man shot at him five times... FIVE TIMES, with one pistol. Incredible. He felt lucky to have escaped in one piece. His shoulder still throbbed where the man had shot him, but it was not seriously damaged. He was fortunate that the bullet did not damage bone or blood vessels. He could still play.

But here he was. The future was looking rosy. He may even be able to make a living as a musician. He contemplated the possibilities and drifted off to sleep.

Sunlight came through his window and awakened him. He got dressed, noting that he should get other clothes—ones that matched the time and were clean. He would need to find a place to sell his gold coins and get the appropriate currency. He had no idea how much he had overpaid for the room, but he wasn't about to go through the same negotiations for his next meal.

He went downstairs to the lobby. Breakfast was being served in a dining room just off the lobby. Just past the hostess stand was an upright piano. The room was not busy, it being late for breakfast and early for lunch.

Silas walked over to the piano and sat down. He played some Mozart. He then thought of the music he had heard in the tavern last night and began to work out the tune. It was kind of exciting; it was unlike any music he had ever heard and he was able to play it!

He finished the tune and looked up. Almost everyone in the dining room had stopped eating and burst out into applause when he stopped. A big man with a a round face and a long scar along his left cheek came up to him. He was wearing a broad brimmed white hat and a pinstripe suit. The big man said to him, "Hey, that's Jimmy Johnson's Harlem Strut. He's in town this week. We went to see him last night. You do a good rendition. What is your name?"

"Silas Smoot," said Silas.

Smoot, eh; that is an unusual name. Must be Russian or something. He paused and finally said, "Have ya eatin' yet?" Silas just shook his head no. "You should join us." He held out his hand, "My name is Al."

Silas happily joined Al and his friends for a free breakfast. Breakfast was good and it was plentiful. There were biscuits, eggs, bacon, fresh fruit and plenty of coffee. He ate hungrily and gratefully, listening to his hosts' discussion. During the meal, he learned a lot about the era in which he was now living. The most stunning thing he found out was that alcohol was actually illegal. When he told his new friend, Al that he had been in an establishment that sold liquor and expressed surprise at the flaunting of the law, everyone at the table burst out into laughter.

Al leaned back and lit a cigar. He said, "Prohibition has made nothing but trouble. But it has presented certain opportunities. This American system of ours, call it Americanism, call it capitalism, call it what you will, gives each and every one of us a great opportunity if we only seize it with both hands and make the most of it. The folks who owned the establishment you were in were simply seizing an opportunity."

"But what about the law?" Silas asked.

This brought about more laughter. Al assured him that the law was not a problem, if you handled it correctly. "After all, it is the law of supply and demand that is important. And people tend to demand that the law leave their liquor supply alone," he said with a smile, puffing on his cigar as the others at the table laughed.

"So clearly you never been to a speak," Al said. "Where you been for the last seven years?

"Virginia," said Silas.

"Must be good, law-abiding people in Virginia," said Al. Then he changed his focus and said, "You got some talent. You working anywhere?"

"You mean playing music?" asked Silas hopefully.

"No, laying brick," said Al. "Yes, I mean playing music."

"Um, no," said Silas.

"You be willing to work in one of those illegal establishments?" asked Al.

Silas could hardly believe his good fortune. He was about to get paid for playing music. Clearly, that jazz music he had picked up was what they were interested in. He would have to hear more than the two songs he had heard last night. "Why yes, I would," said Silas. "Seems silly that they have banned alcohol. Why do the people stand for it?"

"They don't," said Al. "And *that* has provided us with a very nice living." The others at the table nodded and laughed.

Silas accepted the job. He was to start tomorrow night. He told Al about his gold coins and Al took them off his hands for $50 apiece—since they were about the size of an American $50 gold piece. That gave Silas nearly $1000. Al also gave also gave him an additional $300 advance on his salary and told him to get some clothes that weren't so goofy looking. He was, after all, going to be working in a classy place. Al gave him a card for a tailor shop that he highly recommended. They said their goodbyes. Silas was very excited, but he had a lot to do. He had to buy some clothes and he had to learn how to play some new jazz songs.

Chapter 37
September 3, 1776

The Trial of Ezra Collins

Collins' trial was scheduled for the next day, which was the 3rd. There was some difficulty finding 12 people for a jury. In fact, not all trials had juries because of the difficulty of getting enough people with free time to sit in a jury. All of the jurors had to be men, which automatically eliminated 50% of the population. Most cases were tried before a magistrate, but since this was a capital case, a jury was needed. Andrew, Alexander, Allen and Albert were all selected for the jury. A search went out and eight other men were found.

On the day of the trial, Eddie and Angie were not allowed in the courtroom until it was time to testify. They sat in a room that was off the entryway to the courtroom, where they could not hear the proceedings. They sat there for more than an hour when a man came and asked for Eddie.

The courtroom was a large room with six rows of what looked like church pews. It really wasn't a lot different from courtrooms he had seen on TV, the jury was behind a low wooden wall, seated in wooden chairs. All of the jurors were men. The judge's bench was raised higher than the rest of the court, much like in modern courtrooms. The thin man that he had met earlier sat at the judge's bench. A wig covered his thinning hair. The one difference was the area for the witness was off in a corner and very high. He was directed to go to the witness area. There was no place to sit, he just stood behind a barrier that was chest-high on him.

The prosecutor was a small framed man about 5' 8" tall, with reddish brown hair that peeked out under his white wig. Eddie was sworn in. Eddie was asked to state his name and he did.

The prosecutor asked, "Can you tell us about the events that occurred two days ago, at midday on the King's Highway?"

Eddie noticed Collins seated in the front row of the pews. He stared at him for a moment, transfixed. It did not appear that he had a lawyer. He looked terrible. His blackened bruises now had tinges of green and yellow. His left eye was swollen and puffy. He still had the large ink stain, although it had faded a little. His nose was crooked from being broken by Angus Van Auken.

"Young man?" said the prosecutor.

"Um, yeah, sorry," said Eddie. "I saw two men shot and killed."

"Do you see the person who shot them in this court?" asked the prosecutor.

"Yes," said Eddie, pointing to Collins. "That man right there, Lieutenant Collins."

"Can you describe what you saw?" asked the prosecutor.

"Captain Goodman had turned his back to get into our wagon. He had apparently said something that upset Collins, because Collins drew a pistol and shot him in the back of the head. The other fellow, Miller, I think his name was, became upset. Collins then shot him in the chest, to keep him from telling the British about him killing their Captain Goodman. He then dragged the bodies off the road. My sister and I were tied up in the back of the wagon. He drove away with us in the back, intending to kidnap us."

"You are absolutely sure that you saw THAT man do these two murders?" said the prosecutor, pointing to Collins.

"No doubt in my mind. He killed them and then kidnapped me and my sister," said Eddie.

"No further questions," said the prosecutor. Then to Collins, "You may examine the witness."

Collins got up, turned toward Eddie and said, "Are you or are you not a fugitive from the British army?"

Eddie said, "I don't know. I do know that you have been chasing me and my sister for nearly a week, claiming to work for the British army. We actually first met you in General Washington's camp. You told us you were a lieutenant in the Continental army then."

Eddie's answer flustered Collins a little, but he gathered himself and proceeded with his line of questioning. "Do you know why the British army wants you?" asked Collins.

"I do not know THAT the British army wants me. I know that you seem to think that my sister and I know Washington's war plans," said Eddie with a little derision in his tone. He looked at the jury and grinned as if it was the most ridiculous idea in the world. He put his palms up and shrugged his shoulders, as if to say, "The guy is a loon. What can I say?" The jury laughed.

The laughter unnerved Collins a little. He said, "What year were you born in?"

Eddie said, "I am 16, so that would be 1760. I'm an Aquarius. What's your sign?" He laughed and looked at the jury. The joke fell flat.

Collins said, "Remember that you are under oath. Weren't you born much later than that—say in the 21st century?"

Eddie said, "Oh, that's right. I forgot that you think that I am from the future." He looked over toward the prosecutor and said, "Is insanity a defense for murder here?" He was silenced by the magistrate's hammer.

"You are lying," shouted Collins.

The magistrate hit his hammer on the bench. "One more outburst and I will have you hauled out of here in chains," he said to Collins.

Collins turned toward the judge and said, "Your honor, he is a fugitive from the British army. I was merely trying to bring him to justice."

The prosecutor said, "That does not explain why you killed two of his Majesty's officers."

The magistrate tapped his hammer and said, "Alright gentlemen, that is enough. Mr. Collins, do you have any questions that you have not already asked?"

Collins slumped his shoulders in defeat. He shook his head, "No, your honor," he said.

Eddie was led back to the room with Angie. He said to her, "Don't say anything about the future, you are from Connecticut and were born in 1766. Collins is going to push the point about us being from the future."

In a few minutes, the man came for Angie to testify, leaving Eddie alone in the room. She wasn't gone 10 minutes and the man brought her back. She gave Eddie a thumbs-up sign and he relaxed.

The jury deliberated for less than an hour and came back with a guilty verdict. As the proceedings were breaking up Eddie and Angie found Andrew and his sons. They were anxious to get going. As they were leaving the courthouse, they noticed a column of 10 British soldiers heading for the courthouse.

Eddie said to Andrew, "Sir, we had best get going—with your permission. Those soldiers may want to talk to us." Andrew agreed and the group hastily departed. His nephew, after all, was a Continental soldier.

The soldiers, it turns out, were there for Collins. He had killed one of their own and it was felt that he should face British military justice. They had been sent after the bodies of Goodman and

Miller arrived in the British camp, and to bring Collins to face military justice. The officer in charge, a young lieutenant named Bigby, who looked like a slightly smaller and younger version of Captain Goodman. He had been told about the children and to bring them back to camp if he saw them.

But the soldiers did not see the children, who were on their way out of town with the Simmons family. Eddie kept looking behind the wagon, down the road as they traveled. He was worried that the soldiers would come after them. It was evening by the time they got back to the farm. Dinner was a hearty stew that Ann had reheated for them and served it with pieces of brown bread. Lucius and Billy joined them.

Eddie said, "I can't believe that idiot Collins tried to convince the jury that we were from the future and were Washington's secret weapon."

Angie broke away from watching Billy long enough to say, "He tried that with me, too. I am just glad that he is out of the picture. It's like he kept getting angrier and crazier. I was really scared being in that wagon with him. I am so glad you and your dad came along, Alexander."

Andrew said, "Glad to see that he will get what he deserves." He then turned to Lucius and asked, "How is that arm, young man?"

Lucius said, "That officer was right, it really is just a scratch. I'll be fine. It hurt my pride more than anything, being taken by surprise like that."

"How about you, Billy?" Andrew asked

"It's still a bit sore, but I'm getting better," said Billy Simmons. "We'll be heading out in the morning. I am good to travel. We'll take our time; I'll be fine."

They talked a bit longer and Billy, Lucius, Angie and Eddie made their way to the barn. It was a pleasant, warm evening.

Chapter 38
June 23, 1974

Sol and Vernon Do Some Exploring

Sol and Vernon appeared in front of what looked like an oversized house on a busy rural thoroughfare. Up the street and through some trees, Sol could see sun glistening off the waters of a lake. The road was flanked with woods. This was the only building in sight, other than some nearby houses. In front was a wooden cigar store Indian. The house was very old, but the door was new, made of metal and glass. Above it was a blue neon sign that said Wilson's Roadhouse.

Sol and Vernon stepped in. It was dark inside the bar and it took a few minutes for their eyes to adjust. The decor looked like the 1970s. The carpet was burnt orange. The bar was copper plated. There were chrome lights and the prints on the wall looked like Peter Max knockoffs. The walls were paneled with a light grey wood with the slats lined up at 45 degrees.

The two sat at the bar. The place was empty. The clock on the wall said 11:05; the place had probably just opened for lunch. The bartender was a young man in his 20s with brown hair that covered his ears and collar and a nicely trimmed mustache. He wore a wide, brightly colored paisley tie that was tied in a full Windsor knot. He wore a white shirt, black pants and a white apron. He was polishing the bar. The copper shone where he had finished. He was cleaning the last couple of feet of bar, which was dull and stained. Definitely the 1970s thought Sol.

Vernon said, "That must take you a couple of hours."

"Start at 10, usually finish by opening," said the bartender. "Can I get you something?"

Sol ordered two draft beers. They were 85 cents apiece. He found an old looking $5 bill and told the kid to keep the change.

Vernon asked, "What is today's date?"

"June 23rd," replied the bartender.

"What year?" asked Vernon.

"You kidding?" asked the bartender. "1974. If you don't know what year it is, maybe I shouldn't be serving you beer."

"He's just messing with you," said Sol. "Isn't that right, Vernon."

"Guilty," said Vernon with smile for the bartender and a tilt of the head. He then whispered to Sol, "That is very close to what I figured." The bartender just looked at him with a puzzled look.

"How close?" asked Sol.

"Within six months," said Vernon. "Location is still up in the air." Then to the bartender, "Where are we?"

The bartender gave him another strange look. Vernon said, "We've been driving all night."

"New Castle, Wisconsin," said the bartender.

Vernon was looking over towards the far side of the dining room. The wall opened and an old woman emerged from it. She was dressed in a 1930s style dress that went down to mid calf and a bright red hat that looked like a derby with a bow on it. "Who is that?" Vernon said.

"Ms. Janie Wilson. Her family owned this place for decades. When they sold it, part of the deal was to keep the name, let the old lady live upstairs and feed her in the dining room. She comes down every day at this time to get lunch. The place used to be a speakeasy during Prohibition. It's honeycombed with passages." He reached behind the bar and pulled out a picture. He said, "This was taken during Prohibition days. He pointed at the figures and said, "That is Janie Wilson—she was a looker back in her day. And that there is Al Capone."

Sol looked at the picture and said, "Who is that in the back?"

The bartender said, "I don't know, but some say that it is a ghost. People who were in the room swear that he was never there—at least that is how the story goes."

Sol showed the picture to Vernon, "Look familiar?" he asked. The figure in the back was Eddie.

Sol and Vernon finished their beers and thanked the man. They stepped out into the bright sunlight. So said, "This is a very solid lead, we have an image of Eddie, in New Castle Wisconsin during Prohibition." Vernon said, "I want to try another test. We may be very close to being able to predict the time we arrive."

He looked up and down the road. There was no traffic. He and Sol linked arms, Vernon touched the screen, and as always, they disappeared.

Chapter 39
September 4, 1776

The Journey Continues

Philadelphia was about 40 miles away. If things went smoothly they could make the trip in just over a day, Billy Simmons told the others. They left mid morning after eating breakfast and saying goodbye to Andrew and his family.

The ride was pleasant. Billy drove and Lucius sat in back with the children. Lucius was a little heartsick, missing Sadie. Angie wanted to make sure that he went to look for the treasure in North Carolina. She was really enjoying her role as Cupid. "Eddie and I can stay in Philadelphia and wait for you. We can go to Mt. Vernon when you get back. We will have to go through Vernon's notes anyway," she said. Then she giggled and said, "Vernon's notes were at Mount Vernon. What are the odds?" Then she gathered herself and said, "You can go back to Sadie a rich man. Go with Billy, it will be safer for you." She then hollered up to Billy in the front, "Billy, you want to be rich, don't you?"

Billy turned back and said, "Yes ma'am. But this does sound like a pipe dream."

Billy looked doubtful. Eddie said to Angie, "Stay in Philadelphia? We need to get to Mt. Vernon. We would be wasting time. We can wait for them at Mt. Vernon AFTER we get Uncle Sol's notes."

Angie said, "Eddie, what is your hurry? We have a chance to meet ALL of the Founding Fathers. A lot of them are still in Philadelphia, working on the Articles of Confederation. Also, if Uncle Sol has more information, he would have left it with people we would know about—like Jefferson or Franklin. If Uncle Sol really has figured out the machine, we could be back in Wisconsin the day after we left. We can stay as long as we like and still be back to Uncle Sol's before Mom and Dad get home. We may never get an opportunity like this again."

"I just want to get home." said Eddie. "Plus I am a little worried that you may never want to leave."

"Please, I really want to do this," said Angie. "I promise to go to

Mt. Vernon with you and help you figure out how to use the CKD if you just do this one thing for me."

Eddie said, "Help me with the CKD AND leave with me, right?"

Angie remained silent. "Right?" repeated Eddie. Angie shrugged. "You can't be serious. We HAVE to go home."

"And why is that?" asked Angie rhetorically. "Because it is soooo wonderful in the 21st century?"

"It's home, Angie. That is where we belong," pleaded Eddie.

Angie just shrugged again. Eddie knew he couldn't force her to go and that arguing would just make her dig in her heels. He let it go.

When the wagon reached Trenton there was still a fair amount of daylight left. Billy said they were almost half way to Philadelphia. If they kept going, they could make it to Bristol, Pennsylvania before dark. From there it would be a short ride to Philadelphia.

They were just outside of Bristol at dusk and it was decided that they would make camp rather than to try to make it into town. It was a warm night and the weather was dry. They were near a body of water, Falls Township Lake. They made a fire, and fed and watered the horses. Billy had shot a couple of rabbits, which they cooked over the fire.

When they settled in to eat their meal, Billy said to Eddie and Angie, "So tell me more about the future."

Eddie took a bite of rabbit and said, "For one thing, the trip we just made would have taken about half an hour. You could get to England in about eight hours by flying there."

Billy said, "It's amazing to me that men can fly in your time. I still find it hard to believe."

"Absolutely," said Eddie. "You could fly from New York to Philadelphia in about an hour."

"What a wondrous time you live in. You must miss it terribly," said Billy.

"I don't know, Billy, I think it is pretty wondrous here," said Angie. She sighed, he really was nice looking. "It really isn't all that 'wondrous' in our time; for one thing, it is a lot more crowded and dirty," said Angie. "It is much better here."

"But it IS home, Angie," said Eddie pointedly. He was beginning to feel like Angie didn't want to leave. He had to work on convincing her, but he wanted to avoid a direct confrontation.

Angie ignored him, "What else do you want to know? We already told you about movies, automobiles and airplanes. Oh, and a long time ago, before we were born, a man landed on the moon.

And, they were able to bring him back. For some reason we stopped going there, but there are space stations that orbit high above the earth."

"The moon! That is truly amazing," said Billy. "What is it like up there?"

"It's smaller than earth, so there is not much gravity. You can jump 50 feet at a time. There is no air and it can get very hot or very cold, depending on where the sun is," said Angie.

"How were the men who went able to stay alive?" he asked.

"Special suits protect against the temperatures and they carry the air they breathe with them," Angie explained.

Billy nodded. "Astounding."

"You say that the Colonies win the war," Lucious said.

"Yes," said Angie, "In 1783, with help from France and Spain."

"Then this would become a vast nation, going all the way to the Mississippi River," said Billy.

"And later, it becomes vaster than that—all the way to the Pacific Ocean," said Eddie.

"Are there other wars?" asked Billy.

"Oh yes, lots of them," said Angie. "The only one you will see is when America goes to war with England again in 1812, but they win. During most of the 19th century there are wars with the Native Americans—you call them Indians, but in our day you're not supposed to say that."

"Except for that jerk football owner who insists on keeping the name Redskins for his team," interjected Eddie. "It's a racial slur, but he calls it tradition."

Billy said, "I don't understand. I hear that term all of the time."

Angie sighed and said, "I'm sorry I brought up the whole 'politically correct' thing. Eddie, let's not get into a big discussion about how we are supposed to express ourselves in the 21st century. Let's just say that in our day people get really upset if someone says the wrong thing and leave it at that."

"Like when you curse in mixed company," offered Billy.

"Close enough," said Angie. "We were talking about wars. The War of 1812 is probably the only one that will concern you; but America wins."

Billy asked, "What is this 'football' that you speak of?"

Eddie said, "You have to understand that cites are MUCH bigger than they are now. New York City, in our time, has more than 8 million people living in it. It has more people than there are in all of the Colonies combined. There are people who make their living playing games like baseball, football, basketball and hockey. Football is a game where 11 men try to move a ball 100 yards with 11 other men trying to keep them from doing it. Literally millions of people watch them doing this."

"Sounds like a waste of time," said Billy.

"No argument here," said Angie.

"Anyway," continued Eddie, ignoring them, "They play these games in huge stadiums—bigger than the Coliseum in Rome. There can be as many as 50,000 or 60,000 people watching the game in the stadium, plus millions more watching at home on television."

"What is television?" asked Lucius.

"Television is a box or a panel that shows something that is going on someplace else. For example, someone at the stadium can point a camera at the game going on in the stadium and people with television sets can see everything that the camera points at. It is like being at the game," said Eddie. "You can literally watch something that is happening hundreds of miles away without ever leaving your home."

"Not only that, we carry devices, like the one I showed you in New Rochelle. You can watch movies, sporting events and even TV anywhere," said Angie.

"How do people have time for this?" asked Billy.

"People don't work as hard as you do in our day," said Angie. "We don't have to haul water, make candles, or make our own clothes. Clothes washing is done in a machine and only takes about an hour. Very few people farm. People work about 40 hours per week and the rest of the time they are free. They take vacations, watch television, go to plays and sporting events and go to gyms to exercise. Also, it does not take as long to get from place to place. In 2014 we could have gone from New York to Philadelphia by automobile in less than a couple of hours."

Lucius said, "Sounds like a wonderful time that you live in."

Angie said, "Some things are better, other things are not. Day-to-day life is much easier. We can communicate with anyone in the world instantly. We can go anywhere in the world in a day or less. We have a lot of gadgets and conveniences, but it is crowded and the air and water are polluted. We have a lot of crime. There are weapons that can literally kill millions of people at a time. Here you have to work hard and you don't have many conveniences, but the air and water are clean. It's quiet—even with a war going on."

"I would like to see the world you live in," said Lucius. Billy agreed. They talked a little longer and eventually drifted to sleep.

Chapter 40
September 24, 1883 and June 10, 2014

Sol and Vernon Learn More About the CKD

Sol and Vernon appeared on the street of a city. There were horse-drawn carriages and people dressed like it was the late 19th century. Women wore long dresses and hats. They were cinched at the waist and had bustles. Men were dressed in a variety of ways. Those who were dressed well, wore derby hats, broad lapels on their suits and cravats.

"Late 19th century," said Vernon pointing. "Those are gas lights."

A man walked by reading a folded up newspaper. Sol stopped him and asked, "Sir, may I look at your newspaper for a quick minute?" The man handed Sol the newspaper. He glanced at the date and thanked the man.

"September 24, 1883, New York City," said Sol. Vernon nodded. He linked arms with Sol and they were gone with a "pop."

They appeared almost instantly in the barn. They headed back to the trailer. Vernon sat at the table and began scribbling furiously. He spoke as he wrote, "Both trips were within six months of what I had predicted. We will need a better sampling, but I created a grid, like Cartesian coordinates. Each square is about 100 years. They are divided into 100 smaller squares; each represent a year. But it is not absolute, the year is predicted in relation to the bright dot that represents our time/location of the barn. That point is moving ahead in time and notice how it moves through the grid. If it is on the outside of the circle, the predicted years are different from what they will be if the bright point is in the center."

Sol said, "I see, everything is relative to the bright spot and at any given time, and we only have a limited number of time choices."

"Yes," said Vernon, "But if you wait long enough the time options change. Eventually you will be able to get to the time you want—within a few months. You kind of have to calculate on the run, because the points are always changing. We can always get home and we can arrive approximately when we want to. But if we want a specific location, we lose accuracy on the time—kind of like the Heisenberg Uncertainty Principle."

Sol said, "You know what they say, 'Heisenberg might have been right.' Can you write all this up, so that Angie would understand?"

Vernon said, "Yes."

Sol said, "Then we should make copies and drop one off every decade or so."

Vernon asked, "Drop off to who?"

Sol said, "I guess we go back in time and meet people and decide who can be trusted with the information. We have a good start. You can't get much more reliable than George Washington. My guess is that Angie will seek out people that history remembers—like Washington. I know the odds are not with us, but we have to try. I have some photos of Angie and Eddie; we should include them with the packet."

Vernon still busied himself with his papers and said, "We should try to go back in time at least one more time. I want to make sure of the predictability of these calculations. I want to try the 18th century again; I think that is our best hope of reaching them."

"Wait a minute then," said Sol. "Let's copy your notes and these two pictures. If we are going to the 18th century, we should at least leave a packet that they may find." He got up and Sol stood with him in the middle of the kitchen. They locked arms and Vernon touched the screen and with a loud "pop," they were gone.

Chapter 41
June 5, 1925

Silas Smoot Goes Shopping

Silas went to the tailor that Al had recommended. When he told the man who had sent him, the man couldn't do enough for Silas. "Mr. Capone is a very special customer. I'm gonna take very good care of you," he said.

Silas told the man that he needed clothes for tomorrow night, and that seemed to present a problem. He told Silas that he could rush and have three custom suits in a week, but to have something for tomorrow was going to be a problem.

He thought for a minute and snapped his fingers, saying, "I have someone who is about your size. He never picked up his suit. I will alter it for you and have it tomorrow."

He found a selection of shirts and ties that fit Silas as well as two pair of pants that fit well enough, one tan and one black. He also picked two pair of shoes that fit very well. Silas was able to leave the shop in clothes that were contemporary and fitting for the job. He also purchased underwear and socks. He spent nearly all of the $300 Al had given him. He changed his clothes, discarding his old garments. The man gave him a bag with six shirts, the spare pair of pants and the spare pair of shoes and instructed him to come back tomorrow after 3 pm for the suit.

He left with his purchases and decided to explore the city. It was an incredible place. He had never seen so many people. There were no horses, only metal carriages that were powered on their own—amazing. There were tall buildings everywhere. Above head was a trestle with a long conveyance on it. It was similar to the horseless carriages he had seen on the street, but the carriages were MUCH larger. They could hold dozens of people and several of the conveyances were hooked together. Literally hundreds of people could travel (at what Silas thought was a very high rate of speed) anywhere the trestle went. When the carriages turned, they screeched and wailed loudly. Stairs led to the top of the trestle and people got on the conveyance. It took them to other places in the city. The street he was on was called "Wabash" and the trestle covered the entire street. Even though it was a bright sunny day, it was shady on Wabash Street.

He walked another block to State Street. There he came upon what must have been a store; but it was unlike any store he had ever seen. It took up an entire city block and it was several stories high. There was a clock that was easily the size of a carriage protruding from the building. A sign in front said "Marshall Fields." He went inside. It was fantastic. All manner of goods was on display. There were clothes, perfumes, women's purses, jewelry, watches and something called radios. He looked up and he could see five stories of the building looking up in the open central area. There were stairways that moved; they could take you upstairs without walking.

He heard music above and headed toward the sound. He came to an area where machines that produced music were on display. People could buy cabinets that played music. He went over to the area where the machines were. There were cabinets that stood chest-high and there were others that were not much bigger than a loaf of bread. A man showed him that by turning a dial on one of the cabinets, you could hear different what he called "programming." Silas listened for a while to someone telling a story, then the man turned the dial and there was music.

There were other boxes with a kind of funnel attached. Silas asked what they were and the man, with a surprised expression on his face, said that they were phonographs. Silas had no idea what that meant, so he asked the man to demonstrate how they worked.

The man took out a shiny black disc that was not quite a foot in diameter and placed it on the device. It began to spin. He placed a metal arm with a round head and what looked like a needle on the edge of the disc as it spun. Music began to play from the funnel. Silas stared open-mouthed at the device; it was the most wonderful thing he had ever encountered.

The discs were called records and they apparently stored music. Any kind of music that you wanted was stored on one of these records. The machines that played the music varied in size and price. A machine called a Victrola looked like a large wooden cabinet and cost several hundred dollars. Silas found one that was about one-foot square and worked fairly well. It cost $25; he bought it. He asked the man about jazz records and there were a lot to choose from. He asked if he had anything by James P. Johnson. The man said, "Oh—the Charleston—I love that one." He sang: "Charleston,

Charleston," as he did a little dance. Silas just stared at him. He asked for other music that was popular and purchased 20 of the records. Burdened with his purchases, Silas made his way back to the Metropole Hotel.

When he got to his room, he set up the record player the way the man had showed him and began playing his new records. He listened carefully to all of the songs. He would be ready for his new job tomorrow.

Chapter 41
September 3, 1776

Collins Makes Another Move

In New Brunswick the lieutenant in charge of the small troop of soldiers went into the courthouse, seeking the magistrate. His name was Bigby and he was Goodman's cousin. He was younger and a little smaller than Captain Goodman, but he had the same Patrician good looks and grey eyes. He was under orders to ask about the presence of two children, a red-haired girl and a dark-haired boy. The courthouse was clearing and he managed to find the magistrate in his chambers, through a door in the back of the courtroom. The magistrate explained that the two children left shortly after the trial, but he was not sure where they were headed. He thought that they were going to Virginia, but could not say for certain.

Collins had already been taken back to the Gaol, hands bound behind him and awaiting the executioner. The room wasn't a barred cell, but was a windowless room, large with a brick fireplace. This time there were three other inmates with him. They were awaiting their trials for much less serious crimes.

Collins backed up to the corner of the fireplace and began moving his bonds back and forth over the bricks. He did not want to break free just yet; he only wanted to make so he could easily get out of them. He would break out when he was transferred or when the jailer brought food. He felt pretty confident that the other inmates would not interfere. He wore the ropes down to a few fibers and sat down in the corner.

A few minutes later the door burst open and three British soldiers entered. A tall lieutenant with dark hair and grey eyes was at the front of the group. Behind him were two privates. The lieutenant stepped into the room and bellowed, "Which one of you is the murdering scum Collins?"

Collins looked up, feeling that owning up to his identity might not be a good thing. Lieutenant Bigby spoke again, "Where is Collins?" A skinny, gaunt man who was awaiting trial for public drunkenness was seated across the room from him. He clearly was miserable and nursing a hangover. The man lazily pointed at Collins.

The captain strode across the room and stood in front of Collins. He barked, "Collins?" Collins looked up at him. There was hatred in his eyes. This was not going to go well, but there was no way that he was going to escape being identified. He simply nodded at the man.

"You murdered my cousin," said Bigby in a low, menacing tone. "I am going to have the pleasure of watching you hang. You are to come with us. His Majesty's army will be dispensing the justice that you so richly deserve."

Collins studied the man for a minute. He could see the family resemblance to Captain Goodman. He looked into those angry eyes and got the feeling that hanging would be a welcome relief after a journey with this man.

"Get up!" barked Bigby.

Collins slowly rose. The lieutenant stepped forward, putting his face within inches of Collins. "You are an ugly bugger, aren't you?" he said. He punched Collins on the side of the face, knocking him to the floor. "Get up! We don't have time for you to lie around." Collins got up, with some difficulty since knee was throbbing and his hands were tied. He walked slowly toward the door.

As he approached the door, one of the privates took the lead with the second falling in behind. The angry lieutenant followed. They made their way down the stairs and into the street. When they emerged from the Gaol, the other seven soldiers fell in around them. They were about 200 yards from the river, where the soldiers had left their boat.

When they got to the boat, the soldiers took their places near the oars. Bigby and Collins stood on the dock. The captain said, "Get in there, in the middle." Collins managed as well as he could with his hands tied. The captain kicked him. Collins took the opportunity to launch himself to the far side of the boat. He stood on the edge for a second, on his good leg and went over the the side and into the water. Adrenaline had given him the strength to break the last fibers of the rope that bound him. He was grateful that the lieutenant was focused on punishing him and not on making sure his bindings were secure. He swam underwater. He could hear the musket fire from the surface and he hoped he was deep enough. About 50 yards upstream was a marshy area that was full of cattails and reeds. He swam under the boat, staying underwater. He felt like his lungs were going to burst, but he fought off the urge to surface. He got under the dock, but only for a few seconds to get air. He submerged again and swam for his life underwater. He made it to the reeds, surfacing slightly, only enough to catch his breath. Hiding behind the reeds, he managed to break off a hollow reed and breathe through it, laying on the bottom of the river.

Above he could hear shooting and shouts. He lay completely still and waited. It seemed like much of the activity was toward the dock, but he could not be sure. He was terrified, and would stay underwater all day if necessary. He would stay there and hope that the soldiers would figure that he drowned. He slowly worked his way deeper into the reeds.

On the surface, the captain had his men fan out along the shore, searching for Collins. He had two of his men strip to their pants and go into the water. Lucky for Collins, he had them go upstream, figuring that Collins would swim with the current to try to get away. Also, if the prisoner had drowned, that is the direction that the river would take him. After two hours, they came up empty. They searched for another hour then gave up.

None of the soldiers went into the reeds, but the lieutenant had them fire several volleys into them, hoping to kill or wound Collins if he were hiding there. Fortunately for Collins, the soldiers did not know that a bullet fired into water loses speed very quickly and is not effective beyond a couple of inches. Collins did not know it either and the sound of the shots and the bullets hitting the water terrified him. The lieutenant's reluctance to send his men into the muck of the marshy area saved Collins' life.

Collins lay perfectly still at the bottom of the marsh for what seemed like an eternity. He would wait until dark if necessary. After a very long time, it seemed to become silent. There were no shouts and no shots fired. Of course there could be sentries posted along the river, so he carefully surfaced, just peering above the surface of the water. The reeds afforded enough cover so that he could not be easily seen.

The lieutenant did post two sentries, one at the dock and another about 100 yards upstream. He and the other soldiers made their way back to Clinton's camp with their two fallen comrades. The men were instructed to watch the river. Another two sentries were to relieve them in two hours. They were to watch the river in two hour shifts throughout the night.

After several hours, Collins decided to risk moving. The cattails and reeds offered him some cover. It was near dusk, but he could still see the two sentries down river. If they looked closely enough, they could see him. He had to be absolutely quiet. He looked upriver and there was no one. He slowly and silently made his way upriver. The marshy area extended for several hundred yards and offered him cover as he moved away from the soldiers. He waited for darkness at the edge of the marshy area.

After dark Collins slowly make his way upriver beyond the cattails silently, without drawing the attention of the soldiers. He finally made it to a bend in the river and was out of the line of sight of the soldiers. He then quietly made his way onto shore.

He climbed onto shore. He was cold, wet, covered in mud and he had lost a shoe. But he was free! He quietly walked away along the river. Now to find those children and exact his revenge.

Chapter 42
June 10, 2014

Sol and Vernon Continue Their Efforts

Sol and Vernon were in the kitchen, making copies of Vernon's notes and putting them into packages. They were convinced that the late 18th century presented them with the best opportunity for contacting the children. Sol made the point that the children might decide to leave the 18th century, in which case they could be anywhere and in any decade.

Sol and Vernon sat at the table, looking at the pattern of lights on the disc. Vernon had drawn the x and y coordinates on a piece of graph paper with the time formula and a pencil sketch of dates in relation to the light representing the barn in 2014. They formed a pattern that resembled a spiral. Vernon said, "None of the points stay fixed, so you have to watch and calculate on the fly. With practice, you can get pretty close to the time you want to arrive. If you want to get to a specific place, you lose accuracy with the time."

They worked for several hours making copies and filling envelopes. Vernon said, "The whole thing is less than precise, but if they get one of these packages there is a reasonable chance that they can learn to travel close to any point in time that they choose. It will take learning and practice, but eventually they should be able to come home."

"IF we can get a package to them," said Sol. "Deciding who to give packages to will also present a problem."

"Not an ideal situation, for sure. We can try for historical figures who we know to be honorable. George Washington believed you, and will become more convinced as the predictions you made for him become true. If he runs into the children, I am sure he would help. We just need to recruit more such people to help us. Every contact increases the chance of Eddie and Angie finding someone who will help them to get home," said Vernon.

"It's a long shot, but it is our best hope," said Sol.

They gathered up about 20 of the envelopes along with their weapons and duffels. They linked arms and Sol said, "Take us somewhere lucky, Vernon." He touched the screen and they were gone with a "pop."

Chapter 43
June 5, 1925

Silas Smoot Gets Ready for Work

Silas Smoot sat in his hotel room, transfixed, looking at the record player and listening to the amazing jazz music. After a couple of hours, he went down to the dining room. It was between lunch and dinner and the piano sat unoccupied. He sat at the piano and began to play.

Within 15 minutes, he had a small crowd standing around and listening to him. He had a passable singing voice and had memorized the words of a couple of the songs. He started a new song (one that seemed to be popular), called The Charleston and began to sing:

"Charleston, Charleston
Made in Carolina
Some dance, some prance
I'll say there's nothing finer
Than the Charleston, Charleston
Oh how you can shuffle
Every step you do
Leads to something new
Man I'm telling you
It's a lapazoo

"Buck dance, wing dance
Will be a back number
But the Charleston
The new Charleston
That dance is surely a comer

"Sometime
You'll dance it
One time
The dance called the Charleston
Made in South Carolina"

There was a group of about a dozen people standing around him. One couple started dancing. One man opened a hip flask and took a sip. He offered some to the man next to him, who also took a sip. As the impromptu party picked up steam, two men approached from the lobby. They were tall and dark, with dark hair and dark eyes. Both were broad shouldered. They wore dark suits and wide brimmed hats and looked like they could be brothers. They moved over to the piano, edging a couple of the patrons out of the way, but they politely waited for Silas to finish his song.

When Silas finished playing, the people in the group noticed the dark men and quietly moved away. Silas looked up at the two men who had crashed his little party. They had a menacing look about them, but did not seem to be angry or intend him harm. He just knew that he didn't want to get on the wrong side of either of them.

One of them spoke with a heavy accent (Italian), that Silas did not recognize. "You Smoot?" he asked. Silas nodded. "Boss wants you to a come with us. Start you new job."

"I thought I didn't start until tomorrow," said Silas.

"Job no in Chicago. Up north, you work for Gerry B. He one of the Boss's business associates. We take you there," the man said. His partner remained silent.

"I have to go get my things," said Silas. "Also my suits are not ready yet."

"Suits will be brought to you tomorrow. Get you things, we wait," said the dark man.

***

Silas Smoot sat in the back seat of a Cadillac, marveling at the speed, comfort and smoothness of the ride. His record player and records sat next to him. The two dark men were in the front seat. "How far is this place?" he asked.

"Coupla hours," said the talkative one from the front passenger seat. The silent one was driving. "Relax, take it easy. We be there before you know it."

They were moving fast, a couple of hours could find them a hundred miles away, thought Silas. He leaned against the door, stretched out and watched the scenery fly by; it was absolutely amazing. His companions said nothing more and they rode in silence for nearly three and a half hours.

They arrived at dusk in a heavily wooded area. Silas could see a lake peering through the trees on the left, about 100 yards from where they stopped. "We here," said the dark man. "Get you stuff." Silas gathered his belongings and climbed out of the car.

They were in front of what looked like an oversized house. Next to the door was a wooden Indian. Above the door was a big wooden sign that said "Wilson's Roadhouse."

The three men entered, with Silas struggling to balance the record player and stack of records. They entered a large dark room full of tables. There was a bar running along the right wall. There were a few patrons, sipping from coffee cups. A mirror ran the length of the wall behind the bar. A man in a white shirt and a white apron stood behind the bar pouring drinks into coffee cups from what looked like a silver coffee pot.

They were greeted by a woman who Silas thought was the most beautiful woman he'd ever seen. She was nearly as tall as Silas, 5' 10", and had jet black hair that was cut very short. Her big, luminous, light green eyes seemed to light up the room. She had very long legs that emerged from a very short dress (it embarrassed Silas to look at her as he was still not used to seeing a woman dressed this way). The dress was covered with short strips of a silvery fabric; it shimmered when she walked. Silas just stared at her, dumbfounded. She said, "I'm Janie Wilson, I run this place. Can I help you?"

The talkative dark man looked at Silas and said, "Hey Smoot, close you mouth. You gonna catch flies." Then to the woman, "Al sent us. Here you new piano player," motioning with his head.

"Of course," she said, smiling at Smoot and running her finger along the front of his shirt. "You any good?" She leaned in toward him and winked.

"I, er, um, well..." stammered Silas.

She turned toward the dark man, and said with a smile and a wink, "Let's hope he plays better than he talks." Then to Silas she said, "We got a place set up for you above the carriage house in back." Silas managed a nod. She led them through the dining room and through two double swinging doors that lead into the kitchen.

At the back of the kitchen was a door to the outside. They went through it and into a parking lot. On the far side of the parking lot, about 50 yards from the back door stood a large carriage house. She took them across the lot to a side door in the carriage house. It opened to a single narrow staircase. They went upstairs.

The upstairs of the carriage house was a large open room. It was like a big studio apartment. There was a stove, a wooden icebox and a sink with some cabinets against one wall. A small table with two chairs was nearby. There was a bathroom in the corner, next to the kitchen area. Silas happily noted that it had a bathtub. Across room was a single bed and next to it was a dresser. There was a big easy chair in the middle of the room. Silas noted that it was bigger than his cabin back home. "This is very nice," he said sincerely.

"He speaks," said Janie. "Yeah, it's the flippin' Taj Mahal. Make yourself at home, you start tomorrow at eight. You can eat lunch in the kitchen before 11 and dinner before five. You're on your own for breakfast. We're about five miles from town, there is a diner there, as well as a grocery store, if you prefer to cook."

Silas put his burden down on the table and sat at one of the chairs. "Thank you," he managed to say to her. He was really going to like it here.

Chapter 44
September 5, 1776

Philadelphia at Last

Angie was the first to wake up as the first rays of morning light shone through the trees. There were still some hot embers from last night's fire. She stirred them and added some wood to get the fire going. By the time the other were awake, she had hot water for tea and had gotten out biscuits and dried meat for breakfast.

Billy said, "We should eat up and get going. We have about another 20 miles to go. It is early enough that we could make Philadelphia in daytime."

They ate, loaded up the wagon and were on their way before 7 AM. As they traveled south, the road had fewer ruts in it than it did further north and they were able to travel a bit faster. "Smooth going," Billy said. "We should make it to Philadelphia in a few hours."

It was a beautiful summer day, clear with a few wispy clouds in the sky. The temperature was in the upper 70s. They were not too far from the Delaware River; you could see it through the trees every so often. Occasionally you could see a deer through the trees. Angie thought it was the most beautiful place in the world.

"So are you two homesick?" Billy asked Angie and Eddie, looking over his back.

"You have no idea," said Eddie. "When I get home I am going to take a hot shower and play some video games."

Billy just shrugged, not knowing what a video game was. "How about you, Angie?" he asked.

"To tell you the truth, this is the most beautiful place that I have ever been," she answered. She looked at Billy, sighed and said, "And, I am really enjoying the company. In our day, this little stretch of land between New York and Philadelphia is full of cars, noise, air pollution, shopping malls, businesses and factories. All of this beautiful countryside is gone. To tell you the truth, I'd rather stay here."

"I bet you miss all of your fancy machines and your conveniences. Sounds like life is easy in your time," Lucius said.

"Amen to that," said Eddie. "It's fun for now, Angie. But I think you'd eventually be miserable here." He had to keep trying to get her to see that staying would be a big mistake.

"I don't know," said Angie. "It is so beautiful, clean and peaceful here. There is too much of everything at home. Too much noise, too many people, constant news and communication. I like it better here; but I do miss showers."

"Peaceful," snorted Billy. "There's a war going on."

"Even so, it is quieter here than in our day." Angie said. "If we stop the wagon and listen, we won't be able to hear a thing other than birds and other nature sounds. Billy, you cannot appreciate how noxious our air is. The air here is so clean, that breathing actually creates a kind of euphoria."

"There's no Cheetos or pizza," said Eddie.

"That IS unfortunate," said Angie. "But I have to say, I have a LOT more energy and my clothes are getting looser."

"Tell me you're not wanting to stay here," said Eddie. "You DO want to get back home, don't you?"

"I started out that way, but the more I think of it, the more I want to stay here," said Angie.

"You can't be serious!" cried Eddie.

"Don't worry," said Angie. "I will help you to get Uncle Sol's notes."

"And you will come with me?" Eddie asked pointedly.

Angie just shrugged. Eddie let it go for the time being.

They ate a cold lunch in the wagon. Billy wanted to keep going, so he had them eat while traveling. His persistence paid off. Shortly after lunch they could see the city of Philadelphia from a hill just outside of the city.

Chapter 45
September 3 & 4, 1776

Bigby on a Mission

Bigby made it back to Clinton's camp with five of his men and the two corpses. He arranged for burial for his cousin and for the other man. Then he reported directly to General Clinton, who was very interested in the whereabouts of the two children. He pointedly asked Bigby about the children and their whereabouts.

"No sir they left town as we were arriving. It is possible that they are on their way to Virginia." He cleared his throat. "On a more serious note, I am sorry to say that the criminal, Collins, escaped." He said sheepishly.

"Bad news, that," said Clinton. "No reprimand coming from me. You have suffered a terrible loss. I was fond of your cousin; he was a fine officer and gentleman."

"Yes sir. Thank you, sir," said Bigby.

"Perhaps you can redeem yourself. I need you to bring me those children. Unless I miss my guess, Collins is after them as well. Follow the children and you are very likely to find Collins. If you do come across the murderer, there is no need for you to bring him back here. Simply carry out his sentence. He has already been convicted and he deserves to be hung, but shooting may have to suffice. I think you are correct about the children going to Virginia. Your cousin's last report stated as much. Take one man with you and leave in the morning."

"Yes sir," said Bigby. "If given a choice, I would choose Sargent Woodruff. Good man. He's a tracker and a crack shot."

"Good choice. The man was with Roger's Rangers during the last conflict with the French. By all means, take him with you," said Clinton. "Get to Philadelphia as quickly as you can. The children will probably stop there; they may even stay a while. There is also a good chance that Collins will be there as well. He is obsessed with those children."

"Yes sir!" said Bigby.

Bigby and Sargent Woodruff arrived in New Brunswick around noon, dressed in civilian clothes. Woodruff was about 40, 5'10" tall and looked like he was made of leather. His face was brown, with more than a few wrinkles and he kept his hair short. He wasn't big and powerful looking, but he was solid muscle. Words that would be used to describe him would include hard, craggy, and grim. They went to an inn, The Sign of the Red Lion, and had lunch. Bigby said, "Those children have a head start and are probably almost all the way to Philadelphia by now. If they spend time there, we will find them. If not, it will be easy enough to catch them on the road to Virginia. If we come across Collins, we will carry out the sentence as necessary." Woodruff nodded. The two of them ate their meal and were on their way early into the afternoon.

Chapter 46
September 3, 1776

Collins Improves His Situation

Collins made his way upriver away from the town. Although his situation was greatly improved, it still was not a good one. He had no money, no weapons, he was wet and cold, he was missing a shoe and it was dark out. He was wanted by civilian law enforcement, the American army and the British army. Not good. For now, he just wanted to put distance between himself and New Brunswick.

He walked along a trail that followed the river for about an hour. It was dark and getting hard to see when he noticed a fire through the woods. He could hear voices. He slowed his pace and quietly crept toward the fire.

There were two men. They were talking and enjoying a meal. The food smelled wonderful; he was starving. There was a gnawing pain in his stomach. He had not eaten all day. His trial had been held at lunchtime and the British soldiers fetched him before he could be fed.

He crouched in the dark, about 30 feet from the fire, out of sight. He was trying to think of a story that he could tell that would make him welcome by the fire. Maybe he could say he was ambushed and robbed; that could work. He was working out different scenarios in his head when one of the men got up and started to walk toward him. Had he been discovered? He found a large rock near his feet and picked it up. He flattened himself on the ground to avoid being seen.

The man did not come too close. He walked past Collins, about 10 feet to his left without noticing him. He stopped in front of a tree and began to relieve himself. Collins got up and quietly moved close to the man. The man sensed, rather than heard Collins. He turned around and Collins hit him in the head with the rock, swinging with all of his might. The man collapsed in a heap.

Collins then circled around behind the second man. He had to move fast, before the man became curious about his friend. He was about 20 feet away, behind the second man. He crept up, as quietly as he could. The man heard him when he was about 10 feet away. Collins lunged for the man, hitting him with a glancing blow on the side of the head. They both went down. The man was not unconscious and struggled. Collins managed a second blow, then a third. The man stopped moving.

There was some meat on a spit. Collins took it and hungrily ate. The second man was about his size, so Collins stripped of his wet clothes and took the clothes belonging to the man. Even the boots fit. He threw his old clothes in the fire. There was a purse with some coins in it. The man also had a pistol, powder and shot. Collins helped himself to the booty. He went to the first man, who also had a purse and a pistol. There were also two horses, bedrolls and food. He gathered up all of the valuables, mounted one of the horses and shooed the other one away.

Now he was ready to find those two children. They would be on the King's Highway. Maybe they had gotten to Philadelphia by now. He knew that they were headed toward Virginia. He would find them and get even. He was tired, but he had to put some distance between himself and the two men.

Collins rode the horse slowly, making his way east and south. Eventually he would come to the Kings Road. For now, he just wanted to put a few miles between himself and his victims. He would have liked to find an inn and stay the night, using some of the money in the purses he stole, but that would be dangerous. He was not that far from New Brunswick, and was worried that he was a little too close to that town to remain anonymous. It was possible that word would have gotten out about his escape. There may even be people searching for him. It would be safer to camp. He was exhausted, but had to keep going for at least a little while, just a few miles more. He would make camp. It was warm, so he would forgo making a fire. Better to stay hidden.

He traveled a few more miles and found a nice clearing near some water. He dismounted, tied up the horse and retrieved one of the bedrolls. He needed sleep; he was exhausted. He felt safe enough. It was far from any settlement and it was unlikely that anyone would come upon him. It was even more unlikely that they would know who he was. He was also far enough away from the two men he had robbed in the woods. It was unlikely that they would be able to track him. In fact, he pretty sure they were not alive. Perhaps he should have made sure they were dead. Oh well, too late now.

Chapter 47
October, 1752

Sol and Vernon Make a New Contact

Sol and Vernon had chosen cotton clothing that was simple and could pass for garb during the Colonial era. They carried with them their duffels, their weapons, a new stash of gold coins and the envelopes with instructions for Eddie and Angie. They arrived to their destination with a "pop" and found themselves on the streets of an 18th century city.

"This is probably Philadelphia," said Vernon. "I am not sure about the year, we lost some of the timing accuracy by narrowing down the location. It was a tradeoff."

"This is the place to be, if we want the Founding Fathers involved with our search," said Sol.

Vernon nodded, "I think you are right. If Angie is in the Colonies in the 18th century, there is a good chance that she will seek out the Founding Fathers."

They were near a print shop. "That is the likely publisher of the local newspaper," said Sol. "Let's see if we can determine the date." They headed toward the shop.

Sol noticed a stack of newspapers near the entrance. It was October of 1752. "Early," muttered Sol. In the back of the shop they saw a bald headed bespectacled man in his forties, with shoulder-length hair. He was busy setting type.

Vernon noticed the man in the back and said in amazement, "You're Benjamin Franklin!"

Franklin looked up from his work, smiled and said, "I must be in the prime of my senility, because you know me, but I surely do not remember you."

Sol said, "You do not know us, Mr. Franklin, but there is an important matter that we would like to discuss with you."

"Very well," said Franklin. "Let me finish my work; then we shall have dinner together and you can discuss your issue. In general, mankind, since the improvement of cookery eats twice as much as nature requires," he continued, looking down and patting his protruding belly. "I fear that I am no exception. Make yourselves comfortable and I will be right with you."

Sol and Vernon found a couple of chairs at the front of the shop and awaited their host. Sol picked up a copy of the newspaper, the *Pennsylvania Gazette*, and began to thumb through it.

He read aloud, "Monday Night last a man was taken up, and sent to prison on suspicion of being James Rice, alias Dillon, one of the Murderers described in this paper, having a woman with him who was also taken up the night following; but it appears that his name is James Talbot, and he is a convict runaway servant, belonging to Major Washington, on Potomac River, in Virginia; and that the woman's name is Mary Belly, also a servant to the same gentleman. They offered a silver spoon and other things to sale here supposed to belong to their Master."

"Sounds like Major Washington needs to keep better track of his servants," mused Sol. He showed the paper to Vernon. "Not very fond of periods, are they?" Vernon noted. "That is a very long sentence." Sol shushed him, noting that the author was probably Franklin, who was in earshot.

Sol continued, "Last week Nathan Smith and Richard Skinner were committed to the jail of this city for stealing a coverlid and tablecloth from Isaac Ashton of Abington Township." He added, "Those bounders!"

Franklin finished his work and came to the front of the shop. "The issue is finished. Energy and persistence conquer all things. But now we shall go to my home where my missus has made what is no doubt an excellent meal and we shall discuss your business." He put on his coat and motioned for the two to follow him out of the door. He locked up his shop and headed up the street. His home was a few doors away from the shop. He entered the door and shouted, "Deborah, we have guests."

A girl of about nine ran out and hugged him. "Daddy!" she shouted. He picked her up and swung her around. When he put her down, she noticed the two strangers. "Hello," she said, "I am Sarah Franklin, who are you?"

"I am Sol Fitzgerald and this is Vernon Greene," said Sol with a bow.

Sarah curtsied and said, "Pleased to meet you."

"Now Sarah, why don't you help your mother with the dinner while we talk," Franklin said. He motioned for them to go to a sitting room to the left of the entryway. Sol and Vernon each took a seat. Franklin poured some wine for each of them and said, "Wine is constant proof that God loves us and loves to see us happy." He handed each of them a glass and took a seat. "What is this important business that you want to discuss with me?"

"What I am about to tell you may seem a little farfetched," Sol began. "We are from 262 years in the future." Franklin just looked at him impassively, saying nothing. "I don't expect you to take us at our word," Sol continued. He reached into his duffel and pulled out an iPhone. "Technology has come a long way." Sol took a few minutes to describe air and space travel, television, computers and the internet. At the end of his speech he said, "We travel on paved roads in machines that are capable of going over 100 miles per hour Although we are not allowed to drive that fast." "Doesn't stop you," Vernon interrupted him. Sol continued," Of course, I cannot bring all of these technological marvels, but I can show you a sample."

Sol had begun to video his little speech, scanning around the room. He took about two minutes of video and walked over to Franklin and played it for him. Franklin leaned forward and stared in amazement. "This is fantastic," he said. "I have so much to ask you about. How long can you stay?"

Sol said, "Unfortunately we have to get going. We have a favor to ask of you. At some time in your life you may come across two children." He gave the descriptions of the children and told the whole story. Franklin agreed to help, in exchange for one hour of questions. Sol handed him an envelope and they discussed the future, talking about inventions and technologic achievements. Sol mentioned the war for independence, which Franklin thought was an absurd idea. "Things will change," Sol told him.

Sol and Vernon had a second glass of wine with Franklin, but did not stay for dinner. They said their goodbyes, and Sol and Vernon linked arms and were gone with a "pop." Franklin's wife and daughter came into the room when they heard the "pop" and asked where their guests were. "You wouldn't believe me if I told you," Franklin said.

When they were back in the barn, Sol said to Vernon, "That was a good contact. He believed us and he's a scientist. Plus, he's famous; there is a chance that Eddie or Angie would want to meet him if they did land in Colonial America." He sat at the lab bench, going through his duffel and counting the envelopes. Vernon joined him.

"This could work. He may not see the children for another decade, but it won't matter. The meeting could happen within days of their arriving in the 18th century," Vernon said.

"Crap!" exclaimed Sol. "I think I gave him one of the old envelopes. One of the ones we created before you figured out how to estimate the time of arrival."

"It doesn't matter," said Vernon. "It's a numbers game. We will put out dozens of envelopes. Even if they get the old one, they may eventually get one of the new ones. Plus, as we gain knowledge, the information we put in the envelopes will become increasingly useful. One thing, maybe we should not be giving the people we contact too much information about the future. I don't believe we can change history, but it may be prudent to be more tight-lipped."

"Agreed," said Sol. "But he is a man of science and I was pretty excited to meet him. I talked more than I should have."

Chapter 48
September 4, 1776

Collins Renews Pursuit

Collins slept very soundly and was very late in the morning when he had awakened. He felt refreshed, although his knee still throbbed and he had trouble breathing through his nose. He got up, ate a breakfast of dried meat and biscuits from the supplies he had stolen.

He finished breakfast, gathered up his belongings and mounted the horse. He could push and possibly make it to Philadelphia after nightfall, but opted instead to set a leisurely pace and arrive on the following day. Better to arrive in daylight. He figured that those two children would make it to the city later today, he would be one, or possibly two days behind.

Little did Collins know that by the time he had awakened, British agents were on their way to find him. He figured that he had made a clean getaway. There was too much area to search and there was a war on, so he felt safe. It was a false sense of security; he never figured that Clinton would send men after him based on his knowledge of the children's destination.

Chapter 49
September 5, 1776

Eddie and Angie Meet Benjamin Franklin

As the wagon rode past Independence Hall, Eddie looked at it and felt a little emotional. This was literally where the United States of America was born. He never thought of himself as particularly sentimental or patriotic, but he became a little misty-eyed looking at the building.

"What's up with you?" Angie asked, noticing the expression on his face.

"Nothin'," Eddie said, turning away.

"We should find a place to stay," said Billy.

They found an inn just over a block away from Independence Hall, but it was full. Delegates were still in town. The proprietor of the inn told them of woman at the edge of town who took in boarders, and that she might have some room for them. They got back into the wagon and headed toward the east side of town where the woman lived.

As they headed up the street, Billy stopped for a rotund, bald headed man with shoulder length hair and allowed him to cross. Eddie looked at the man and exclaimed, "Hey, you're Benjamin Franklin!"

Angie admonished him and said, "You're such a celebrity gawker."

The man looked at Eddie, noticing the others in the wagon and said, "Hey, you're Eddie Fitzgerald!"

Eddie's mouth fell open and he stared for a moment. Then he said, "You know me?"

"I know *of* you. Your Uncle Sol sends his best wishes," Franklin said. "He left something for me to give you, a rather large envelope. It was more than 20 years ago, but I remember it like it was yesterday."

Eddie could hardly contain his excitement, "You saw Uncle

Sol!"

Franklin nodded and motioned for them to come over.

"We were going to General Washington's home to get another envelope that Sol left for us," said Angie.

"I was under the impression that your Uncle left many such envelopes. My guess is that the contents of my envelope is much the same as General Washington's," Franklin said.

"When can we see it?" Eddie asked.

"We were just going to get a room at Mrs. Davis' house, can we meet you later?" asked Angie.

"Get a room, nonsense!" exclaimed Franklin. "I have plenty of room in my house. The children are grown and my lovely Deborah, God rest her soul, is no longer with us." He climbed up into the front of the wagon with Billy and said, "Just go ahead to that next street and turn left."

He did not live very far away at all, thought Angie. Even though Philadelphia was the capital of the new nation, it wasn't very big; it was probably about the size of the Wrigleyville neighborhood in Chicago. The house was another two blocks away. Franklin directed Billy and Lucius to a livery stable nearby where the horses and wagon could be kept.

Billy and Lucius took the horses to the stable after everyone got out of the wagon. It was a short walk back to Franklin's house.

"We can't thank you enough for letting us stay with you," said Eddie.

"Nonsense," said Franklin. "It is I who should be thanking you. You will have to pay rent, of course," he said with a chuckle. "You will have to put up with my incessant questions about the future. I had a very interesting discussion with your uncle a few years back and I am anxious to continue to learn more."

He motioned them to come inside. They were greeted at the door by a thin black man, an inch or two shorter than Franklin, with short grey hair. "George," he said, "We have guests."

"He has a slave?" Eddie whispered to Angie.

"No, Franklin freed his slaves," Angie whispered back. "He's an abolitionist now, although he never really fought to ban slavery in the constitution."

"George will show you upstairs to your rooms. You gentlemen will have to share and you, young lady will have your own room," Franklin said. "It's a little tight, but Mrs. Davis would only have had a single room for the four of you."

"Can we see the package Uncle Sol left?" Eddie asked.

REVOLUTION TIME

"Of course, of course," said Franklin. "But first get settled in your rooms and come downstairs for some supper."

George led them upstairs. He gave the boys extra pillows and bedding for their room. Eddie opted to sleep on the floor.

They washed up and went downstairs for dinner. Franklin was already seated, drinking a glass of red wine. He offered some to Billy and Lucius from a decanter. Lucius declined, but Billy accepted.

On the table were chicken, potatoes, sliced tomatoes, bread and peas. They helped themselves and dug in greedily. "It is wonderful to have a home cooked meal after the last two days on the road," said Eddie.

Franklin said, "Hunger is indeed the best sauce—eat up." He took a sip of wine and said, "So the two of you are from the year 2014; according to your Uncle Sol, so many marvelous things had been invented by then. I was fascinated by flying machines. Can you tell me how they work?"

"Of course," said Angie. "Flying couldn't really happen until the development of the internal combustion engine because it had enough speed and power without being weighed down with coal and water the way steam engines were."

"Yes, Sol told me about internal combustion engines. Genius, really," said Franklin.

"The second thing was the design of the wing," said Angie. "The bottom of the wing is flat and the top of the wing is curved. The air at the top of the wing moves faster than the air at the bottom of the wing and therefore has less pressure. As the airplane moves faster, it creates a force called 'lift' on the underside of the wing."

"Fascinating," said Franklin.

"I would have thought you would be more interested in electricity," said Eddie.

"Oh, I plan on asking you all about electricity," Franklin said.

Just then there was a knock at the door. George opened the door and led a man to the dining room. He was about 40, with a high forehead and graying hair that emerged from the sides of his head in tufts. He was what could be described as "stout," not really fat. He was short and a little thick through the middle.

He stepped into the dining room and nodded an abrupt, "Good evening" to the group.

Franklin rose and said, "John, I would like you to meet my new friends. The two young ones over there are Angie and Eddie Fitzgerald. This gentleman is Billy Simmons and this other gentleman is Lucius Freeman. Everyone, this is John Adams, one of the delegates to the Congress."

"Wow," said Angie. "You're John Adams."

"Um, yes. Have we met?" Adams asked.

"John, why don't you join us for a little supper?" Franklin asked.

"I've eaten," Adams said.

"Some wine then," said Franklin, pouring a glass.

Adams took the wine and sat down. "You have, no doubt, heard of the disaster on Long Island last week," he said.

"Yes, a disastrous defeat and quite a tragedy," Franklin said. "Yet I somehow think our new nation will survive." He winked at Angie.

"General Howe wants to discuss peace with some members of the Congress. It has been suggested that the two of us go," said Adams.

"He figures that adversity will make us give up and that we will trade our liberty for a little safety," mused Franklin. "Of course anyone who would give up liberty for a little safety deserves neither. Although I suppose it can do no harm to talk to the man. Tell the others that I will consider it."

Angie said, "You two go to speak to General Howe in a few days, but nothing comes of it."

John Adams stared at her in amazement. "She's psychic," Eddie said.

Angie took the iPhone out of her pack and gave it to Eddie and whispered, "I am going to stand over there by John Adams. Take our picture." Eddie nodded in agreement.

Adams finished his wine and said, "It was a pleasure meeting all of you, but I still have a great deal of work ahead of me, so I will bid you all a good night." Angie ran over and put her arm around him. Adams was startled, but Eddie got the picture. Angie held out her hand and said, "Such an honor to meet you, Mr. Adams."

Franklin escorted him to the door. They chatted for a few minutes then Adams left. Franklin came back to the table. "He has one of the finest minds in the America. Hard worker, too. He must be on every committee involved with writing the laws for the new government.

"He wants to speak to General Howe. He truly believes that reason can still prevail—even at this late date. He is a good, rational and sincere man who, unfortunately, assumes everyone else is also good, rational and sincere. I fear that this war has taken us beyond reason. The British will cling to their pride and authority and will not want to make any concessions to a bunch of rebels who had the audacity to challenge the authority of the King. I am much more hopeful that he will be more successful at securing aid from the French when he goes there than he will be in securing peace from General Howe."

"Well, you're going to France with him, aren't you?" said Angie.

"Me? No, I am too old for such a trip," said Franklin.

"You have to go!" exclaimed Angie. "The French will think he's a pill. You won't get the aid unless you yourself go."

"Pill?" asked Franklin, not being familiar with the term. "Mr. Adams has a fine mind and is a skilled diplomat and lawyer."

"They will find him boring and judgmental," said Angie. "They won't like him very much at all. For that matter, he will not care much for the French. They will find you interesting and charming. The French will love you. You have to go. America will not get aid from the French unless you go. Mr. Adams can go, but he joins you later. You go this winter."

Franklin took a long sip from his glass. "Paris, eh?"

Chapter 50
June 11, 2014

Sol and Vernon Narrow Their Focus

Sol and Vernon had distributed the remaining 20 envelopes at various times throughout the 18th century. They had left packages in each of the colonies with prominent people. They arrived in the barn and headed toward the trailer.

Vernon said, "We have the 18th century pretty well covered. Do you want to put together some more packages?"

Sol said, "We should really eat and get some rest. I guess I have been a little too frantic about this. We've been burning it at both ends. It's just that I am just desperate to get them back before the summer ends. But we cannot keep up this pace. We should get a good night's sleep and start again in the morning." He thought a minute. "I am really intrigued by that picture we saw in New Castle, Wisconsin. That may be our best hope of finding them yet. We have a very specific geographic location and a time span just a little over a decade long. I like our chances of finding them there. The picture had to have been taken some time between 1920 and 1932. That is when Al Capone was in Chicago. It is safe to assume that a picture of him taken in Wisconsin would have been during that period."

"It's hard to believe they were with him. I hope they're safe," said Vernon.

"They would be safe with Capone unless they decided to set up a competing bootleg operation, a prospect that I find highly unlikely," said Sol.

"The fact that they were in the 1920s means that they used the device. Maybe that means they have a set of notes," said Vernon.

"Maybe they had notes or maybe they felt threatened and made a jump. If they stay a while in the 1920s, it gives us a narrow time and place where we can actually find them. If we can do that, we can physically bring them home," said Sol. "I should go to Lucy's house and let her know that we still may be a while."

"Lucy, huh," said Vernon, with a knowing look. "I will stay here and let you two be alone."

"Don't be silly, Vernon. There is nothing going on between us," said Sol.

"Yet," said Vernon.

"I want to see how Sam and Dave are doing," Sol said, but he looked a little sheepish. "When I get back we can eat, rest and then take a look at Castle Rock, Wisconsin in the 1920s."

Chapter 51
September 6, 1776

A New Day at the Franklin House

Angie slept very well and was the first one downstairs, other than Benjamin Franklin, who was sitting at the table eating a roll and drinking some tea when she arrived. She had so much more energy lately. She put her hands on her waist. She had never weighed herself or paid much attention to her weight for that matter, but she could notice that her waist had gotten smaller. There was no junk food here and she and Eddie were on the go all of the time. The funny thing was that she did not miss the junk food; and she felt good.

"Good morning, Angie," Franklin greeted her. "Have some tea and rolls with me." She took a seat across the table from him and helped herself to a roll. Franklin poured her a cup of tea, "Milk or sugar?" he asked. She opted to drink it plain. She was beginning to like the taste of tea.

"Mr. Franklin," she said, "I was hoping to look at Uncle Sol's notes today."

"Ben," he said, "Please call me Ben. I admire your manners, but I expect that we will become good friends. So you should call me Ben."

"Ben," she said, "Could I please see Uncle Sol's notes?"

"Of course, of course," Franklin said, "I have them right here." He walked over to a desk in the next room and retrieved the envelope. He came back into the dining room and placed the envelope in front of Angie. She took a sip of her tea, opened the envelope and began reading.

Just then Eddie came downstairs. He yawned, grabbed himself a roll and sat down next to Angie. "Whatcha got?" he asked.

"Good morning, young man," Franklin said. "Help yourself to some breakfast. I have a nice pear tree out back, and I will bring in some pears to have with breakfast."

"Uh, thanks," said Eddie. "Good morning to you Mr. Franklin." Franklin stepped through the kitchen and out the back door.

"These are the notes from Uncle Sol and Vernon. It says that we can locate the exact place and time that we are now occupying and mark it on the machine. That way, no matter where we go, we can come back here," Angie said. "They have found a spot on their CKD that allows them to return home any time they want. They are going to continue to look for us so they can bring us home with their machine. They are also going to continue to leave clues and we should contact famous people or, preferably, people we know who are going to become famous in the future." Angie did not know that this was an old set of notes and that since then Sol and Vernon had gotten proficient at coming to within a few months and within some miles to a desired location. She said to Eddie, "I will help you figure this out, then you can try to get home."

"WE can try to get home, you mean," said Eddie.

"Actually," said Angie, "I was going to ask Mr. Franklin if I could go to Paris with him. It would be a wonderful opportunity."

"Angie, you can't be serious," said Eddie.

"I am, and you can't force me to go with you," said Angie.

"This is crazy," said Eddie. "You don't belong here. We both belong at home." Angie just shook her head and refused to continue the conversation.

At that point Billy and Lucius came down and the argument stopped. Everyone said their good mornings and Franklin bid them to have tea and rolls. Angie continued to read the notes. Inside the envelope was what looked like a flash drive. Eddie paced behind her. The notes explained that Sol and Vernon had used a computer to "mark" a spot on the machine. Vernon put information on the flash drive to interact with the hard drive of the CKD and enable them to do the same thing.

"This should be pretty easy," said Angie. "All we have to do is mark some stones, use the program to mark a spot on the machine, then send the stone away. If one of the stones lands nearby, that is 'home' and we can leave the mark on the machine."

"How do we get back to Wisconsin in 2014?" asked Eddie.

"They didn't get that far, but they are working on it. They know we are in the latter part of the 18th century. Uncle Sol says that once we create a home base, we can try to see if we can get home because if we end up somewhere undesirable, we can always get back to where we started."

Franklin, who had just come in from the kitchen, holding a bowl of pears, said, "It looks like you have quite a project for yourselves. Let me know if I can be of any assistance. I was thinking that I could show you around our city this morning and you can get started on your project this afternoon."

Lucius said, "That would be very nice, Mr. Franklin. I would like to see the city."

"Me too," said Billy. Eddie just nodded.

"Call me Ben, please," said Franklin. "Finish breakfast and we can get going."

Billy and Lucius said that they were grateful for the hospitality, but that they were going to follow up on Angie's idea and go to North Carolina to get the treasure. It was over 500 miles away, and Billy said that they should get going soon after Mr. Franklin's tour.

Franklin was very interested in the story about the treasure. Angie took out the newspaper article to show him. When he finished reading it, she gave it to Billy, with a shy smile. Franklin said, "You are planning to take that wagon all that way. You will have to cross water to get there, why not go by boat?"

Lucius said, "Cost, for one thing. We have some money, but we have to be conservative in order to complete the journey. Also, we would need to be able to trust the captain and crew to not rob us and throw us overboard."

Franklin was a shrewd businessman. He made a proposition to the two men, saying, "I can solve both problems for you. I will invest in your little venture. I will give pay to hire a ship and to cover any incidental expenses for, let's say 10% of the treasure. Also, Captain Beaumont is a good friend of mine and a good, God-fearing man. He has painstakingly put together a crew of like-minded men. He will take to your destination for a fair price and you will be as safe as you are in this very dining room."

"One thing," said Angie. "They promised not to take all of the treasure. They have to leave at least half for the university researchers to find in 2014."

"Not a problem," said Franklin. "I am sure that we will all be adequately compensated."

It was agreed. Franklin went into his study to get some money. He gave some to Billy. "This is for any incidental expenses you may have. I will strike a deal with Captain Beaumont and pay him to accommodate you. We will tour the harbor in a little while and I will take you to Captain Beaumont's ship."

Chapter 52
June 12, 2014

Sol and Vernon get Ready for the Next Journey

It was close to midnight when Sol returned to the trailer. Vernon was already in bed, but heard him come in. "Nothing between you and Sally," he thought, silently chuckling. He did not hear Sam and Dave, and figured that Sol had prevailed upon Sally to keep the dogs a little longer.

They both slept in, being exhausted. Vernon arose at nine and Sol got up a few minutes later, smelling the bacon and eggs Vernon was preparing. He sleepily sat at the table as Vernon piled eggs, bacon, potatoes and toast onto two plates. He poured coffee for each of them and joined Sol.

"Late night?" Vernon asked.

"Sally had a little wiring problem. I was able to help her out. It was the least I could do, considering that she is taking care of Sam and Dave." Sol took a forkful of egg and potato.

"I see," said Vernon. "Good thing you were available." He took a bite of his food, finished chewing and said, "So what is the plan today?"

"I figured that we would try to go to 1920s New Castle. Clearly, Angie and Eddie were there. We could try to talk to Janie Wilson before the dementia set in," said Sol.

"Great," said Vernon. "We can leave after breakfast."

"I need to go into town first," said Sol. "We need to get more gold coins."

"I have a better idea," said Vernon. "Let's go back in time 10 years and buy them then. They will cost you half as much. Actually, if we go back to 1975, it will be even better."

"Good idea. I will need to get some cash in the form of old bills first," said Sol.

"Try to get bills older than the early 1970s," said Vernon, "Gold was much, much cheaper in the 1970s before prices took off. In 1975 it was less than $200 per ounce. It went to over $500 by the end of the decade. We should shoot for mid-1975. There was a run on precious metals starting in late 1975 that drove the price up."

Sol looked at him in amazement, "How do you know that? You were six."

Vernon said, "I remember hearing about it when I was a kid. I remember everything."

"Sounds like a good idea. Gold is nearly $1200 per ounce right now." Sol snorted a laugh. "Funny, if we had nothing better to do, we could accumulate a lot of money."

"Yeah," Vernon laughed. "We could become some high-end antique dealers or buy and sell stocks."

"Sounds boring," said Sol. Vernon was Sol's business partner and they were both already very wealthy. "Let's buy the gold in 1975 though; it kills me to pay today's prices. They seem artificially inflated."

Sol went into town to his bank. His request for bills older than 1975 was unusual, but they accommodated him because he was by far their biggest depositor. He was also thought of as "eccentric," so no one even batted an eye at the request. They were able to scrape together a little under $10,000 in old bills for him. Sol was careful not to raise any flags with the federal government, and taking out more than $10,000 would force the bank to alert federal authorities.

When Sol got back to the trailer, Vernon was waiting for him wearing a powder blue leisure suit. Sol looked at him and said, "Are you kidding me?"

"Halloween from three years ago. I figure it'll help me blend in," said Vernon.

"Very stylish," said Sol. He went to the center of the room and Vernon took out the device. They locked arms. Vernon touched a point on the screen and they disappeared with a "pop."

Chapter 53
September 6, 1776

Exploring Philadelphia

Benjamin Franklin led his little brood out of the front door of his home. "We are on Market Street," he said. "The State House is two blocks to the west and one block to the south, on Chestnut Street." They went about a block and Franklin said, "On the left there is Mrs. House's boarding house." He laughed, "As far as I know she did not change her name when she got into the business. But now if anyone asks for a house to stay in, we are obligated to direct them there," he said, chuckling. "It is a bit more expensive than Mrs. Davis' house where you originally wanted to stay."

Billy noticed the masts of ships in the Delaware River about 500 yards from Franklin's front door when they stepped outside, and said, "You live very close to the harbor."

Franklin said, "Yes, one stop and then we shall go and get you acquainted with Captain Beaumont. First, let me show you the State House where we are working on a document to outline the laws for our new government. The result will not be very satisfying, I am afraid. For now, we are putting together a loose association of states without much of a federal government. It will have to do until we win the war. Securing agreement between the states is our chief concern for the time being. If we do not leave most of the power with the states, some will leave the union. The Articles of Confederation is not an ideal document. Truth be told, it is a terrible document. Unfortunately, it is the best we could hope for during this war."

They turned a corner and went another block. Independence Hall came into view. Franklin walked up to the door and said, "Let's go inside and see if they are accomplishing anything."

They entered in the doorway under the bell tower. They walked through an entryway that led to a hall flanked by Greek style columns and archways. To the right of the entry way was a staircase leading to the top. Down the hallway, on either side was an entry to a room. Franklin led them through the room on the left. Inside were 13 desks. There was a smattering of delegates seated at the desks. Some were pushed together, like when doing a project at school, Eddie noted.

They saw John Adams seated with three other delegates and walked over to him. Franklin said, "John, you remember my friends from last night." He looked over Adams' shoulder, "How is it going?" Franklin asked.

"This business of some of the states claiming Western lands is going to present a problem," Adams said.

"The result will be at best temporary," said Franklin. "From what I've seen of the document, it is more like we are forming a club than forming a nation."

"I agree," said Adams, "But we have to leave most of the power with the states if we are to have any hope of ratifying the thing before the war is over."

Franklin bade Adams and his colleagues goodbye and the group left Independence Hall. "It's a nice day, Eddie, would you like to walk down to the wharf and see some ships?"

"Yes, please," said Eddie. "Then we should get back and work on mapping the machine."

"You can begin after we get back and you have some lunch," said Franklin. Then to Billy, "I will introduce you to Captain Beaumont. He sets sail tomorrow. You and Lucius can gather your things and get on board this afternoon. He is on his way to Jamaica, but will take you to your destination and wait for you for a price. You will have to go to Jamaica with him, but overall this is safer and faster than trying to take that wagon there."

Chapter 54
September 5 & 6, 1776

Collins Closes In

Very late in the afternoon, Collins had come across the King's Highway a little way south of Bristol. He was about 20 miles from Philadelphia. It was getting late and he decided to camp and leave for the capitol early tomorrow morning. He once again opted to not start a fire. It was not cold and he did not want to attract any company. He ate some dried meat and biscuits and went to sleep.

His knee still hurt, but not as bad as earlier in the week. The headaches had stopped. His face was beginning to heal, but the purple of his bruises were taking on a multicolored look. There were areas of green and yellow interspersed with the purple. The ink spot had faded a little, but overall, he looked more grotesque than he did earlier in the week.

Collins awoke to the first rays of the morning sun. He felt surprisingly refreshed considering all that he had been through. He had overcome a lot because of his singleness of purpose. Anger and adrenaline worked to minimize his discomfort. He was going to get even with those two. Especially the boy who had twice injured and humiliated him. It was their fault that he was a fugitive. Had they not escaped, he would have gotten paid and been done with this affair. But their escape had shaken General Clinton's faith in him and caused him to be saddled with the insufferable Captain Goodman.

There was a very good chance that the children would spend some time in Philadelphia, having spent a several days on the road. They would rest and get supplies. Collins was sure that they would leave him out of any story they told; it would create too many questions. If that were the case, it was a probability that no one in Philadelphia would know who he is or what crimes he had committed.

Collins packed up his things and mounted his horse. He could be in Philadelphia by early afternoon. He would find a quiet place to stay, get cleaned up and set about the task of finding those two children. He touched one of the pistols at his side and patted it. He would find them.

Chapter 55
May, 1975 and 1929

Sol and Vernon Raise Some Traveling Money and Run into an Old Acquaintance

Sol and Vernon appeared in Chicago in mid-1975. It was warm out and there were leaves on the trees, so they figured it was late spring or early summer. "Our timing should be pretty close to perfect, as far as getting a good price for the coins." said Vernon. "It's funny, Americans were not allowed to own gold from the time of the Great Depression until 1975. Prices more than double by the end of the year."

They found a phone booth. "When was the last time you saw one of these?" said Sol. They went inside, looking at the Yellow Pages for coin dealers. They found one with a very large ad that was only two blocks away.

They walked to the dealer. It was in a storefront on south Wabash Street, under the el tracks. There were bars on the windows and a sign that said, "Gold Bought and Sold." The Yellow Pages ad was certainly more impressive than the store was. They went inside and negotiated with the dealer. They settled on a price of $182 per coin. Considering the look of the store and the surrounding area, Sol was surprised that the proprietor could supply him with the 54 coins his $10,000 was able to purchase. The purchase was worth about $60,000 in 2014.

They completed their transaction and turned to leave. Looking out on the street and the various characters that were milling about, Vernon stopped and said, "Maybe we should go directly home from here." Sol agreed and they were gone with a "pop." The owner stared in amazement.

A moment later, they appeared in the barn and made their way to the trailer. They packed duffels with supplies and were ready to go. Vernon studied the screen of the CKD for a few minutes as they stood together with their arms linked. Finally, he touched the screen and they were gone with a "pop."

They appeared in front of Wilson's Roadhouse. It was cold out and there was still snow on the ground. Vernon said, "I went for the end of the decade. It is either 1929 or 1930. That way, if they were here earlier, there may have been witnesses."

"It's a starting point," said Sol.

They stepped inside the bar. It had a very different look than it had in the mid-1970s. The walls were covered with a dark wood paneling. The place was dimly lit and the walls were lined with booths. There was a piano bar at the wall farthest from the doorway, and a small dance floor to the left of it. On the other side of the piano bar was a booth. A man sat at the booth eating; he was the only person in the place.

The man looked strangely familiar to Sol, who stood in the entryway looking at the man, with his eyes adjusting to the dimness. The man looked up and rushed toward Sol, who recognized him too late. It was Silas Smoot, and he was moving fast toward Sol. Sol panicked and lifted his leg and tried to reach his gun in his ankle holster, but the man was upon him before he could reach it. They collided and the man grabbed him in a bear hug, knocking the wind out of him. Sol was standing on one leg and would have fallen if the man did not have such a tight grip on him.

"My good friend!" he exclaimed. "How can I ever repay you the kindness you have done me?" Sol was a big man, but Silas managed to lift him off his feet and swing him around. "Have you eaten?" he asked. "Come, join me. It is so good to see you."

He walked back toward his booth, motioning for them to follow him. He motioned for them to sit at the booth and went through the swinging doors into the kitchen. He came out with two plates piled high with roast beef, mashed potatoes and sweet peas. He dropped off the plates before going to the bar and grabbing two beers for his guests.

"You won't believe it," he said, "But alcoholic beverages are ILLEGAL here. They might as well outlaw breathing. The funny thing is that it absolutely has done nothing to stop people from drinking." He took a bite of his roast beef. "The food here is excellent. Anyway, what the law has managed to do is make criminals organized and wealthy. These are some terrifying people. A few weeks ago, in Chicago, seven men were murdered by men dressed as policemen. They were shot with machine guns—guns that shoot so rapidly you can't hear individual shots. It sounds like a roar."

He took a sip of beer. "I was a criminal, but not like the criminals they have here. I never harmed anyone. These men, however, are dangerous."

He took another bite of roast beef and continued, "But thanks to you, my good friends, I now make a living playing music. I am hired by these same dangerous men, but they leave me alone and I do not interfere with their business. They pay me to play my music. Selling illegal alcohol pays them very well, so they pay me very well. I have money; I have a place to stay and I even make money off something called phonograph records. At home, I could never make money from my music; it is why I turned to crime. Those days are over. I am a law-abiding citizen now—well except for the liquor. That doesn't really count, does it? By the way, I am so sorry that I robbed you—but you did shoot me. Water under the bridge I say."

Vernon and Sol had taken to eating their meals, being unable to get a word in edgewise. Smoot was talking rapidly and animatedly, using hand gestures. He finally paused and said, "I owe you so much, yet we really have never formally met."

"I am Sol and this is Vernon," Sol said. "We were wondering if you could help us."

He held out his hand. "Silas Smoot, and I am happy to do anything I can do to assist you."

They shook hands. Sol took out a picture of Eddie and Angie and showed it to Smoot. "We are looking for these two children. We have reason to believe that they were in this establishment sometime between 1920 and 1932," Sol said, handing him the picture.

Smoot took the picture and studied it. "No, I have never seen them. It is unlikely that children would come to an establishment like this."

"Actually," Vernon said, "We saw a picture of them that was taken in this very dining room."

"I am here most nights," said Smoot. "I did not see them."

"Could you keep the photo and ask around?" Sol asked. "We can come back in a few months and see if you were able to find anything out."

"It is the very least I can do," said Smoot.

Sol handed him one of the envelopes, and said, "If you see them, give them this."

"Happy to help," said Smoot, taking the envelope. "Anything you need, really."

Sol and Vernon thanked him. They took a final sip of beer and left through the front door. Once outside they circled around to the back of the building and made sure no one was looking. They linked arms; Vernon touched the colored point on the screen and they were back in the barn.

Chapter 56
September 6, 1776

Billy and Angie Learn Something About the CKD

Franklin took everyone on a tour of the harbor. At the end of the tour, they found Captain Beaumont's ship and climbed aboard. Franklin introduced him to everyone. Franklin then took Captain Beaumont aside. They spoke quietly together for several minutes. When they finished speaking, Franklin pulled a stack of bills from a coat pocket and handed it to the captain. The captain went over to Billy and Lucius and told them that they were to gather their things and come back aboard later this afternoon. By the time the transaction was finished, it was getting close to lunchtime.

Franklin said to Billy and Lucius, "You two are all set. The ship will anchor off Burton Woods and wait for you. They will send you ashore with some men and a dingy. You can gather the treasure and return to the ship. You will have to take a little side trip to Jamaica before returning to Philadelphia. Hopefully, we will all be rich."

Eddie said, "Can we get back now? I really want to go over the notes and see if we can get out of here."

"Is my company that objectionable?" asked Franklin.

"Oh....um....no, of course not. We just want to get home," said Eddie.

"Relax, child. I am just jesting," said Franklin. "Of course we should get back, eat some lunch and you two can get to work."

Angie said, "I'm in no hurry."

They arrived at Franklin's house and he bade them to sit at the table as he went into the kitchen to make some ham sandwiches. When he came out of the kitchen with a platter of sandwiches, Billy and Lucius ate very quickly then went upstairs to pack.

Franklin went into his study and emerged with two leather pouches. He brought them into the kitchen and gave them to Angie and Eddie. "What is this," Eddie asked.

"Something that may help you on your journey," said Franklin.

"Just some coins. It is not a lot of money today, but in the future these coins may be rare and worth something. You shouldn't be traveling without money."

"That is very generous, thank you!" said Eddie. He opened his pouch; there were at least three dozen coins. He looked through them. Some were silver, some were copper and all were very new looking.

"Yes, thank you," said Angie.

Angie sat at the table and removed the CKD and Vernon's notes from her backpack. Eddie sat across from her. She said, "Eddie, go outside and gather some pebbles."

"Why do I have to go and do the grunt work while you work on the important stuff?" complained Eddie.

"Fine," said Angie, and she handed Eddie Vernon's notes. Eddie took the notes and began reading, with a perplexed look on his face. After a minute, he handed them back to Angie and said, "I'll be right back."

Franklin emerged from the kitchen with a platter of sandwiches and tea. Angie reached into her backpack and retrieved her iPhone. She turned it on and said, "Mr. Franklin, can I ask a favor?"

"Of course," he said.

"I want to get a picture of us together," she said. She stood on a chair next to him and leaned her head towards his, holding the iPhone at arms length. "Smile," she said and took a selfie. "I figure that if we are lost for a while, I may end up with quite a collection. I already have you, Mr. Adams and General Washington." She powered down the phone, took a sandwich and sat back down with the notes.

While she was reading, Billy and Lucius came downstairs with their belongings. Angie looked up from her reading and suddenly became very sad. She got up and hugged Lucius and said, "I am really going to miss you two. Lucius, say goodbye to Sadie for me. You two are going to make a wonderful couple. And please, apologize to Angus for me."

"Anything for you little lady," said Lucius. "If you are right about this article, I am going to owe you a great deal."

Angie hugged Billy and sighed. She was still taken with him and did not know what to say. Finally, she said, "Be careful, Billy. And thank your cousins and uncle for saving us."

Billy said, "Thank you, Angie. I believe that good fortune awaits and I will owe it all to you."

"Wait, I want to get a picture of us together," Angie said. She had the three of them pose for a selfie. "Make sure you stop and say goodbye to Eddie when you go outside." The two men nodded and left the house.

Angie was alone with Franklin in the kitchen. She thought for a minute and got her nerve up. "One other thing," she said. "Would it be possible for me to go to Paris with you?"

Franklin's eyes opened wide in surprise. "Don't you need to go home with your brother?" he asked.

Angie said, "He is anxious to get home. I actually like it better here."

Franklin said, "I have no objection, if it is alright with your brother. But think carefully. Family is your most precious possession."

That made Angie sad, because she knew that Franklin and his son became estranged over the fight for independence. William Franklin was the acknowledged illegitimate son of Benjamin Franklin. He was the last Colonial governor of New Jersey and a staunch loyalist. When Benjamin decided to take up the patriot cause, he tried to convince William to join him, but the son stayed loyal to the Crown. That strained their relationship to the breaking point. William Franklin continued as governor until January of 1776, when colonial militiamen placed him under house arrest. In fact, he was being held by the patriots at this very moment. He was later incarcerated in Connecticut but finally released in a prisoner exchange in 1778. He moved to New York City, which was still occupied by the British. Active in the Loyalist community of New York, Franklin became President of the Board of Associated Loyalists. In 1782, William Franklin departed for England, never to return.

During negotiations in Paris for the peace treaty, Benjamin Franklin became known for his uncompromising position related to not providing compensation or amnesty for the Loyalists who left the colonies. His son's reputation as a Loyalist may have contributed to his position. He and his son never spoke after the war.

Eddie came in with a handful of pebbles and placed them on the table near Angie. Angie said, "According to Vernon, we need to create a colored spot on the machine. Once it is created, we place a pebble on it and that pebble will travel in time. If it lands nearby, then we keep the color on the spot we used to send the pebble; if not, then we remove the color. If a pebble lands nearby, it means that if we ourselves touch that spot, we will return to where the pebble landed." Angie then placed the flash drive into the time machine, created a colored spot and placed one of the pebbles on it.

The pebble disappeared with a "pop". They listened in the room for another "pop"; there was none. Angie repeated the process another dozen times with no result.

Franklin was watching them intently. "So those pebbles are being sent to a different time and place?" he said in a questioning tone. Angie nodded, she was eating a bit of her ham sandwich.

"Yeth," she said through a mouthful of sandwich.

"Fascinating," said Franklin.

"It will probably take all day, according to Vernon's notes," said Angie as she placed another pebble. They heard a loud "pop" in the kitchen. Eddie raced back to the kitchen and came back with the pebble. "That's it!" he exclaimed.

"What's it?" asked Franklin.

"We can start to try to get home," said Eddie. "Because no matter where we go we can always get back to here."

"Hopefully you can stay a visit a while before you go leaping through time," said Franklin.

"Of course," said Eddie. "But, you know, no matter where we go, we can get back to your kitchen. Even if we find our way home, Uncle Sol can set our CKD up to return home. That means that we could visit whenever we wanted to."

"Eddie, you should go on alone," Angie said.

"We need to stay together, Angie," Eddie said.

Chapter 56
September 6, 1776

Collins Goes to Philadelphia

Collins was just a few miles outside of Philadelphia at the same time Angie and Eddie were making their discovery. He passed a few travelers on the road, but no one recognized him. To his knowledge, no one carried any news about what had happened in New Brunswick. He hoped he could spend the necessary time in Philadelphia anonymously.

He would be there for no longer than a day. He would stop at an inn or boarding house, eat, rest and search for those blasted brats. He would dispatch them and be out of town by the following afternoon. If they had left town, it would not take a long time to find out. They stood out. He would be able overtake them on the road to Mt. Vernon. In many ways, that was the preferable scenario — no witnesses.

He arrived in Philadelphia at three in the afternoon. After making inquiries to a passerby, he was directed to a boarding house on Chestnut Street that was owned by a Mrs. Davis. He left his horse at a livery stable nearby. He asked about the children at the stable, but the proprietor had not seen them.

It was a short walk to the boarding house from the stable. He knocked on the door to the boarding house and Mrs. Davis answered. She was a dumpling of a woman, not too old, maybe 40. She was about 5' 2", plump, with bright blue eyes. Her dark hair was tied up behind her and she seemed to have a perpetual smile.

"Can I help you?" she asked. "Oh Good Lord! You poor man, whatever happened to you?"

"Some men tried to rob me outside a tavern a few nights ago. I fought them off, by they got their licks in," said Collins in his most polite tone. "I am seeking a room for the night. Possibly for a few nights."

She quoted him a price and said that it included breakfast and dinner. He paid her with some of the coins from his stolen purses. She took him in and showed him the room. She said, "Alexander

Hamilton had this room during the early part of summer when they were working on the Declaration."

Collins nodded appreciatively and said, "Ma'am you would not have happened to see two strange children about? One is a chubby girl about the age of 10 with red hair the other is a tall dark haired boy about the age of 12. They would have arrived in town yesterday or the day before."

"Funny you should mention it," said Mrs. Davis. "Two such children are staying with Mr. Benjamin Franklin. Why do you ask?"

"They are my cousin's children, Ma'am. He said that they would be arriving in town with another relative and a slave. He asked me to look in on them."

"Well," she said, "They seem to be staying with Mr. Franklin. He lives just two doors over."

"Why, thank you, Ma'am," Collins said with a grin, "You have been most helpful."

She told him that dinner was in two hours and he could rest in his room and clean up. Collins retired to his room, cleaned up and took a nap before dinner. He wanted to be fresh and rested when he found the children because he may have to leave town in a hurry afterwards.

Chapter 57
1920

Sol and Vernon Begin to Search the 1920s

Sol and Vernon arrived home and prepared for another jump. They had decided to go to the early 1920s and try to find the children there. Silas had said that he had arrived in Chicago in the spring of 1925. They decided to start with 1920, in case the children arrived before Silas. They would go to 1932 and talk to Silas and see if the children arrived between 1929 and 1932. They were a little off in their calculations and ended up in Chicago. "Not a big deal," said Sol. "We can get a car and drive to New Castle. It is only a few hours away."

"The automatic transmission has not been invented yet," said Vernon, "You don't drive a stick shift, and I don't drive."

"How hard can it be," said Sol. "Let's stop and get some currency of the day." They were near a bank, so they entered. Sol arranged to sell the gold coins for $32 apiece. They netted a little over $1700. It was enough for an automobile and a place to stay. They found an automobile dealer a few blocks from the bank. Sol picked up a slightly used Ford Model T for $250. They got into the car and Sol prepared to drive away. He had no idea how to start the car or how to operate it. Not only did the car not have an automatic transmission, the controls were nothing like any vehicle either man had seen.

There were two handles on the steering wheel, neither of which had anything to do with changing gears. There were three pedals on the floor, but none of them was a gas pedal. He and Vernon got out of the car and asked the salesman to show them how to operate the vehicle.

It was quite a complicated procedure. Operating a Model T is nothing like driving a modern car—even one with a stick shift. For one thing, starting the vehicle was accomplished by engaging a crank at the front of the car. If the car backfired, it could cause the crank to move suddenly backward with enough force to break an arm. You had to be careful to use the left arm and to not wrap your thumb around the handle. It took a good half hour before Sol could start the car, put it into gear and change gears. Acceleration was accomplished by a throttle, which was one of the levers on the steering wheel. There were three pedals on the floor. One was a brake and the other two enabled you to change gears. There was no gas pedal. Reverse gear was accomplished by depressing one of the pedals. They practiced driving around the car lot and finally pulled out into traffic.

"It will take us a few hours to get to New Castle," said Sol. A little way out of town they stopped to buy gas. It was 18 cents per gallon. "Unbelievable," Sol said as he paid the attendant. It was late in the afternoon when they arrived at their destination. They drove past Wilson's Roadhouse and found a motel about four miles to the west of it. There was a small town a little further up the road. It had a gas station, a grocery store, three churches and a sundries store. They drove through town, then doubled back, got themselves a room at the motel. Sol showed the proprietor a picture of Angie and Eddie. The man was amazed that the photo was in color, but had not seen the children. Sol offered him $1000 if, when they returned in a few months, he could help them find the children. They walked into town and made the same inquiries to the proprietors of each business, and making the same $1000 offer. No one had seen the children. They drove to Wilson's Roadhouse and made their inquiries; they had no success there either.

They got back to the room and Sol said, "We can spend a few days and pass out photographs, offer the reward and then we can come back in six months and repeat the process."

Sol and Vernon spent three days in New Castle. They spread money around, they showed pictures and they offered the $1000 reward. The plan was to come back in a year and see if anyone saw the children. If not, then they would repeat the process and come back the following year. They would do this, every year between 1920 and 1934 if need be.

They spent some time in Wilson's Roadhouse. They met with Janie Wilson, the woman who managed the place. She was a strikingly beautiful woman. She was tall her dark hair peeked out from a large tam-o-shanter hat, luminous light green eyes and reminded Sol of Adriana Lima, the girl in the KIA commercials.

Wilson's Roadhouse was a speakeasy. Janie ran the place, though her father, Frederick Wilson, owned it. A year earlier, gangsters came into town. Gerry Bongiovani, or Gerry B as he was known, was a friend of Al Capone. He came in and just took over the roadhouse. Her father was old and in frail health. Gerry B had two of his thugs move with him into the apartment on the third floor of the roadhouse. They "persuaded" Mr. Wilson to sign a "lease" and rented the roadhouse from him for a pittance. Gerry B let Janie stay on, and even paid her a salary. She said that he was creepy and that she shuddered to think of why he wanted her around. At least he didn't force himself on her; it was like he was courting her. "Creepy," she said.

Sol thanked her for the information and offered his reward. She replied that the only reward that she wanted was to get her place and her father back. Vernon said that they might be able to help her with that. They got up to leave.

Outside of the roadhouse Sol asked Vernon, "Why did you promise to solve her problem? We are not 'muscle' and would not stand a chance against these guys."

"Simple," said Vernon. "Drop them, one at a time, into the American wilderness at various points during the 17th century. Let them interact with the Native Americans without the support of numbers. Some may actually survive, but they would never be able to organize into a criminal organization and I doubt any would have an influence on history."

"If she can put us in touch with the children, I guess that I would take that bargain," said Sol. They went back to the hotel, gathered their things and disappeared with a "pop," leaving the car. Sol had given the ownership papers to the Model T to Janie.

Chapter 58
September 6, 1776

Bigby and Woodruff Arrive in Philadelphia

Bigby and Woodruff arrived in Philadelphia a few hours after Collins' arrival. They came upon Independence Hall on Chestnut Street. "This is where the traitors congregate," said Bigby. "We need to be cautious here; we will not find many friends. If we can take the children indoors and quietly we shall do so. If they are in public, we will have to content ourselves with watching and following them until an opportunity presents itself. We can't afford to cause a disturbance."

"What about Collins?" asked Woodruff.

"I picked you for this mission because you are good with bladed weapons. Kill him silently, if you get the opportunity. He won't know you, so you can get close. He might recognize me, so I will try to keep out of his sight. If he sees me, I will shoot him if I have to. In that event we will have to make a hasty retreat."

They turned a corner and found themselves on Market Street. They had traveled about a block when Bigby motioned for Woodruff to stop. About half a block ahead they saw Collins, sneaking into a home. The two men dismounted, drew their weapons and approached the house.

Chapter 59
September 7, 1776

Collins Takes Action

The morning after discovering their "home" spot on the device, Angie awoke early and went downstairs. Franklin was already seated at the table, drinking tea and eating a roll. He motioned for her to sit down and help herself.

"I have to go speak with the some of the delegates this morning. I also have to speak to John about our upcoming trip to see General Howe," Franklin said. "You are welcome to come with me."

"Eddie and I are going to test the device when he gets up," Angie said. "Is it alright for us to be here with you gone? Eddie may be gone; I plan on staying."

"Oh, absolutely not a problem. George will be here if you have need of anything," Franklin said. "I actually hope that you will stay a while and make yourselves at home. I would like to examine it. But think long and hard about whether you want to separate from your brother. Do you have the device with you? "

"Eddie has it," Angie said. "I could go up and get it, if you like. Otherwise he will probably bring it down with him when he gets up."

"Oh, no hurry," said Franklin. "I trust you will be here when I return."

"Oh yes," said Angie. "Uncle Sol said that once we have established a 'home base,' which in our case happens to be your kitchen, we should be able to get there no matter where or when we are. Eddie and I are going to test that theory by first trying to go from elsewhere in the house to the kitchen. We will spend the rest of the day getting comfortable with the machine."

"Then I look forward to visiting with you and your brother later this afternoon. And, please, come and go freely. You two are family and you should stay together," said Franklin. The clock in the hallway chimed. Franklin said, "It's getting late. I must be off."

Angie grabbed herself a second roll and poured some more tea. She reached across the table and helped herself to the newspaper

Franklin had been reading. Breakfast and a newspaper, not so different from home, she thought. Thankfully, there were no limp bran flakes.

Collins had been standing on the porch of Mrs. Davis' house when Benjamin Franklin left his house. He stood and watched him walk down the street. Franklin being gone meant that there was a good chance that the children were in the house alone. He ran up to his room and retrieved the pistols. He put them in his belt and put on a frock coat to hide them. The weather was a little warm for him to be wearing the coat, but no matter.

He walked toward Franklin's house, but ducked between buildings before he passed in front of the house, making sure to crouch and keep his head below the level of the windows. He stepped past a window and stood up slowly, peering in. It was the window to the kitchen. There was an old black man standing to his right. He appeared to be cooking. Straight ahead and a little to the left was a doorway that went into what appeared to be a dining room. There was someone seated at the table. When he saw who it was, his heart raced. It was the red haired girl.

Collins ducked down and circled around to the front of the house. Drawing one of the pistols, he opened the door and stepped inside. He closed the door, but did not latch it. Silently, he stepped into the dining room, which was on his right.

Angie was looking through the newspaper. One page was entirely devoted to ships that had arrived and the contents of their cargo. There was a gossipy piece about Agnes Mullins running off and leaving her husband, Thomas. There was another article about an escaped murderer. Angie read the article and gasped. It detailed the "…daring escape of Lieutenant Ezra Collins, formerly of the Continental army. Collins was being transported from New Brunswick Courthouse by soldiers stationed in New York to be hanged for the murder of Captain Aubrey Goodman and an unknown American." Angie gasped and felt a sudden tinge of panic. "Could Collins find them here?" she wondered.

"Well, if it isn't my lovely 'daughter,' " Collins said with a sneer, leveling the pistol at Angie. Angie gasped, eyes wide with terror.

George stepped out of the kitchen, holding a large iron skillet. "Fire that gun and you're gonna have to deal with me."

Collins drew a second pistol, cocked it and said, "Not a problem for me."

"I throw this, you gonna miss," said George, leveling a steely gaze at Collins.

"I won't miss the girl," said Collins. "Now, dear 'daughter,' won't you tell me where your brother is?"

"He went with Mr. Franklin. He'll be gone all day," Angie said.

"That is a LIE," said Collins in a loud voice. "I saw Mr. Franklin leave, and he was alone. You are quite a liar, aren't you? You lied to that farmer in Musketa Cove. You lied to General Clinton. You lied at my trial. You are lying now." He leveled one of the pistols at her and prepared to fire.

Several things happened at once. Collins felt someone grab him by the coat. There was a loud "pop" in the dining room. George threw the frying pan, which put a large dent in the plaster of the wall behind where Collins had been standing. Collins disappeared. Eddie and Collins appeared in an alleyway in Chicago in 1925. The pistol went off. Eddie touched the screen immediately after depositing Collins in the alleyway and he disappeared with a "pop."

When Collins' gun went off, it killed a man standing directly in front of him. The man was carrying a Thompson submachine gun that he was preparing to fire at three men standing in front of him. Hearing the shot, the men turned around. They drew guns of their own. Collins stood there with a smoking flintlock pistol, in shock. He looked around. Nothing was familiar. The men in front of him were dressed strangely. It was dark out, but there were bright lights at the end of the alley and rapidly moving carriages. He was dumbfounded. The girl was gone and he was in this strange place.

A heavyset man in a white, wide brimmed hat stepped forward. He looked down at the dead man, and nodded with a tight-lipped smile, making an appraising face. He said, "He's as dead as Abraham Lincoln. Nice work." He then looked Collins up and down and said, "Jeez, what happened to your face? You look like you kissed a meat grinder. You are one strange looking guy, but you know how to handle yourself, I'll give you that."

Collins just stood silent. The man took the fired flintlock pistol from Collins' hand and studied it for a moment. He turned and looked back down at the dead man. He shook his head, laughing and said, "Thank you. You saved my life with this museum piece. I owe you." He reached into his pocket and fished out a big wad of bills. "This doesn't begin to cover it." He handed the money to Collins and said, "Name's Al Capone. I owe you, and I always pay my debts."

The man studied Collins' face and said, "You look like a guy who likes to mix it up; I can always use a guy like you." He poked him in the ribs, winked and said, "I bet the other guy looks worse, am I right? Yeah, you know how to take care of yourself. You come around to the Metropole Hotel. You need a job, you need money, you need help—anything you want. You got a friend." He turned and left, calling back, "Remember, Metropole Hotel, Al Capone—stop by; anything you need."

He kept the gun and walked away, showing it to his associates, "Get a load of this thing. Guy went up against a chopper with it with it AND WON." Capone was laughing and shaking his head. "Ugly bugger, though." Collins just stood there and watched them walk away. He looked at the bills in his hand, it was some kind of money—a lot of it.

Chapter 60
September 7, 1776

Eddie and Angie Discover that Philadelphia may not be Safe

Eddie had panicked and acted on impulse when he saw Collins pointing the gun at Angie. As soon as he and Collins landed in that alley he randomly hit the screen of the machine. He just wanted to get out of there. He appeared in a darkened bar or restaurant. In front of him was a group of people seated, posing for a camera. A flash went off. Eddie looked to his left, there was a bar and the man seated at it looked like Collins in a dark business suit. Eddie studied the screen of the CKD for a minute, found the colored spot and appeared back in Benjamin Franklin's kitchen.

Less than two minutes had passed since Collins was threatening Angie. Eddie stepped into the dining room. Angie was really upset. George had his arm around her and was comforting her. He walked up to them. "Angie, he's gone," Eddie said.

He grabbed her in a tight hug and said, "I really don't want to go anywhere without you. We are family and should stick together. I know I have been mean to you, but Angus is right; we are family and really all each other has. I'm really very sorry. But can we try to get home—*together*?"

"Sorry?" she mouthed, tears welled up in her eyes. "You saved my life. Angus was right, we are family and should stick together."

"I've never been very nice to you," he said, still hugging her. "Angus said I should cherish you because you cannot be replaced. Collins could have killed you, and I would never have said how much you mean to me."

"We can't stay here," Eddie said. "We are rid of Collins, but the British may actually send agents to find us. They sent Captain Goodman; they may send others."

"I told Mr. Franklin that we would be here when he got back," said Angie, still sobbing. "But if you want to go after that, I will go with you. I so wanted to go to Paris with him."

"It would be best, even if you don't want to go home. Collins may have enlisted help." said Eddie. Angie just nodded.

"You should wait for Mr. Franklin," George said. "He would be sorely disappointed if he missed you. I think the British army may be a way off in coming."

Angie had collected herself. "They take the city is September of 1777, next year." She was still shaken. "He was going to shoot me!" she said.

"But he didn't, thank God. He's gone now," said Eddie.

"He'll never pay for his crimes."

"You don't know that," said Eddie. He paused and softened. "We can wait for Mr. Franklin, if you like. We should be fine here for a while. We're safe. Collins was probably alone. After all, who would help a jerk like that?"

Angie nodded, "Especially when you consider what happened to the last two people who worked with him. Waiting for Mr. Franklin would be nice," she said.

Just then, Bigby and Woodruff burst into the house with their weapons drawn. They leveled their guns at Eddie and Angie. Bigby spoke, "You two are to come with me. Where is Collins?"

Eddie didn't hesitate. He grabbed his sister and touched the screen. They were gone in a "pop," leaving Bigby and Woodruff to stare in utter confusion.

Chapter 61
August 25, 2014

An Unexpected Homecoming

Sol and Vernon appeared in the barn with a "pop." They had spent most of the summer looking for Eddie and Angie. They had made dozens of trips to the 1920s and to the 18th century, but with no luck. Time was running out. Soon they were going to have to face Ellen and Ben, who were arriving at O'Hare in three days.

Sol was seriously thinking of relocating to the 1950s. He and Vernon had discussed it. Vernon was against the idea, but Sol absolutely did not want to face Ellen and give her the news about Eddie and Angie.

It was twilight, just beginning to get dark. There was enough light for them to find their way back to the trailer. As they approached it, Sol said to Vernon, "Did you leave any lights on?"

"No," said Vernon. "I made sure everything was shut off when we left."

"It appears that we have visitors," Sol said.

"Maybe it's Lucy getting supplies for the dogs," Vernon said. "We have been gone a few days and she does have a key."

They approached the door to the house. Sol entered first. He was charged by a red-headed blur who grasped him is a hug so tight he could not move. "Uncle Sol!" exclaimed the person, who continued to hold him. "It's us! —Angie and Eddie." She held him for a few minutes, then released her grip. Sol felt a great sense of relief wash over him, until he got a good look. The two of them looked very different from when they left. Angie was thinner and Eddie was taller—they had grown.

Angie had developed into a tall, slender and attractive teenager. Eddie, that small and skinny kid, was about six inches taller and was a little more muscular. "Hi Uncle Sol!" he said.

"All I have to say is the most common cliché spoken by uncles," said Sol. "My how you have grown."

Eddie said, "With all the time travel it was kind of hard to figure how long we were gone. We received the notes you gave to Benjamin Franklin, and made his house our home base. The problem was the British. They seemed to know we were there, so we did not return. We had some problems with the machine, but we finally created a new home base."

"This is going to be hard to explain to your parents," said Sol.

Angie said, "Don't worry, Uncle Sol. We'll cover for you. Kids get growth spurts all of the time. We'll just tell Mom it was a lot of fresh air and exercise. Besides, she'll be so happy that I lost weight, that she won't take issue with our growth."

"Not such a bad idea," said Vernon. "This can work. It beats living in the 1950s."

Angie said, "Boy, do we ever have a lot to tell you."

OTHER ANAPHORA LITERARY PRESS TITLES

PLJ: Interviews with Gene Ambaum and Corban Addison: VII:3, Fall 2015
Editor: Anna Faktorovich

Architecture of Being
By: Bruce Colbert

The Encyclopedic Philosophy of Michel Serres
By: Keith Moser

Forever Gentleman
By: Roland Colton

Janet Yellen
By: Marie Bussing-Burks

Diseases, Disorders, and Diagnoses of Historical Individuals
By: William J. Maloney

Armageddon at Maidan
By: Vasyl Baziv

Vovochka
By: Alexander J. Motyl

CPSIA information can be obtained
at www.ICGtesting.com
Printed in the USA
FFOW02n0833070416
23034FF